What the World Doesn't See

MEL DARBON

USBORNE

What the World Doesn't See

"Poignant, tender and utterly absorbing, I defy you not to root for Jake and Maudie."

Lisa Williamson, author of *The Art of Being Normal*

"A brave and tender book about loss, family bonds and not judging on first appearance."

Joseph Elliott, author of *The Good Hawk*

"An important and beautiful story about the tight bond between two siblings, and looking beyond a person's disabilities."

Susin Nielsen, author of *We Are All Made of Molecules*

"An incredibly moving read, this beautifully told story explores grief, family and love in a powerful and impactful way... This book deserves a wide readership."

Secrets

90710 000 561 856

To my brother Guy.
You made the world special just by
being in it. RIP.

First published in the UK in 2023 by Usborne Publishing Ltd., Usborne House,
83-85 Saffron Hill, London EC1N 8RT, England, usborne.com.

Usborne Verlag, Usborne Publishing Ltd., Prüfeninger Str. 20, 93049 Regensburg,
Deutschland, VK Nr. 17560

Text copyright © Mel Darbon, 2023

Cover illustration by Adams Carvalho © Usborne Publishing, 2023

A CIP catalogue record for this book is available from the British Library.

FMAMJJASOND/23   ISBN 9781474937849   04620/01

Printed and bound using 100% renewable energy at CPI Group (UK) Ltd, Croydon, CR0 4YY.

CHAPTER 1

Maudie

Mum said one word when I asked her why she was sitting in the shed: "Sorry". Her voice was soft and shaky. I couldn't get my head around her being out there, in the dark, on a half-empty bag of compost, clutching the oily rag my dad used when he fixed the lawnmower.

One minute she'd seemed fine, eating dinner with us, and the next she'd bolted out the back door leaving me and Jake, open-mouthed, staring at her empty chair and half-eaten plate of lasagne. We always have lasagne on Saturdays – it was Dad's favourite. He and Jake liked to eat it on their laps watching the football.

While we eat we usually discuss what we're going to do on Sunday, but tonight Mum was too distracted. I thought she was just tired, as Jake had got up twice the night before. Plus, I was too busy texting under the table to my best friend

Liv to really register what was going on. Normally Mum would have taken my phone away. I was actually glancing up to see if she was checking on me when she dropped her fork onto her plate with a clatter and ran into the garden.

Mum didn't say another word after "Sorry", which was freaky, and she didn't seem to want to come out of the shed. So I'd had to leave her there while I went to help settle Jake for the evening, otherwise he would have got anxious. I tried calling Eve, Mum's sister, to see if she could come and talk to Mum, but she was on night duty at the hospital. By the time I got back out to the shed, Mum's hands were ice cold and she was shivering.

Eventually I persuaded her to come inside and got her into bed. And then I didn't really know what to do so I tried to get some sleep as well, but my brain wouldn't stop buzzing. I couldn't block out Mum's white face as she said sorry, her eyes focused past my left shoulder.

That word is on repeat inside my head now. *Sorry, sorry, sorry.* I want it to stop.

I've spent hours thinking back over the last few weeks to see if there was anything that might have shown me this would happen. Sure, Mum's been a bit tense and snappy, but she always gets like that when she has a deadline for work, especially a wedding dress.

This is different though.

Thinking about it, Mum didn't watch a film with me, Liv and Jake on Friday, which she always does. She spent the evening looking through old family photo albums instead. And when my Aunty Eve invited her out for a drink last week, on one of her rare nights off, Mum didn't want to go.

I even had to help her put her pyjamas on last night, which was off-the-wall weird. She was wearing Dad's favourite chunky Fair Isle jumper that comes down to her knees. At least she lifted her arms above her head, which Jake usually refuses to do because he thinks it's funny.

I don't get it – Mum's always in control.

I'm really scared. What if she still can't cope today?

CHAPTER 2

Jake

Mum gave me salad. With my pasta. I hate salad. I got upset. Maudie ate it for me. She's a good sister. She helped me get to bed. Mum always does that.

I didn't want blue pyjamas. I wear red Arsenal pyjamas on Saturdays. Maudie knows that. She said they were in the ironing pile. My pyjamas got tangled. It made my head muddle up. Maudie helped me. Then she read me a story. I have two books at bedtime. Maudie said, "Not tonight, Jake." I don't know why.

It's very dark in my room. The dark puts monsters in my head. Oh dear. I can hear Mum crying.

"Mum? Mum! Jake will make it better."

Mum's not answering me. I can hear my sister knocking. Maudie's talking to Mum. The crying has stopped. Mum's not talking back. I can see my door opening.

"Hello, girl!"

"Hey, Jake, did you call me?"

"He wanted his mum."

"We need to let Mum rest, Jake."

"Mum was crying. Jake heard her. Is his mum okay?"

"Yes, I think she's asleep now. Can I sit on your bed?"

"BE CAREFUL! Don't drop his bag. Keep it safe!"

"I know – here it is."

"Mum didn't say goodnight. She kisses Jake's head at bedtime. It makes the monsters go away. Why didn't Jake's mum do that?"

Maudie holds my hand. I don't like it. It prickles my skin up. Maudie has a sad face. Her mouth is upside down. I can hold her hand. I can do it.

"Do you remember when we went on that long, long walk by the lakes, with Dad?"

"Yes he does. Maudie got stung by a wasp-bee. Ow!"

"I did! How could I forget *that*?"

"Maudie got a big nose."

"Yeah – huge. Dad couldn't stop laughing. I was so angry at him. Do you remember we walked so far you sat on a rock and refused to budge, because you were so tired?"

"Jake's legs stopped working."

"They did, and it's a bit like that for Mum tonight. She's exhausted because she's been working so hard, I think her whole body has stopped working. Do you get what I mean?"

"Mum's legs won't work. Like Jake's."

"Exactly! All Mum needs is a good night's sleep, then she'll be fine tomorrow. Let's get some sleep ourselves. I'll kiss the monsters away for you. There, night night."

"Bugs bite."

My head is worried. I don't know if Mum's legs will work in the morning.

CHAPTER 3

Maudie

I check my phone to delay going downstairs. There's nothing from Aunty Eve but about six texts from Liv, wondering where I got to last night and if I'm okay. We usually spend most evenings chatting for hours and Liv had promised she'd call after she'd been for her driving lesson last night.

I quickly tap in a reply to her.

Sorry. Shit night. Mum went to pieces. Need to speak later xx

A reply pings straight back.

Hugs ♡

That's why I love Liv, she just gets it.

I groan when I see the time, it's gone ten and I must

get up. We often go bowling on a Sunday, which Jake loves – we all do. Mum seemed okay when we went last Sunday, didn't she? We had such a laugh. I'm sure we will again today. I cross my fingers, like I did when I was little.

I go downstairs to find, not Mum, but Eve sitting at the kitchen table, trying to stop Jake fitting a whole sausage into his mouth. He shoves her hand away, startling her.

"Hey, Jake, try cutting that up, then you won't choke." I smile at him.

He drops it onto the plate. "He doesn't know where his mum is."

Eve jumps straight in. "She's having a lie-in, Jake. She's really tired." She looks flustered as she waves a hand to me in greeting.

I raise my eyebrows in question at Eve, but she's now rummaging in the cutlery drawer. My heart thuds erratically in my chest. I never managed to get hold of my aunt last night, which means Mum must have called Eve herself. She must be shattered coming here straight after work. Why didn't Eve wake me up? I feel a bit sick. I should ask her straight out what Mum said to her and why she's here, but I can't. I have a feeling I might not like the answer.

Jake pushes his plate away from him. "Jake has full English on Sunday."

"Oh dear, sorry. I'd forgotten that, Jake." Eve looks strained.

"It's fine, Eve. You're only missing the mushrooms, Jake."

"Jake likes mushrooms."

"Don't worry, I'll make sure we have them next Sunday." I turn to Eve. "It's my fault, Mum and I cook breakfast together on Sundays now. I should have got up earlier."

"Maudie's fault." Jake looks at me intently.

I hover near Eve, who's focused on cutting up Jake's food, until I finally pluck up the courage to ask her, "Why are you here?"

Eve picks up Jake's fork and stabs it into a piece of sausage, offering it to him.

Jake turns his head away. "He's not a baby, he doesn't need feeding."

Eve grimaces. "Argh! I know that, Jake, I'm just not thinking straight. I thought it might help." She smiles apologetically at Jake and gives him the fork. "I had a very difficult baby delivery last night that ended in an emergency operation. I need a gallon of coffee to get my brain going this morning."

She really must be tired; Jake loves her, but on an unpredictability scale of one to ten he's an eleven, and he'd have lobbed that sausage at her if she'd tried to get it in his mouth.

Eve hasn't answered my question and her face looks grey and drawn, which gives me a horrible feeling in the pit of my stomach.

"Where's Mum? Have you seen her this morning?" I look around the tiny kitchen, as though she's going to magically appear from under the sink or something.

Jake prods me with his fork. "She's having a lie-in. Eve said that."

I look at Eve, who has turned bright red and refuses to hold my eye. The knot in my stomach gets tighter. Can't Mum get out of bed? Is she still feeling like she did last night and can't get up?

Jake opens his bag and pulls out the ripped front page of a *London Bus* magazine and holds it up to show me. Half my brain is still distracted with worries about Mum, but I take a deep breath and try to sound enthusiastic.

"That's such a great open-top bus, Jake. One of your favourites."

He hands the ripped cover to me but changes his mind as I'm about to take it and snatches it away again. "It's all broken."

"That's because you rip them up, Jake."

He shakes his head. "Jake made a leaflet. He told you that last week."

"You did. Sorry."

"Maudie wasn't listening."

He raises a disapproving eyebrow at me, just like Mum does, then arranges his leaflet on the bottom of his bag, making sure it's flat, before hooking the handles over his knee. He lines all the coasters evenly along the middle of the table.

"I'd forgotten how specific everything has to be. I really

am being useless this morning." Eve keeps her eyes on the table.

I sit down next to her and rest my hand gently on her arm. Eve looks up at me and gives me a wobbly smile. I'm shocked at how rough she looks. She has huge dark circles under her eyes and an angry spot is coming up on her chin.

"Eve? Did Mum call you?"

She takes my hand in hers. "Maudie." She lowers her voice. "I... Well, there's no good way of saying this..."

I glance over at my brother, who's now murmuring under his breath and picking at his nails, which are ripped down to the skin, bleeding at the edges. Not surprisingly, Jake's anxious too, and our feelings are only going to make that worse.

I pass him the sports section of the newspaper to help distract him. "There are some good photos here of Arsenal players."

"Jake loves football." He spreads the pages out on the table.

"Eve, please tell me what's going on, or I'll go and ask Mum myself."

She pinches the bit between her eyebrows and swallows hard before blurting out, "You can't, Maudie. Your mum has gone."

"GONE?"

Eve nods.

"That girl's too loud. It hurts his ears. Where's his mum gone?" Jake anxiously looks around the kitchen.

15

"Not sure, Jake, but there's nothing to worry about," I reassure him. "I expect she's gone for a walk or something."

He seems happy with this for now. I lower my voice. "But Mum can't have gone. I put her to bed."

"Your mum rang me at five this morning, asking me to come over urgently. I got here as fast as I could. It took me a little bit longer, as I detoured home first from the hospital to change out of my stained uniform. By the time I got here she'd left," Eve whispers. "What the hell am I going to do? I've got Ed's parents round for Sunday lunch." She drops her head in her hands. "God – what am I saying? Who cares about bloody lunch when your mum's... Sorry, I didn't mean that."

"What did she say? Will she be back later? She hasn't gone for long, has she?"

"I honestly don't know. I don't think so, but she didn't say." Eve sniffs and wipes her nose on a piece of kitchen roll. "I feel so bad. She's a single mum, full-time carer and seamstress. And she still misses your dad so much. I don't know how she manages, because she's always working."

Guilt silences me. Mum's always running around after me and Jake, and the hum of her sewing machine often lulls me to sleep at night. She never stops. "She's just having a day off, yes?"

"I guess." Eve shakes her head.

I hear the doubt in her voice.

"I feel just as bad. I mean, I'm living with her." A huge

16

lump forms in my throat. I feel terrible. So much for me trying to be the perfect daughter; working hard at school, focusing on my art portfolio, never getting home late, when I should have been helping Mum out more to make life easier. Why can't I get it right?

Jake pushes his plate to the other side of the table. "Stop talking! He doesn't like this bag. He wants the pink one."

There are beads of sweat on Jake's forehead.

I push down the lump in my throat and get all practical, like Mum does when Jake gets agitated. "Hey, Jake, I'll get your other bag in a sec," I say to him, then turn back to Eve. "We can manage on our own today, Eve, no problem. Can't we, Jake?"

"No problem. Can Jake see the boats?"

"Of course!" I tell him. "Mum totally deserves a day off."

Eve's voice cracks as she lowers her voice again to speak to me. "Honestly, I don't know if it is just a day, Maudie. I don't know what's going on – she hasn't texted me or anything since she called. Where could she have gone? I'm really worried about her."

I am too, as it isn't like Mum at all. I swallow hard to stop myself crying. "I'm going to check her bedroom. There might be some sort of clue in there as to where she's gone." My voice wavers. I know I'm clutching at straws.

Eve swallows hard, her eyes glassy. "Maybe. Don't get your hopes up, sweetie."

"I have to check." I hear the desperation in my voice.

"Jake wants Marmite." He pushes the jar towards me.

"I'll do that now." Eve scrapes her chair back, eager to keep busy.

"Love it or hate it," Jake booms at her.

"Yuck – I hate Marmite." Eve laughs.

"Jake and Maudie love it." He lifts his hand up to high-five me as I go past. We smack them together.

I walk out of the kitchen and stand at the bottom of the stairs, afraid to go up. "Mum?"

There's no answer, of course, but I still climb each step one at a time and linger outside her bedroom door, which is open just a crack. I knock, just in case. But the silence tells me what I already know.

CHAPTER 4

Jake

Aunty Eve's in my house. I want her to go home. She doesn't listen to me. She didn't put cold water in my tea. My tongue is hot and burny. Ow!

Mum isn't here. She's gone out. Me and Maudie can go and find her. I'm good at hide and seek.

CHAPTER 5

Maudie

My eyes scan the room for any clue as to where Mum might be. There's a horrible air of desolation in here.

She left in a hurry. Dad's T-shirt that she wears at night is lying in a heap on the floor, and the top drawer of her pine chest is open, with a pair of tights hanging over the edge. Mum hates mess, but even her bed isn't made. I grab my phone from my pocket and press Mum. It goes straight to voicemail. I'm hurt she doesn't answer and chuck my phone on the bed. That's when I notice a piece of folded paper on one of the pillows, with my name on it. I snatch it up.

I know you'll understand this when you're older, Maudie, but I can't stay here any more. I'm sorry to be leaving you and Jake, but I can't keep trying to make sense of what happened to your dad. I'm so tired. Take care of each other while I'm gone. Sorry.
Mum xx

Sorry again. She must have planned leaving last night. How could she not tell us?

And how long will she be gone for? Today? A couple of days? She wouldn't leave us for longer, would she? What she's written makes me scared she won't come back for ages.

What if she's not planning to come back at all? No, I can't let myself think that. Of course she'll come home soon.

I look on the back of the paper. Nothing. I flip it back over and read it again. I stare at the words, which start to merge into each other, then separate again.

Mum walks out on us and this is all we get?

I screw the note up into a tight ball and hurl it on the floor. It lands pathetically on the rug, so I kick it hard, my emotions overwhelming me.

I scan the room for any signs of how long Mum might be gone. I only see a couple of empty hangers in the wardrobe – that's good, she can't be planning on being away too long after all. But then I notice her silver suitcase with the wonky wheel has gone from the top of the wardrobe. This is not just a day trip.

I hear Eve calling my name. I grab the screwed-up note off the floor and make my way back to the kitchen.

Eve sees the expression on my face and snatches the note from my hand, scans it and looks at me in horror. "Shit – shit!"

"Uh-oh. She said 'shit'. Derrick says you mustn't swear." Jake shakes his head from side to side. "Uh-oh."

"Fuck." Eve sinks back down on her chair.

"Uh-oh uh-oh uh-oh. Fuck. Uh-oh uh-oh."

I snatch the note back and rip it in half in a sudden fury. Then I'm really upset I've destroyed it. My anger deflates like a punctured balloon, and I feel myself sag.

"Oh dear, Maudie's broken it up. That's naughty," Jake tuts. "Maudie didn't make a leaflet."

"This isn't happening. Where's Mum gone?"

"He doesn't know. He doesn't like it. Why's Maudie sad?" Jake looks at me, confused.

I take a deep, deep breath. "I'm alright, Jake, just a bit upset. Don't worry, Mum will be back soon." I quickly swipe a tear from my face.

He frowns. "Don't be upset, Jake's here."

"That's so lovely, Jake." Eve's smile wobbles as she says it.

I slump in a chair and bury my face in my arms. Eve wraps her arm round my back. This time last Sunday we were heading off to the bowling alley. We were happy, or so I thought.

I go straight through the automatic doors after Liv, Mum and Jake. He's talking at the top of his voice because he's excited. He marches up to the girl at the ticket booth, who's slightly distracted by the noise. She smiles at Jake and says a cheery hello.

"HELLO!" he booms back, which gives Liv the giggles and sets us all off, including the ticket girl. Jake looks very pleased with himself.

Mum sorts the tickets while Liv and I head over to the lanes with Jake. The overpowering smell of popcorn, burgers and sweaty bodies hits us.

"God, it smells like my brother's bedroom in here." Liv wrinkles her nose up in disgust. "I can't wait until next year and freedom."

"It's going to be the best. Let's hope we get a place on the foundation course at Saint Martins. Then we have to think about where we're going to live in London."

"It's so expensive," Liv says gloomily.

"We can find part-time jobs." Nothing is going to ruin our dream of art college.

Tinny pop music blares out over the speakers, alongside the occasional, "Strike!" and a loud PWOCK as the pins explode when the ball hits them. Jake usually hates confusing noise, but he loves it here. I scan the rows and see our empty lane at the end.

"Hey, Jake, there are some of your friends from school."

I turn him in their direction. Jake raises his arm in a salute to them, and his classmate Sam, who is about to bowl, forgets to let go of the ball and stumbles part way along the lane before dropping the ball, which slowly rolls to a stop in front of the skittles. He gets a huge cheer from his friends and the lane next door. Jake picks up his own ball, gallops down the lane, flattens all the skittles at once and bellows, "STRIKE!" at the top of his voice. You can barely hear the warning over the loudspeaker, everyone is clapping so loudly.

"Hey, Jake, you haven't got your slippers on!" I remind him.

He ignores me, he's enjoying himself too much.

Once Liv has recovered from nearly wetting herself, she nudges me with her elbow.

"Oh god, that guy who asked you out a few weeks ago is here!" She points over to the cafe when I look blank. "You know, the one who told you to feel his jacket, as it was 'boyfriend material'." She makes a retching noise.

"Don't point at him! He'll think I'm interested."

Liv snorts. "In his dreams. I can't believe he said that."

We both collapse with laughter again.

Mum comes over with our bowling shoes.

"What are you two giggling about?"

"That guy, with the world's worst pick-up line. Remember him?"

"Yes, I felt a bit sorry for him actually."

I raise my eyebrows heavenward. "Only you, Mum."

Mum ignores me. "Let's get these on, Jake, then we can play."

Jake refuses to wear bowling shoes, so we bring his slippers.

"No, Maudie do it." He pushes Mum's hand away.

"Please," Mum reminds Jake.

"PLEEEEEASE!" Jake yodels at her, then pats her head. "Jake was funny."

"Very funny," Mum says wryly, passing me Jake's slippers.

"Sit your butt on that chair then," I tell him.

"Ha ha! Maudie said 'butt'."

Once we're sorted, we grab the end lane and get set up. Jake takes bowling very seriously, whereas Mum, who's hopeless at ever getting a strike, tries to be funny and always does some silly walk from an oldie TV show called Monty Python's Flying Circus, which apparently she and Dad used to crease up over. It's so cringy. Even Liv, who adores my mum, pretends she's not with her. Sometimes it makes Jake laugh, other times he acts as though he doesn't know her too.

Jake starts the game and manages a strike with his second ball. Liv manages to throw the ball down the gutter and I knock six down. Then Mum launches into her funky-chicken strut up the lane, swinging her ball, which gets her a warning over the loudspeaker to get off the lane or she'll be removed.

Luckily Sam causes a commotion by standing right next to his bowling pins and refusing to budge, so Emma Jones, Sam's girlfriend, gets very cross with him and threatens to go out with Jamie Manson if she can't play. We all double up with laughter when Sam moves away from the skittles immediately.

Mum looks round at us all, laughing too. She grabs me and gives me a hug, then everyone else wants one too. Mum can't stop smiling.

I feel a hand rubbing my back and Eve's soft voice saying, "It's alright, darling, we'll get through this."

"Mum seemed happier last weekend than she had for ages. I just don't get what happened, Eve." Or was it just that me and Liv were so happy, and I didn't notice how Mum was really feeling? "We haven't talked as much recently, but that was because of my exams and Mum's work building up."

Well, that's what I'd thought. If I'm honest, her moods had been a bit erratic, sometimes swinging from totally over-the-top happy to hardly speaking. I'd been too wrapped up in discussing our chosen art foundation course with Liv to pay much attention.

Eve is checking her phone for messages. I grab mine and see if Mum has texted me.

"No message from your mum," she tells me.

"Me neither." I want to call her but don't want to be rejected again.

"Oh god, Maudie," Eve groans. She holds up her phone to me, showing the date.

"Today's your mum and dad's wedding anniversary – March fifteenth. It went right out my head. She must have been really struggling."

"And it's Dad's birthday soon." Suddenly it's all too much. I burst into tears.

"Oh no, Maudie's crying again. Don't cry, girl, here you are." Jake hands me his half-eaten piece of toast. "Jake make you better."

"Th...thank you."

As I take it, Eve's phone pings and lights up. She snatches it up.

"It's your mum."

"What does she say?" I try and grab the phone from her.

"Hang on." Eve scans the screen. "That she's okay, but she needs time."

"Just that?"

Eve nods miserably. I turn my own phone over.

There's nothing for me.

CHAPTER 6

Jake

I looked for Mum. I couldn't find her. I didn't find Dad. He never came back. That was lots of time ago. It made me full of sad. Then the bees came. Inside my head. They wouldn't leave me alone.

Buzzzzzz.

Sometimes I can't stop them.

I want Mum back. She knows what to do. Aunty Eve doesn't. I tried to tell her. She wouldn't listen. She got soap in my eyes. I broke the shower. I didn't mean to. The monster in my head told me to do it.

Maudie watched television with me. We saw bats. I like animals. They don't hurt you. Then Maudie cleaned my teeth. The brush makes my teeth prickle. I put the toothbrush down the toilet. That monster is very bad.

I'm going to school tomorrow. Derrick's my teacher. On Thursday we sat in the music room, but we didn't sing. A funny lady came. She had orange hair. She said my name. I didn't look at her. She had a green bobble hat. I don't like green. Aunty Eve was there. I couldn't see Mum.

That lady is coming back. Derrick said I'm having a holiday. I don't want to stay in that lady's house. It's too big. Eve said it's lovely. It's not my house. I'm going to push it out my head. I'm not going there. Who will chase the monster away?

CHAPTER 7

Maudie

Izzy, Paz, Will and Theo are walking home with me and Liv after school. We've finished early as we have study leave. Their shouts and hoots of laughter hurt my head. The boys are trying to see how many Pringles they can cram into their mouths at once. They think it's hilarious. Liv and Theo are deep in conversation, probably planning their first proper date, and Izzy is desperately trying to get Will's attention. He's winning the crisp competition though. I feel I'm on the outside of them all, looking in, wondering how I'll ever be part of it all again now Mum's gone. It's just under two weeks since she left.

Izzy elbows me in the side. "Why didn't you say anything in English today?"

"Yeah, thanks to you," Paz teases, "we actually had to do some work!"

I feel like answering back, *Isn't it obvious?* but I don't have the energy. My friends were sympathetic when I told them what happened, but they can't really understand how my mum leaving affects me and Jake. I wish Liv did English with us, she totally gets it.

She hooks her arm through mine. "You okay?"

"Missing Mum," I whisper. "And Dad too actually."

"Didn't your dad die over two years ago, though?" Izzy butts in, then realizes what she's just said and looks horrified. "I'm sorry, I didn't mean…"

I feel like she's slapped me. Doesn't she get it?

"The pain never goes away, Izzy, it feels as raw as the day he died," I try to explain. "We were just learning to live with it, and now Mum's gone too."

Izzy sounds upset when she says, "I get it, I really do, and I didn't mean you shouldn't care any more." The over-earnest way she says it doesn't sound like she gets it at all.

I can feel the tears threatening to burst out. "You think it will get easier, b-but—"

Liv takes my arm and pulls me away. Izzy is about to say something else, but Liv shakes her head – No – at her.

I start to cry. I suddenly feel so alone.

Liv shuts her bedroom door and makes me sit on her bed.

"You should have stayed at home today. One more day wouldn't have made any difference, especially being today. We're mostly revising at school anyway."

I nod. "I know."

It's Dad's birthday. March twenty-eighth. He'd have been fifty. A milestone that must have been so apparent to Mum. I keep checking my phone to see if she has contacted me. She must know how I feel today, since she must be feeling the same herself: heartbroken. I feel in my pocket for the note she left us when she disappeared. I stuck it back together with Sellotape.

"Why don't you phone her?" Liv always knows what I'm thinking.

"I'm going to, it's just I was hoping she'd call me."

"I'm sure she'll call you later."

"She would've called or messaged by now if she was going to."

Liv sits next to me and rests her hand on mine.

"I just wish I didn't feel so alone – you're the only person who understands any of this. The other guys are great, but I'm sure they think I'm some sad loser. I tried telling Izzy how I felt but I could see she was still thinking *What's the big deal?*"

"She didn't mean it – she just opens her mouth and says the first thing that comes into her head. And the other guys don't think you're a loser, they just don't know what to say, that's all. Perhaps if you properly opened up to them they'd understand better?"

I shake my head. "I'm scared if I tell them how I really feel, I'll totally fall apart."

"You know, it's okay *not* to be okay, Maudie. You don't have to be Miss Perfect all the time." When I don't respond she nudges me with her foot. "Don't ignore me."

I sit up on her bed and pull her hand-knitted wattle-stitch throw around me. It took her six months to make, and no one is allowed anywhere near it except for me, and only when I'm in a crisis.

"Maudie! Look at me."

Her blue eyes hold mine. I look away first but then straight back. I owe it to Liv to be honest, as she's been there whenever I've needed her. She's stayed at my house a few times in the two weeks since Mum left. She's listened to me talk about it late into the night, even when I knew she wanted to sleep. Liv's always been there for me.

I explain the best way I can. "I have to keep it together. I have to be strong for Jake. I can't fall apart now."

"Mauds, you can with me." She wraps her arms around me.

"I know it's been tough for Mum, but how could she ditch us? Me and Jake are hurting too. Some days the grief is unbearable. Sometimes I wake up and I've forgotten Dad died and I'm happy again. Then I remember – and it hurts so much it's almost a physical pain."

"I know, Maudie, I know." Liv hugs me tighter.

"It never gets better, not like people say. You just learn to live with it. People expect you to switch off your emotions after a certain amount of time and act like it never happened.

33

But I want Dad back, Liv, and I want my mum. You know, I'm not even sure what Jake understands about Dad dying, even though I talked to him about it. But it's totally messed me up, so it must've done the same to him?"

Liv nods. "For sure."

I rest my head on her shoulder. I remember the morning I talked with Jake so clearly.

Night turns to day, as the sky gets brighter. The rising sun tints the edges of the clouds pink. How can it keep rising after what's happened? Birdsong and the occasional barking of a faraway dog break my thoughts up.

Jake is sitting up in bed, flicking through a family photo album that I made for him since Dad died. I still can't get my head around it. The pain is so raw I feel as though my heart has been crushed. One minute Dad was there, the next he was gone. I didn't realize cancer could work so fast. I thought he'd have longer.

"Hey, Jake, you okay?" I say this softly, as we don't want to wake Mum up. She's asleep for the first time in three days.

"Dad's not here. He's in Jake's book." He holds the album up to show me. "Jake doesn't know where he's gone."

I've been trying to work out the best way I can explain it to Jake. "Dad isn't going to be here any more, Jake. He died." My voice cracks, but I breathe slowly in and out to stop myself sobbing. "Do you remember when you grew that tall sunflower, that was bigger than Dad?"

34

"Jake won the competition." He claps his hands, then stops. "Oh, Jake mustn't wake his mum up."

"You did win it. Do you remember that after a while the flower went brown and dried up – and died – it was all gone. All living things grow, and every living thing dies. Then it's not there any more. Like your sunflower."

"Jake's flower went away. Mum said the mud took it back. Jake was sad."

"You were. People die too, sometimes before they're meant to."

"Jake doesn't know what die is."

I suddenly feel overwhelmed. I know Mum tried to explain it to Jake, but he just thought she meant Dad was playing hide and seek and kept looking for him in the places Dad used to hide from him.

"Dying means you stop breathing." I place my hand on his chest. "You stop talking and moving and feeling. Then the people left behind – you, me and Mum – are sad and lonely. Are you feeling sad about Dad and…and maybe a bit lost without him? I am."

"Jake's sad. Jake's dad isn't here. He's gone away. When Jake played hide and seek, he found his dad. Jake can't find him any more. No one wants to play with Jake except Maudie. His mum's too tired."

"Mum has so much to do now she hasn't got Dad. He didn't mean to go away – he loved you so much. He got sick, very sick, and couldn't get better."

"Is Jake's dad coming back?"

I can't say the word "No"; my throat is rigid with grief. I sob silently into my hands.

Jake hugs me from behind. He doesn't say anything, but holds me for the longest time ever and lets me cry. Jake doesn't like hugs most of the time because he says it makes his skin full of prickles.

After a while Jake pulls back, then he hands me his photo book.

"Maudie have Dad. He's in Jake's book. Maudie can see him." He places the book in my hands and rests his own on my head. "Jake will take Maudie's sad."

Did I help Jake? I wish I knew. I only know he helped me. I hold Liv's arm tight and let out a big sigh.

"Mum going means I have to be the strong one now."

Liv makes me look at her again. "You're not the adult here." She rests her forehead against mine.

All I can do is nod, because I suddenly want more than anything not to have to be responsible. Sometimes being seventeen and not-quite an adult is overwhelming. It's so hard trying to work out who you want to be and how to deal with stuff. Without Mum it's so much worse. I feel like a shaded-in pencil drawing of myself that's been rubbed out, so that all that's left is my outline.

"God, those first two days after Mum left were so awful. I still feel bad that Eve and I had to lie to Jake and say Mum'd gone on holiday – but how was I supposed to explain to him that she walked out on us?"

Liv shakes her head. "You can't, but you've been his rock, keeping him in his routine. At least you know your mum's safe."

"I guess, though I'm still so angry that she hasn't contacted *me*, her own daughter."

I twist Liv's blanket around my finger. Liv untwists it and smooths it flat.

"I know how much that must hurt."

"I'm the one who's always been there for Mum, not Eve, so why hasn't she messaged me? She's rubbed me out, just like that. Who does that?" It bursts out of me before I can stop myself, and I feel Liv tense up. "God, I'm sorry, Liv. I'm so wrapped up in myself."

Liv shakes her head. "You're the last person on earth wrapped up in themselves. And you were totally there for me when my dad left. At least I can see my dad."

"It's all such shit, isn't it? You know what really hurts – that after only a fortnight we've already become sort of resigned to the fact she won't be coming back any time soon. Jake is up and down but coping and Eve has managed to get into a routine with us now. She still doesn't get stuff, like Jake's special bags are only to be used by him, though. He freaked out when she was about to pop down to the corner shop for some milk and had his red bag on her arm. She was so cross with herself.

"Eve's been brilliant mostly though – she hasn't done any night shifts this week and has taken Jake to school on her way to work and picked him up most days too. I help out the rest of the time. You'd think with her being a midwife she wouldn't mind taking Jake to the loo and stuff, but she *always* gets out of that. I guess she has enough of that at work."

Liv grimaces. "Can't say I blame her – imagine how many bums she must wipe in a week."

For some reason the thought of that creases us both up and every time we try and get a grip, we start laughing again.

A loud knock on Liv's bedroom door finally stops us. Her mum shouts from the other side.

"Don't forget you're picking your brother up from school soon, Livvy! I've got to drop Mrs Thomas at the surgery. Good to hear you girls enjoying yourselves."

"That's such a mum thing to say." Liv rolls her eyes.

"I heard that." Liv's mum opens the door and pops her head round. "How did the revision go, girls?"

"Fine!" we both chorus.

"How are you doing, Maudie?"

"Not so—"

"You can shut the door, Mother," Liv orders her, which her mum does with a sigh. The door clicks shut. "Mum, I know you're still lurking there, just go downstairs."

"Don't be late for your brother," she shouts through the door.

"I won't be, because you keep reminding me! Why can't he walk home on his own?"

"Just do it please, Livvy."

We hear her run down the stairs.

Liv grimaces at me. "You can come with me, Mauds, or stay here while I'm gone. I won't be too long."

"Thanks, but I promised Jake I'd be home in time to have his drink and biscuit with him after school. He gets upset when he comes home and Mum's not there. I hate it too."

Liv untangles herself from me and stands up. "Your mum will be back. She needs time to sort her head out, I guess, but she loves you both too much to leave you for good. End of."

I stand up too and grab my old-man tweed jacket I wear with the sleeves rolled up. "I couldn't cope without you, Liv."

"We couldn't cope without each other." Liv yanks on her boots with the four-inch track soles. "Call me later. I'm just working on my portfolio for college."

"I won't call until late, as I'm on dinner duty and helping get Jake to bed."

I give her a goodbye hug.

"You need to prepare your portfolio too, Mauds. Have you even started designing your evening gowns yet?"

"No."

"Maudie – you can't give up on yourself. Those fantasy ball gowns were incredible. Even Theo was gobsmacked."

"I know, I know."

It's not like I want to give up on my dream of becoming a top fashion designer, but I'm kind of distracted at the moment. I pick my school bag up off the floor and head out the door.

"Try not to strangle Seb on the way home," I call over my shoulder.

Her pillow thumps me on the back.

CHAPTER 8

Jake

Eve says she's taking me to see that lady. With the orange hair. We're going to her house. I don't want to go. I'm going to have biscuits with Maudie. At our house in Shiplake. She won't know where I am. I'm not getting in Eve's car. I'm going home. To my house. I can run fast. I can run down the road. You can't catch me!

CHAPTER 9

Maudie

I could go straight home but I don't want to yet. I should try and catch up on my schoolwork – I still haven't handed in my English coursework, though Mrs Gould is being really nice about it. The truth is, I feel as upset as Jake about going home when Mum isn't there, so I head across the road to the park and sit down by the pond. The bench is cold and damp against my legs, but I don't care.

I stare at my phone screen, willing it to ring and be Mum. Before I have time to think, I find her number and press it. It cuts off immediately. Oh Mum.

To stop myself from bawling my eyes out I watch a little girl running round the edge of the lake. In the distance I can hear the squeals of kids on the swings and slides, and I can just make out two bigger boys clinging to the rope on the zip wire. I recognize them from school. They're not sixth formers and must be skiving. The wire swings wildly as they judder across the length of the playground. Out the corner of my eye I see the little girl stumble and her dad just manages to grab her before she falls in the water. He hugs her tight as she cries on his shoulder. I swallow a lump watching them. I remember Dad comforting me when I'd hurt myself, and feeling warm and safe. I wonder what he'd make of everything that's going on with us now.

We watched Dad fade away before our eyes. He'd done the typical bloke thing and ignored any symptoms. That went on for months, until Mum finally persuaded him to go to the doctor, who prodded and poked him. What set off alarm signals for the doctor was Dad's weight loss. Ironically Dad had been pleased about that, as he'd got a bit chubby around the middle, from midnight snacking when he was up with Jake at four in the morning.

Before long Mum had to get a nurse in after school and at weekends to help manage with caring for both of them. She hated that.

In the last few months, Dad was often so ill he couldn't get out of bed, let alone take care of Jake, and nothing usually stopped him doing that. Jake couldn't handle it at all – not the cancer, or the fact our dad was dying, or that he was out of his routine; not any of it. He tuned in on everyone's pain and had meltdown after meltdown. I was pretty certain it was because he couldn't make words for his own pain, but Jake definitely got that Dad was no longer the dad he knew and was fading away.

We all got used to dodging missiles.

Jake rarely mentions Dad since he died. That used to really upset me, but now I think I understand; he's boxed Dad away somewhere inside his head and sealed it down with extra-strong black tape, only to be opened in private Jake head space. Because Dad was the one who helped him make sense of his world. Dad was his everything.

He was my everything too.

I remember getting up one night to check on Dad when he was very ill, because I was terrified I might wake up in the morning and he'd be gone. I went into Mum and Dad's bedroom and listened to Dad breathing. He looked so peaceful it was hard to believe anything was wrong. I couldn't bear it, so I crept into Jake's room and lay down next to him, as I didn't want to be on my own. I buried my face in his pillow and silently shook. I felt a weight on my head and Jake's hand stroked my hair. He let it stay there, warm and solid. "Girl be okay," he said, "Jake take care of her."

"You alright?" A lady pushing a buggy peers at me anxiously.

I wipe my eyes, embarrassed I was crying in public. "Yes, thanks, I'm fine – really."

"If you're sure." She hesitates, but a squeal from her little boy, who's waking up now she's stopped moving, makes her walk on.

I glance at my watch. It's two-fifty and Jake will be home

from school at three. I've been here for forty-five minutes just because I couldn't face going home to a house that's haunted by people who are no longer there.

I throw my bag over my shoulder and jog across the grass and around the lake. A flock of crows breaks free from the trees, charcoal cinders spiralling in the sky. The wind ripples the water, bobbing the ducks up and down on the waves. I watch them, searching in my brain for any clues about Mum as I run.

I know it isn't just about their anniversary. For a start, Mum said something when we were eating lunch together on that last Saturday, before she went and sat in the shed for hours. I didn't register it then. But I do now.

"Why don't you go to the cinema with your friends tonight, Maudie?"

"I'm fine, Mum. I like our film nights together. I want to be here with you."

"I really don't mind. You need to be with your friends, not sat at home with your boring, useless mother on a weekend. I'm ruining your life."

I sigh dramatically. "Don't be silly. I'm not even going to listen to that nonsense."

"See! You're even sounding like me. It's not right."

"Mum! I don't want to go out. I'm happy at home with you and Jake."

Deep down inside, a tiny part of me thinks that I would like to be with my friends. But I can't abandon Mum. She lost her husband, her best friend and the father to her children. She needs me.

So I make my voice upbeat when I say, "Sure, I like going out with the gang, but it all gets too complicated, and Paz has been making it clear he would like to be more than friends – not that he's being pushy or anything."

"Wouldn't you like to go out with Paz? He's very cute."

I raise my eyebrows at her choice of words. "I like him, a lot, but just as a friend."

Mum looks at me for a bit. "Are you sure about that? I'd...I'd hate to think you were closing yourself off because of me. You don't need to be here looking after me all the time. Why don't we talk about it?"

"No thanks, Mum, I don't need to."

"Really?" She looks sad. "We used to talk."

I don't think I even answered, just rolled my eyes at her. I didn't want Mum worrying about me. Now I wish I'd talked more; maybe it could have stopped her leaving us.

I run the whole of the rest of the way home. By the time I get there I'm sweating buckets. I practically fall through the front door.

"Jake, you home? Sorry I'm late."

He doesn't answer. He normally shouts out to me,

"Maudie's back. Hello, girl." And I go in and hug him, if he's feeling like he wants one, and ask him how his day went. But Jake's not in the kitchen.

I go out into the hall. "EVE!"

She doesn't reply. She should be here. They both should. The house feels troubled by its emptiness.

CHAPTER 10

Jake

"That's not Jake's house. You said we could go to Jake's house. Jake wants to see his sister."

I'm frightened. I can't see Maudie. I can't see Mum. Who will help me? My head is full of bees.

Buzz-buzz-buzz-buzz.

Make them stop. The monster's getting angry. The bees are stinging him.

"Why don't you come out of the car, and we can sort everything out. Let me do your belt."

Aunty Eve's face is too near me. I don't know what she's saying. The bees are too loud. "Don't touch him! Leave him alone!"

"It's alright, Jake, you do it yourself then. Remember we came here before? Look at me – you liked Wendy's cat and gave her a treat, yes? Hey, it's okay. Take a deep breath in... and out...in and out. That's it."

"Jake can't go in that house."

"Hello there, Jake, Eve."

"Wendy, hi, I could do with a hand. We had a bit of an incident at school. Jake did a runner, but Derrick managed to catch him and calm him down."

"Hello, Jake, how lovely to see you – shall I take your bag for you?"

"DON'T TOUCH HIS BAG! GET OFF HIS BAG!"

"Oh, Jake – NO! Ow! Oh, sweetie, don't pull your hair out!"

The monster told me. The monster told me to do it.

"Jake! Look who's here to see you. She's purring – that means she's happy. Why don't you come in and give the cat some treats? That's it, take your time. Nice deep breaths."

"He doesn't know. Jake can't eat them."

"No, I've got some cake for us, and I have two mugs of tea ready for you."

"She's a nice lady."

"She is, Jake," says Eve. "You follow Wendy and I'll get your suitcase."

"Jake doesn't need a suitcase."

That lady is smiling at me.

"It's not for long, not long at all. I can't wait to hear what you've done at school today."

"Not long." Those bees are going away. They're going back to sleep. "When Jake's had his tea, he can find Maudie."

CHAPTER 11

Maudie

I don't understand why Jake isn't here. Eve would've told me if they were going somewhere else after school. I can't hear the television, but I go into the sitting room anyway. I want Jake to be there, watching *Extreme Railway Journeys*, his bag slung over the arm of his chair.

The empty space weighs in the pit of my stomach.

When Dad first bought it, Jake's chair rounded up into a mound in the middle and you felt you were going to slip off. The dip there now marks it as my brother's chair. The material on the right arm is lighter where he hangs the handles of his bag. A small sound makes me turn around. Eve wavers in the doorway. Her eyes are darting round the room, and she passes her car keys from hand to hand.

My stomach drops.

"Where's Jake?"

"It's...it's for the best—"

"I asked you where my brother is, Eve."

I'm surprised at how unemotional my voice sounds, because I have an overwhelming sense of dread and my heart is pounding.

"It's only until your mum comes back. He's just in specialist foster care until then." Her last words come out in a rush.

I stare at her. I wonder if she's spoken to me in a different language, because her words aren't making any sense. It can't be true. I thought we were doing okay, even if we were muddling through.

I can't speak. Neither does Eve.

The strangeness of the silence is frightening. There's a sense of unreality as I pick up my school bag, wait for her to move away from the doorway, and walk through it, unable to even be near her.

Then I walk back again, unable to leave, anger burning inside me.

"You can't make this decision. I want to see him now." Still she doesn't say anything. "I hate you."

She flinches.

"You didn't even tell me. How could you? You have to get him back. He won't be able to cope, Jake needs his routine. He isn't safe anywhere else. Where. Is. He?"

Her eyes brim with tears, but I don't care. I can't bear to think of Jake in a strange place, thinking he's been abandoned by everyone. I can't seem to get enough air in to breathe.

"How did this happen without me knowing?" I take a

step towards her. Eve steps backwards. "So, you were just pretending to be all nice, acting as though you cared. Of course! You once told Mum and Dad that Jake should go into care, didn't you?"

"That was years ago, before I understood."

"Oh yeah – so why are you doing it now? On Dad's birthday."

Her mouth drops open. She looks horrified. "Oh god, I forgot."

"That says it all. You finally got what you wanted. Dad hated that you said Jake should go into care. He didn't want you around, and Mum only forgave you because you're her sister. How could you do this? What sort of a monster betrays her own family?"

She recoils at the word monster. My heart beats so hard I think I'm going to pass out.

"I'm not a monster. I know you're angry with me, but I had no choice, and I am his guardian when your mum's not around. I'm not the best person to look after Jake. My night shifts are making it too difficult to give you the time you both need. I'm still going to be here with you but Jake's better off with someone who really understands his needs and can take care of him properly."

"Maybe I don't want you here now. We were doing fine. Don't you get it? Jake's not a burden and you're making him sound like he is. Jake's loving and caring and fun. That's what the world, and you, don't see."

Her voice breaks. "I, I…you don't think I really wanted to do this, do you?"

I fling my bag across the floor in frustration. "Then why did you?" I bark at her. "You should have asked me."

"There wasn't time. I made the decision to do this quickly and quietly, with the least fuss for us all. I knew you'd be distressed but I didn't want Jake to hear us arguing – it would have upset him too much."

"Like you'd know what would upset him," I spit at her. "Putting him in care will kill him."

Eve looks shocked, her face flushing red. "That's a little dramatic, Maudie. It's only for a short time."

I shake my head in disbelief. "It might as well be for ever for Jake. He doesn't understand time, remember."

"I couldn't miss any more work, Maudie, I – we, me and Ed, need the money."

"Is that all you care about?" I shake my head in disbelief.

"Maudie, this is not a decision I took lightly, but the bottom line is you're not old enough to legally take care of Jake and I'm the only adult here. It's only until your mum gets back, and you can see him as soon as he's settled. His foster carer is very experienced."

"She's never met him!" I wail.

Eve glances uncomfortably at me, then at the floor.

"Oh, she has, hasn't she? I can see from your face. What, at his school?"

She nods.

"You worked fast. How did you manage that?"

Eve doesn't answer. It feels like a kick to the guts, realizing that all the supposedly responsible adults in my and Jake's lives have been plotting behind our backs. "I want to see him *now*."

"You can't, you have to wait until he's had time to get used to things. Seeing you will unsettle him."

"Just tell me where he is. He's my brother and you can't stop me."

"I know how much this is hurting you, but you've got to think of Jake."

"What? *I've* got to think of Jake? If you'd ever bothered to spend any proper time with my brother, you'd know this will be torture for him. Don't you get it? His routine keeps him safe. It stops him being terrified if he knows what to expect. The world's too bright and too loud for Jake. It hurts his ears, his head, his *skin*. He's *told* me. Because I bothered to ask him. It must be like someone permanently scraping their nails down a blackboard, for him."

My voice is getting louder and louder, so I stop to calm myself down. I want Eve to hear what I'm saying. And if I'm honest, my reaction isn't just about my fears for Jake either. I'm scared of being separated from him. I've already lost both Mum and Dad, so I can't bear to lose him too. I need to get through to Eve.

"Eve, how would you feel if you were ripped from everything and everyone you knew and put in a strange place? It's impossible to imagine what it would do to you, let alone my brother. I need to be with him, can't you see that? He'll think I've abandoned him too."

Her face flushes an even deeper red. "It's all sorted, Maudie. He'll be fine, I promise."

There's nothing more I can say. I shove my way past her and run upstairs to my bedroom and lock the door. I fling myself onto my bed and let the tears take over. I feel like my heart is breaking.

After a while I hear Eve come up the stairs and tentatively knock on my door. "Can I come in? Please? We need to talk."

I don't answer. The handle turns but Eve can't get in. "Maudie, please let me in. Can't we talk?"

"No."

She goes back downstairs.

My phone rings and I scrabble in the gloom to find it. It's caught up in my duvet and by the time I get to it, it's rung off.

My phone pings.

Hey M how are you doing?

Eve's put Jake into care

WTF!!!

My phone immediately rings again. It's Liv and suddenly I desperately need to hear her voice.

55

"Didn't Eve say anything to you at all?" Liv cuts straight in.

"No, I got home, and Jake had g-gone." I sob down the phone.

"I'm coming round."

"Please."

"I can be with you in ten minutes."

She ends the call. I flick through my phone albums at some recent pics of me, Mum and Jake. I try to spot any signs that Mum was about to break down – it's becoming a bit of an obsession. She looks a bit strained in the one at Jake's Christmas show even though in my memory she was so happy. Jake refused to wear his Santa hat for the show, but he'd allowed his teacher to tie a bit of tinsel around his waist. Then during the performance Jake suddenly decided he was going to sing "Happy Birthday" to Jesus, at the top of his voice. The audience loved it and Mum was laughing so much tears were streaming down her face.

The front doorbell rings. I hear Liv talking to Eve and it sounds tense, then the sound of her footsteps thundering up the stairs. I unlock the door and she comes straight in, slams the door shut and wraps her arms around me.

When she lets me go, her face is stony.

"I can't believe Eve did this. I told her that."

"I know, right? She must have been sneaking around for days now, *knowing* she was going to get him taken away. Gave me some crap about how she's the adult and I had no say in it. I'm eighteen in August! Like she could ever know what's best for Jake! I hate her for this."

We sit on the bed, Liv squashing up next to me. Her long legs stick out in front of her. "Poor Jake. When can you see him?"

"Hang on." I blow my nose, so I can speak. "I can't, not until he's settled. Eve said it would be too upsetting for him – like ripping him from his home and family isn't upsetting."

"God, I can't imagine how that must feel."

"I bet Jake wakes up in his bedroom terrified because he doesn't know where he is. His whole routine has gone." I can't stop thinking about how Jake and I love drawing and often work together on a Saturday afternoon. I help him with his pictures, and he tells me if he likes my dress designs. Being apart feels unthinkable.

"Eve won't have put him with someone who doesn't understand, Mauds, surely?"

"Why are you defending her?"

"I'm not! I'm sorry, Maudie, I was only trying to make you feel better."

"I don't think anything can do that."

Liv's voice is small. "It's complete shite, Maudie. I wish there was something I could do."

But what can she do? Everything feels hopeless. The grief from losing Dad and then Mum leaving us was overwhelming and now Jake's gone. He was my reason for getting out of bed in the morning. It was comforting being with someone who was going through the same thing, even if he couldn't put it into words. Now I feel empty and helpless. How can I fix any of this?

"What are you thinking?"

Liv jolts me out of my thoughts.

"I'm losing everybody, Liv. I thought when Mum left it would be a day, maybe three at the most, but now it's been two weeks and I'm starting to think…what if she doesn't want to come back?"

Liv takes my hands in hers and fixes me with her intense stare, the one that's so fierce no one can argue with her. "Don't ever think that! It's not true – she'd lay down her life for you both and you know that. She's only gone because she had to. I don't know why, Maudie, but I know it isn't because she doesn't love you and Jake."

I go over Liv's words in my head, desperate to believe her, but where once I was so sure, now my confidence has crumbled.

"If only Dad was here, Liv, he'd handle things so much better. He would never abandon us."

We sit quietly for a bit, me with my head on Liv's shoulder.

"I'm really, really sorry, Maudie, I'm going to have to go. I've got a final driving practice with Mum before my test first thing in the morning, but I can easily cancel it—"

"Oh my god! I completely forgot it's tomorrow. Why didn't you remind me earlier?"

"You needed me."

"Thank you. What would I do without you?"

"Mum said she'd wait outside. I was going to text her if you wanted me to stay."

"That's so sweet of you but go and practise. You need it. Oh no! I didn't mean that the way it sounded."

Liv shoves me over, but she laughs. "We'll talk later." She hugs me tight again.

"Go!" I push her off me and she runs down the stairs.

A million layers of emotion billow around me. Liv left my door open, so I can hear Eve on her phone. I think she might be crying, but I don't care, I'm too devastated by what she's done.

It's turned dark in my room from the stormy clouds outside. Rain is being thrown against my window. I don't bother to put my lamp on. I pull my duvet over me and tuck my knees up to my chest. Whatever Eve says, he's my brother and I have to make sure he's okay.

So what am I going to do about it?

CHAPTER 12

Jake

I can't see my bus posters. They're in my old house. It's gone away. That lady is staring at me. I want her to stop. Her hair is very red. Red looks angry. I don't know what she said. I can't hear 'cause my head's gone fuzzy.

I'm shouting at her, "Let go of his hand, it's hurting him. Fuckofffuckofffuckoff!"

I mustn't say that word. It's very bad. My head is full of monster bees. They bite me. I can't get them out. *Buzz, buzz, buzz.* They live in this new house. I want them to stop.

I don't like it here. I can't find the loo. I made the floor all wet. "Never mind, Jake." The lady said that. She cleaned the wee up. She tried to hug me. I wouldn't let her. I sat by the telephone. Maudie didn't call me. My heart hurts. I can feel it. When Dad went away my head broke up.

CHAPTER 13

Maudie

I can see my breath in the air. It's the first of April but it's cold and I wrap my arms around myself to keep warm. I should have worn my coat, but I didn't think I'd need it in the car, forgetting Liv's ancient mini doesn't have any heating. We're having to keep the windows wound down too, or the whole car steams up. I don't care – Liv passing her driving test on Friday means freedom for us to do what we want to, without being reliant on anybody else, though she's still a bit nervous driving without an instructor.

It's nearly time for Jake's school to finish. We're staking it out, so we can follow him back to his foster home. It's three days since Jake went into care and I *have* to know he's okay. I can't bear the thought of sitting out another day at home without knowing my brother is alright. I have a plan, one which I hope Liv will help me with.

Liv winds her rainbow scarf tightly around her neck and slides down in her seat.

"How long?"

"About five minutes."

I study the group of people huddled outside the main doors of the school, all chatting to each other, but can't decide out of the new faces who his carer might be.

"Here he comes, Liv!"

She sits up straight, starts the engine up and gets ready to go. Jake comes through the doors. He looks tired and pale, and everything about him is slumped and subdued. He's holding his pink bag to his chest.

"He doesn't take his bag to school, Liv, why has he got it with him? It might get lost or nicked and then he'd be devastated. His carer clearly didn't read the notes I sent her about Jake's routine. I wonder if Eve even passed them on?"

Liv squeezes my hand. I see a middle-aged lady with red hair, a green bobble hat and quilted gilet go over to Jake.

Jake turns his face away and steps backwards.

"He doesn't want to go with her. He must hate this. It's not right, Liv."

The lady finally manages to persuade Jake to follow her. I wish I could hear what she's saying to him. A part of me wanted him to refuse; then I feel bad because I don't want him to be that unhappy. We watch as they walk down the street together and stop at a black four-by-four. It takes some time to get Jake in his seat, but she does eventually. She pulls out into the traffic.

Liv eases her foot off the clutch. Her knuckles are white from gripping the steering wheel. A vintage mini with no power steering isn't the easiest drive. Liv wouldn't listen though. She worked a Saturday job and sold her knitwear as much as she could last year, so she could afford her dream car – and it's her baby. I swear she'd park it next to her bed if she could.

Luckily, we just about manage to keep up with Jake's car, and twenty minutes later we pull in a few spaces up from the house that the car has turned into. It's huge compared to ours and their front garden is bigger than our back garden, with an enormous oak tree in the middle of the lawn. Under the tree is a bird-feeding station, exactly like our one at home. We stop in time to see Jake and his carer go through the pristine white front door.

"Now what?" Liv says.

"Can we wait a bit?"

"Isn't it a bit risky staying here? We might get seen. And you know where he is now, yes, and it looks okay?"

"Yes…but I want to see that *he's* okay…"

"That's impossible, Mauds." Liv's voice is full of concern. "Why—"

"Someone's coming out – it's Jake!"

"What's that in his hand?"

"I think it's a jug."

We both duck down in our seats, not wanting Jake to get upset if he sees us, but I carefully lift my head up, so I can just see Jake over the steering wheel. He's filling the bird feeder from the jug, which makes me want to cry; he does that every day at home. The carer *has* read the notes I sent for Jake then. I miss him so much.

As if he senses what I'm thinking, Jake lifts his head up and stares straight at me. It feels like a fist has slammed into my chest. He lets out a long wail that we can hear clearly through the open window.

Liv starts the engine. "He's seen you – I'll have to go!"

She pulls away from the kerb and puts her foot down. As we disappear around the corner, I can see Jake's foster carer rushing out to help Jake.

I feel terrible. I've made things worse for Jake – he must have already thought we'd abandoned him and now he'll think that's happened all over again. And if Jake tells his carer I was here, I might have to wait even longer to see him properly. He looked so distraught it breaks my heart, but it makes me realize I have to follow through with my plan. However nice this place is, it's not home with me. I can't leave Jake here.

I take a deep breath. "Liv, I know this is a lot to ask, but I need your help."

"Yes."

"I haven't said what it is yet."

"You don't need to. Of course I'll help you."

CHAPTER 14

Jake

I saw Maudie. Maudie went away. In that girl's car. She left me. Why did she leave me?

I ripped my bus book up. That lady stuck it back together. "There, there. There, there, Jake. It wasn't your sister, she's at school." That's what the lady said. "You'll see her soon." I saw Maudie! I told her that.

That lady said she'd make me feel better. I don't want to do cooking. Mum does that with me. She makes biscuits with Smarties. The orange ones are best. I want to go home.

That lady said we'd make rock cakes. I can't eat rocks. Ha ha ha! She's very silly.

I like eating them. I saved one for my mum. I saved one for my sister. But Mum's gone. Maudie's gone. Where are they? My eyes are all wet.

CHAPTER 15

Maudie

"Maudie, are you sure you don't want Ed to stay here tonight?" Eve drums her fingers on the kitchen table.

"No, we'll be fine, thanks. We are seventeen."

Liv and I have private plans to discuss. I gulp down the glass of water I've just filled from the tap. I've got nothing against Ed. He's a good listener and brilliant at IT – he's going to help me set up a website when I start selling my own fashion designs. We used to see a lot more of Eve until Ed came along though. "She's blinded by love," Mum said. "Blinded by lust, you mean," Dad had interrupted.

Eve twists a piece of her hair around her finger, just like Mum does when she's troubled. Her dejected face gets to me, but it's her own fault.

"I've left some vegetarian lasagne for you and Liv, okay?" She tries again.

"'Kay."

It's Thursday, exactly a week since Jake was put into care. I'm ticking the days off on my calendar for Mum *and* Jake now. Mum in green pen, Jake in red. I'm still finding it difficult to even talk to Eve. It's not just because of her betrayal: I'm paranoid that the more I say, the more likely I'll let something slip about my plan to get Jake out of his foster home. Tomorrow.

Eve's just about to leave for her night shift when her phone lights up with a message and she pounces on it.

"It's your mum!"

"What's she saying? Is she coming home?" I try and take her phone off her.

"Hang on, I'll tell you." Eve holds the phone between us. Her face falls. "All she says is she's still safe and not to worry. Could we not just know where she is?" Eve pinches the space between her eyebrows and lets out a deep sigh. "I'm going to try calling her again."

She holds the phone to her ear. I can hear it cutting off straight away.

"At least you get a message." My voice cracks.

Eve tries to hug me. "Oh, Maudie, let's try and get through this together?"

"It's a bit late for that – like you actually care anyway."

"I *do* care, Maudie. We need to talk about your mum and her mental health and how we can help her when she comes home."

"She'll be even more devastated when she comes home and finds Jake's gone."

Eve's arms drop by her side. "I...I..." She covers her face with her hands.

I can't comfort her. I leave her standing in the kitchen and go upstairs. She calls after me.

"I'll see you tomorrow. Call me if you need me."

I don't answer. I can't forgive her, not yet. Not when my heart feels like it's breaking in two. The front door closes. The silence reminds me of how alone I feel and how much it hurts now I know I'm not as important to my mum as I thought I was.

I check my phone for the hundredth time.

Liv was supposed to be here half an hour ago. I hope she hasn't crashed the mini or something. She's going to help me dye my hair for the plan. I'm regretting that idea already, as one time Liv did her own hair it turned out pink – and not intentionally.

I catch sight of myself in my dressing-table mirror: hollow cheeks, wild hair that even anti-frizz serum won't tame and huge dark circles under my eyes from getting no sleep worrying about Jake.

I think back to how Mum and Dad often used to look like this and how, as I got older, I came to understand that they were scared because they didn't know the best way to help Jake or how his life was going to be. Even the doctors didn't really seem to know. Once I heard my parents talking about how Jake had been starved of oxygen just before he was born, and discussing the learning disabilities, the disorders and other conditions it might have caused. But to me Jake has always been just Jake, and all I ever knew was that I adored him. The house has always been filled with his noise and energy and now, without him, it's scarily quiet.

And that's why I must rescue him.

I hear a car revving outside. When I look out the window Liv is trying to park the mini in a space you could fit a car transporter into and failing miserably. I can smell burning rubber from here. After several attempts and one narrow miss of Mrs Davy's red Volvo, she drives off around the corner. Ten minutes later the front doorbell rings and Liv comes rushing in, all red and flustered, with a tractor-tyre sized pizza box in her hands.

"Sorry I'm late! Got us a mushroom pizza with extra cheese and those funny little green things you like." She shoves the box at me.

"Capers, but you don't like them."

"I can pick them off." She throws her black fedora onto the hall table, turns her head upside down and roughs her hair up. "Don't want hat hair!" She grins at me. "Come on, I'm starving."

Liv opens her bag up and pulls out four miniature bottles of vodka and a bottle of freshly squeezed orange. "Ta dah! Why've you got a face on you?"

"It's not that I don't want to, but I can't be a wreck for tomorrow and ruin our plan to get Jake back."

"Der! Why d'you think it's just four tiny bottles, with

uber healthy fresh orange juice and this big-arsed pizza with extra cheese?"

I grin at her. "I'll get some glasses."

After a carpet picnic and watching a bit of *Dirty Dancing*, we head upstairs to do my hair.

"Is this it?" Liv screws her face up at the colour on the box. "Mid brown."

"I'm trying to disguise myself, not attract attention. I might as well have a giant red arrow on my head and a megaphone to announce I'm there if I have fluorescent hair when I sneak up to the foster home."

"True, but Blue Banana would have looked so cool on you."

"It would never look as good on me as it does you."

Liv has amazing long black wavy hair that she's dip-dyed electric blue on the ends. It's always so shiny, unlike my blonde curls that absorb conditioner like a dried-out sea sponge sucks up water.

"I brought the clothes from a charity shop – they're in my bag. And I nicked Seb's Parka he never wears, which will easily fit you as you're so small."

"Thanks, Liv, you're amazing. Won't your mum be furious when she finds out you've stolen your brother's coat?"

"She won't. He hasn't worn it for ages, and it was squashed in the bottom of his wardrobe."

"Oh great, I'm going to smell like the boys' changing room at school!"

Liv grins. "I squirted it with deodorant."

"Gross. Now, are you going to help me with my hair or not?"

I catch a glimpse of myself in my bedroom mirror and do a double take. My blond hair is now dark brown, and I've changed into my disguise clothes and make-up to check out the full effect. I don't feel like me in this parka jacket and Nike trainers. I *never* wear trainers. Liv and I are more into Retro Oxfam finds and quirky outfits from vintage clothes fairs that Mum is brilliant at altering for us.

I block any Mum thoughts and turn to Liv.

"Will I do?"

"It's perfect. No one will notice you."

"I just have to hope Jake doesn't feel upset that I look so different."

"I think he'll just be excited to be with his sister again."

My nerves churn the acid in my stomach. I've never been fully responsible for Jake, not overnight anyway, and I'm nervous. Will we really be okay by ourselves for a few days in a different house? I decide to change the subject, or I'll lose my nerve. "So, what are you going to wear for your big date on Saturday night?"

"It's not a *date* date, it's just me and Theo hanging out like we always do."

"Except this time he's buying you dinner at that fancy pasta place! You know you like each other as more than friends."

"Yeah, okay, but is it risky to try properly dating? What if it all goes wrong and he ends up hating me? Also, I was thinking…" She bites her lip then blurts it out. "I've known him so long, do you think it would feel a bit like sleeping with my brother or something?"

"Eugh! No, of course not. So, you've thought about that then?"

Liv giggles and goes bright red. "No. Yes. A tiny bit." She knocks back the rest of her vodka and orange.

"Yeah well, you've kissed enough times. Doesn't that tell you all you need to know?"

"Hmm…maybe. More?" She unscrews the last of the mini bottles.

We clink our glasses together.

Liv looks at me, a worried frown on her face. Her foot bobs up and down, which means she's going to say something I might not like. "Are you sure you want to do this, Maudie? Won't this be just as upsetting for Jake? I mean, a strange house, without your mum?"

"Why didn't you say this earlier?" I'm a bit shocked and hurt – not my best friend thinking things behind my back too?

"It only just occurred to me, Mauds, and I'm worried about you on your own."

I relax. "You don't have to worry, Liv. I get what you're saying, but he's been on family holidays with us all the time and he's been to your aunt's cottage before, remember?"

"Only once."

"He doesn't like change, but he'll be with me, not a stranger. And I don't have any choice, Liv. I *have* to do something drastic to get Mum to come home, and I'm not having Jake think we don't care and that we've abandoned him. Doing this will get him back with me and get Mum back too."

We decide to go to bed then, the stress of the day wiping me out.

Twenty minutes later, I'm balanced on the edge of my double bed, as Liv is hogging it all, as normal. I can hear her breath whistling in and out of her nose. Once I focus on it, I can't ignore it. Normally I'd thump Liv with my pillow to stop her, but I don't want to wake her because she'll see how scared I am. I wrap my pillow round my head instead.

I try not to think about anything, especially not this time tomorrow…when the police could be looking for me.

CHAPTER 16

Jake

The pillow doesn't smell like me. I left me at my old house. I don't know this Jake. It's very dark in here. There's a snake under the bed. I hate snakes. It wants to bite me. Mum would make it go away. It's here now. Uh-oh. I can hear it hissing. Under the bed.

Hisssss.

I can hear screaming. It's my mouth.

That lady's helping me. She's singing me a song. Ah, that's nice. The bad snake has gone away. I can sleep now. That lady is called Wen-dy. I like that name. I will ask her to take me bowling. On Sunday. Mum goes bowling with me and my sister. I can find Mum there. And Maudie. They can take me home.

CHAPTER 17

Maudie

Liv tucks a stray piece of hair under her grey, knitted beret and fixes her blue eyes on me.

"Are you sure your mum will even get to know you've run away with Jake? No one has a clue where she is."

"Positive! She'll contact Eve again soon, if not me."

Liv rests her hand on mine. She knows how hurt I am that Mum hasn't responded to any of my messages.

"Eve will tell Mum that me and Jake have disappeared. I can't message her myself any more anyway or it will ruin the plan. I need Mum to worry about us so she'll come home…"

I can't say any more. Mum still hasn't tried to contact us. Doesn't she care about me and Jake any more? Will she even be worried when she hears what we've done?

I suddenly feel so worthless and I'm struggling big time. I cringe at how I was on the way home from school last week – it keeps coming back to haunt me. I know my friends are worried about me, from all their messages. When I disappear they'll worry even more, but all that matters to me right now is getting my family back together.

Liv takes my hand in hers. "Look, let me come with you. I can help out and keep you both company."

I want to wail my head off, but instead I lean over and hug her. "Thanks, but I won't let you. Why should you muck up your study time and get grounded or something? I'm *not* going to ruin your chances of getting into art school—"

Liv throws her head back and laughs. "Overdramatic or what! It's only a few days, Maudie, if that. Anyway, I care more about you than my work."

"I'm not letting you miss your first proper date with Theo either. You've liked him since year nine."

"Oh my god, Maudie, it's SO unimportant in the scheme of things. If he didn't want to see me just because I had to cancel our first," she air quotes, "'proper' date, then he wouldn't be worth seeing anyway."

"You don't mean that."

"Of course I do! And I know he'd be cool with it anyway."

It's because they're so sure of each other. I have no idea what that feels like. I'm not interested in a boyfriend or getting into a heavy relationship; there's too much else going on in my life, what with Jake, Mum, studying, focusing on my fashion designs – not that I've done much since Mum left. A tiny part of me is envious of Liv and Theo. It must be great to be that comfortable with someone and feel that special. Liv interrupts my thoughts.

"What about your work, Mauds? You haven't even started your dress designs yet and I know how important getting a top mark is to you."

"It'll be fine. I've talked to my form tutor and got an extension. I can't focus on my work anyway, without Jake t at home. The gap without him is too big to fill."

"I know, Maudie."

"I'm going on my own to Cornwall, though, and that's that. Three of us missing would be easier to track down and I want to be away long enough to worry Mum into coming back home."

Liv nods. "Okay." She bites her bottom lip.

I don't want her to see how nervous I really am, because then she'll insist on coming with me no matter what I say.

"I know you're shit-scared, Maudie, but I'd do the same if it were about getting my family back together. Maybe not with Seb, but another, fantasy, brother."

We both grin at each other again.

We're sat in Tesco's car park, on the far side where no one ever goes unless it's at the weekend and it's packed. I've got a bag of Jake's favourite foods to cover us for the journey: cheesy puffs, Marmite cheddars, raisins in little boxes, three bananas, a packet of squashed-fly biscuits and some apple juice, plus an individual strawberry trifle and a chicken and bacon sandwich for dinner, as it's Friday and the nearest thing I could get to chicken pie.

"God, what if Jake won't come with me, Liv? I really don't look like me."

"Of course he will. He'd know you if you were in a clown suit with a big red nose and an orange curly wig. We need to get going."

Liv drives slowly out of the car park and onto the road to Reading. I pat my coat pocket to make sure our coach tickets are still there.

I check I've got Jake's iPad, charger and headphones, so he can watch his favourite programmes. I have spare felt bags in red, green and pink with a selection of bus magazines – or, rather, ripped-out pages plus two pictures of the Dawlish Coastal train – vital. His mini radio is here too, as he loves his music, plus felt pens, pencils and a drawing pad.

I'm scared.

A small voice at the back of my head kicks in again. *Sure you're doing the right thing? Will it work?* But family comes first...especially now Dad is gone.

I look at my watch. "We should get to Jake's foster home by three, Liv. I'm hoping he'll come out to feed the birds again, as he does it every day at home. It should be the perfect opportunity to lure him out to the mini."

"It will be," Liv agrees.

It felt good to know Jake's carer had read my notes, but it doesn't mean it's the right place for him to be.

"It's so wrong that I haven't been allowed to ask him how he feels. We always talk."

"I know you do, Maudie."

"He really loves telling me about school. Art and music are his favourite lessons, though he hates the triangles. He says they make his ears ping. Sometimes I help him paint his feelings: blue is sad, yellow is happy, though he's never wanted to paint the colours to show how he feels about Dad. Sorry, nervous wittering. I'll shut up now."

"I don't mind, Maudie."

"He still hasn't settled at the foster home according to Eve, so I'm not allowed to see him. Perhaps if they'd let me, we could have sorted something out that works for all of us."

I glance at Liv, who smiles at me. I don't know what I'd do without her.

"I feel sick." I chew my little nail nervously. "It's the first time we'll have been back to Cornwall since Dad died, which is going to be weird. I hope you don't get into too much trouble when your mum discovers you stole her key to your aunt's holiday cottage."

"They'll come around. It's not like you're sneaking down to party, and I know Aunty Jean hasn't got any bookings until after Easter because I heard Mum talking to her a couple of weeks ago."

I twist a bit of hair around my finger. "You're sure your aunt won't be going there with your cousins?"

"Aunty Jean is away on business at the moment in America and heading to the cottage for Easter. You'll be back long before the Easter weekend, so stop fretting."

I fold my arms and stare out of the window.

Liv breaks the silence. "Are you sure you want to be there? You know, it being the last place you went on holiday with your dad."

"I don't have much choice – no money for anything else. I'm on a strict budget as it is. The coach tickets cost half of my savings, and I'll need what I've got left for food and stuff."

"Okay. You do remember the cottage is in the middle of nowhere though, don't you?" Liv sighs and glances at me, a worry frown creasing her forehead. "Will that bother you?"

"No, it's better no one can see or hear us. Anyway, it won't be for long, Mum will come home as soon as she hears, I know she will." Except I don't know that really.

We turn into Hurst Avenue, where Jake is staying.

"Try to park some way up if you can, so we're well out of sight, but not too far away to get Jake into the car and speed off if he does get upset. We can't attract attention."

"If there's a space."

We both hold our crossed fingers up at the same time.

"What exactly d'you mean by 'upset'?" Liv says warily.

"Mum had an epic standoff in the school car park with him once when she had a hire car. Jake refused to get in as it wasn't his car. He made so much noise someone called the police."

"Really? God, I hope that doesn't happen now."

I point over the road. "Quick, that woman's pulling out over there."

"Perfect, and it's a big space."

Liv pulls in and turns the engine off.

We wait nervously.

I clutch Liv's wrist. "There he is!"

My heart thumps erratically, as he follows his carer into the house. I'm so excited at the thought of having Jake back with me. I catch glimpses of him between the tree trunks. He vanishes.

I can't stop my leg jigging up and down and Liv is nervously tapping the steering wheel with her fingernails. I wait ten minutes more before I get out of the car. I tuck my hair under my cap and pull it down over my eyes. I check out the street and start walking.

The afternoon sun peeps through the leaves of the trees that are standing to attention along the edges of the road. I'm struck by the enormity of what I'm about to do. Despite Liv waiting in the car, I've never felt so lonely. My unease grows with every step I take. A boy shoots out from the driveway next to me on his skateboard and fear thunders through me. He might remember seeing me.

Then I see the giant oak tree in the foster carer's garden and a quiet sense of calm comes to me.

I can do this.

I turn the latch on the front gates and push with my hip, but they won't open and clang together loudly. I duck down behind the brick gatepost and wait, my heart pounding. I had assumed I'd simply be able to walk through them.

Then I spot the bolt, which I can easily undo by pushing my hand through a gap, and feel even more silly.

Silently this time, I open the gate and tiptoe over to the oak; luckily its trunk is so thick you could hide two of me behind it.

I lean against the knotted wood, my face burning and breathing like I've been on an assault course. Gradually my heart slows. The bird station is just on the other side of the tree. A fat pigeon lands on it and the feeder swings violently.

I watch and wait.

A few cars swish by and a magpie chatters noisily from a branch, setting me on edge.

Just as I'm about to give up, the front door opens and I see Jake with a plastic jug full of bird seed in one hand and his green bag in the other. He stands on the step and doesn't move. I have to push the palms of my hands into my eyes to stop myself from crying, yet I'm grinning like the Cheshire Cat at the same time. I must look completely dopey.

I shoot back behind the tree when his foster carer appears behind him in the doorway.

"Go on, Jake. You can do it. Go and give the birds their tea, there's a good boy."

She's talking to him as though he's three, not thirteen. A lot of people make that mistake, but she's supposed to know this stuff. My brother steps forwards.

"I'll just be in the kitchen, but I'll check you're okay in a few minutes," the lady says as she goes back into the house.

I have to move fast.

Jake comes over to the bird feeder and places his jug in one of the bowls. "He can't see any birds. He doesn't know where they are. Jake wants to watch telly. Do you, Jake? Alright then. He doesn't like that pigeon."

I'm shaking and my knees feel pathetically weak. I half step around the tree trunk.

"*Jake*, it's me, Maudie," I whisper, not wanting to shock him too much.

He lets out a startled, "Argh!" before throwing himself at me and resting his head on my shoulder and saying over and over again, "Maudie, my Maudie, Maudie's back, my sister came back."

Jake lets me hug him tight. It feels so good to hold him. I notice he doesn't smell of our washing powder, which really upsets me. A part of home has been wiped out.

When he finally lifts his head up, there are real tears in his eyes. He never has tears in his eyes. That tells me everything I need to know; this is one hundred per cent the right thing to do.

"Maudie, my sister Maudie came back."

"Yes, Maudie came back and I'm not leaving you now. Liv has her car here and we're going on holiday together by the sea, which you'll love."

"He likes that. Jake's going to watch *Pointless*."

"You can watch it in the car, okay? On your iPad."

"Okay, girl."

I can see the lady coming back outside. I've missed my chance.

"Shit!"

"Uh-oh, she said shit. You mustn't swear, Jake. It's very bad."

"SHIT." I hiss under my breath.

"Uh-oh, big shit."

I bolt behind the trunk as Jake's carer shouts out to him. I think my heart is going to burst out of my chest. Please make her go back in. I can't fail now. Oh god, Jake will think I've abandoned him all over again.

"What are you doing over there, Jake? You haven't emptied the seed out of the jug. Those poor birds will be hungry. When you've done it, you can watch your television programme."

I can just see Jake's elbow appearing and disappearing.

"Jake's sister. She's all gone. Are you sure, Jake? He can't see her."

I hear crunching across gravel, then silence, then his foster carer's voice loud and clear. "You'll see your sister very soon, I promise. Come on, let's do the seed together, then I'll sit with you and watch *Pointless*."

I have to hold my breath to stop myself bawling my eyes out. I've messed up and I'll have left Jake feeling even more confused and upset than he did before. Jake mutters under his breath; it gets fainter. I dare to peek round the trunk. They're just about to go through the door, when Jake wails,

"His bag, he hasn't got his bag!"

He dropped it on the grass when he hugged me. I duck back behind the trunk.

"You go get it, Jake, and can you shut the door for me when you come back in? I'm just going for a wee."

This is it. My last chance – *Oh god, oh god, oh god, let me do this,* I say over and over in my head. As soon as he's picked up his bag, I step out from the tree and grab his hand. My heart is beating really fast. Jake's so surprised he comes with me without making a sound. We run through the gate and up the road.

Liv is waiting, engine running, passenger door open, ready to put her foot down and go.

Jake refuses to get into the car.

CHAPTER 18

Jake

It's too low. I can't get in. I'll hurt my leg.

"Please, Jake, you can do it."

"NO! NO!"

Why is the car driving away? Why is Maudie leaving me? Don't leave me. Come back, car! That girl's taking my sister.

Uh-oh uh-oh uh-oh. Not again. Girl's all gone. My heart is banging my chest. I can't breathe. Come back, Maudie! Come back! Don't leave me on the road. Huh huh huh.

Breathe, Jake. Mum tells me to breathe. When I'm upset. Breathe in...breathe out. I'll have to run. I can catch the car. I can get them. I can do it. I'm big and strong. Move your legs. Catch the car. There you are! It's slowing up. Maudie's opening the door. I did it!

CHAPTER 19

Maudie

I can barely stand up, my knees are so weak. If Jake doesn't get in the car we've had it – and if they realize I tried to kidnap him they might not let me see him until Mum's home, whenever that might be. That's too awful to even think about.

Jake's bottom lip is pushed out. "You left Jake."

"I'm sorry, I'm sorry, Jake, I had to. You *must* get in the car."

"He can't do that."

I edge him into the seat.

He lets out his booming wail, which I swear the whole county could hear. He generally seems to save those for public places. I'm panicking – surely someone's going to come out to see what's going on, any second now.

Liv frantically waves his iPad at him.

"You can watch *Pointless* if you get in the car," she offers.

"I don't want to leave you again, Jake," I plead with him.

That does it. He lowers himself down, squeezes himself into the seat and slams the door. I'm so relieved, because it nearly broke my heart watching his shocked face as we drove away, but it was the only thing we could do that might get him to go in Liv's car. She clicks his seat belt in.

"Drive!"

Liv speeds down the road.

"That was horrible. I'm never leaving him like that again."

"It worked," Liv says shakily.

"I feel like I've drunk five espressos. You okay, Jake? Your quiz is about to start. Here." I hand him his iPad.

"He likes that."

"Hold it on your lap for now."

Jake grips the tablet in his hands and holds it up in front of his face.

"Your arms will get tired like that."

Jake grumbles at me. "It's alright, Jake. He can do what he wants."

"Okay, hold it up then." I slump back on my seat and shut my eyes.

"You owe me a bottle of wine," Liv says, white-faced. "I was so worried we were going to get caught."

"I'll get you the biggest bottle I can find when all this is over, with two straws, one for each of us."

Tinny music blares out of Jake's iPad. He's turned the volume up full.

"Are you okay with it that loud, Jake? You said it made your ears hurt inside."

"Jake's blocking the bees out."

"Hello, I'm Alexander Armstrong. Welcome to Pointless – the show striving to find the most obscure answers."

"Hello, Pointless." Jake salutes the iPad screen.

"That was super stressful back there." Liv grimaces over her shoulder at me. "Makes you realize, though, if someone was actually being murdered no one would give a shit."

"Yeah, not one person came out to check. Thank god! I'm shattered after that and we haven't got to the end of the road yet."

"Let's say hello to couple number two. Can you introduce yourselves, please?"

"Hello. I'm Ellen, this is Amelia, and we're sisters from Surrey."

"Hello, Surrey. Jake likes her." He sticks his iPad in my face. "They look nice, Jake. Do you want them to win? Yes, he does."

Liv sighs. "You sure you still want to do this, Maudie? It's such a long way to go. We can turn back."

I sit bolt upright. "Of course I want to do it. We need Mum back." I refuse to catch her eye in the rear-view mirror.

"Jake wants his mum back."

"There you go." I try not to look smug.

We spend the rest of the time not speaking, just listening to Jake's TV programme.

"That's a magnificent answer, absolutely terrific."

"He said it's triffic. Jake doesn't know what that means."

"It means it's fantastic, Jake." Liv smiles at him, more relaxed now we're far enough away from the foster home.

"What time will we get to the coach station, Liv?"

"I dunno – it's three forty-five now, so about four fifteen if the traffic's not too bad. I won't go into the station though. I'll drop you in a side street. I googled it earlier. They're bound to have CCTV cameras in the bus station, so best to avoid them as much as we can. You'll have plenty of time to get on the coach and you'll be in Newquay about...twelve thirty, I guess."

I turn to my brother. "You can try and get some sleep on the coach, Jake, or you'll be wiped out by the time we get to Cornwall. We have to go on three coaches altogether, which you'll love."

I'm not looking forward to that. I hope there's no hanging around when we change.

"Cornwall? Jake likes the seaside."

"That's amazing you remember it, Jake!"

"Of course he does." He points at his iPad. "Maudie, shush, he's listening to Surrey."

"Okay, I'll be quiet then."

"Yes, thank you."

"That told you." Liv glances at Jake before giving me a concerned look in her rear-view mirror. "Are you still nervous?" she whispers.

"Yes," I whisper back.

Liv smiles at me over her shoulder quickly. I sigh and watch the grey rain that's now splattering against the window. I wish I could get rid of the angst that's cramping up my stomach.

Jake laughs out loud along with the studio audience. His laugh is so infectious we can't help joining in and it helps ease my tension, reassuring me he's happy to be with me.

We stop and start in the traffic.

"*The other Pointless answers include Ivan the Terrible and finally, Vlad the Impaler. Well done if you got any of those!*"

I watch the time tick by on the dashboard clock. We're going to miss our coach. I wish I had my phone, but I've left it at home, switched off, so that no one can trace me. Liv had the brilliant idea of getting us a couple of burner phones, so we can keep in contact.

"I'm just turning into the street to drop you off." Liv's voice wobbles.

We pull into a parking space. I was so hoping Liv would be able to stay with us at the station until the coach left, but of course that doesn't make sense. Jake's eyes are practically popping out of his head: he's super excited by a blue double decker bus that has just sped past the top of the road.

Liv gets out the car and pulls her seat forwards. I get our bags. Jake flings the door open, he's so eager to see the buses properly. A woman swerves out of the way.

"Watch what you're doing! You could've sent me flying."

Jake struggles to lever himself out of the seat, but something seems to be holding him back. Liv goes to help him while I struggle with the bags. He whines in protest, attracting attention from another passer-by.

"What's happening, Liv?"

"The handle of his bag is stuck on the gear stick knob-thingy. Hang on, Jake, I have to get it off."

"Jake wants to see the buses."

"You will if you let me do this, Jake." Liv tries to unhook the handles. "Don't pull, you're tightening the handle further. That's it, done it!"

Jake shoots forwards, grabbing at the mini's door to stop himself falling flat on his face. It clunks and squeals in protest. Liv gets out the car and anxiously checks it's okay, opening and shutting it a few times.

"Here." I throw Jake's coat at her. "Can you help him do the zip on this, please? It's really stiff, isn't it, Jake?"

"It gets stuck," he tells Liv.

Liv catches the coat. "Here, Jake, let's put this on." He stands quietly, letting her zip it up. Then he salutes a bus that goes by on the main road.

"Evening, bus! Jake likes that one. It's a Berk-shire bus. Do you want to go on that, Jake? Yes, he does. There's a purple one! That's a new bus, Jake. You need a ticket." He grabs my arm. "Can Jake go on that bus?"

"We're going on a big white coach. You can have your dinner once it gets going."

"He can't do that."

"Yes, you can! There's a little table to eat on."

I turn to look at Liv, the enormity of what I'm about to do hitting me. She grabs me in a bear hug.

"Maudie, I don't want to let you go. You sure—"

"*Definitely.*"

Liv nods. "I'll keep in contact as much as I can, just in case the police—"

"Police? You don't really think they'll get involved, do you? I mean, I did wonder before, but—"

"Look, I shouldn't have said that. Don't even think about it now."

I nod. "Yeah, okay." I try to stay calm. "Thanks, Liv."

"By the way, I've put my new number and Eve's number in your phone, just in case."

"You're amazing doing this for us. I...I don't know what to say."

"Then don't." Liv's eyes shine. "Here, this is so you don't get lonely." She hands me a photo. "I'd have made it the screensaver if the phone wasn't so rubbish."

"You think of everything. That's my favourite picture of us." It's me and Liv feeding the pigeons in Trafalgar Square. We look so happy. Just after we took that selfie a pigeon pooped on her hat, and I couldn't stop laughing. "Thank you."

Liv shakes her head dismissively. "Whatever. Here, Jake, present for you too." She hands him a key ring with a little red bus on it. "It's a torch too." She presses a button, and the headlamps light up. "You never know when you might need it." Liv grins.

Jake takes it and holds it up in the air. "It's his favourite. Look what Jake's got." He beams the light in my eye.

I gently move it away. "It's perfect and so are you, Liv. Say thank you to Liv, Jake."

"Thank you, girl." He clutches it in his hand.

Then Liv pushes something in my coat pocket. "Just in case."

She tries to stop me looking. It's five twenty-pound notes. "I can't take this."

"Yes, you can. It's for emergencies and 'cause I love you. Just give me another hug before we both start blubbing, which will make people stare at us." Liv grabs me. "Look after Maudie for me, Jake," Liv says over my shoulder.

"Alright, girl. Jake's going on a bus-coach."

"Miss you already, guys."

"Miss you too, Liv. I love you more, and thank you."

I watch her climb into her car and start the engine. She shoots out in front of a lorry that blares its horn at her. My heart skips a beat.

I force myself to smile at Jake, who's pulling his ear just like Mum does, and I suddenly miss her so much I feel I can't breathe.

Let's hope this gets her back.

CHAPTER 20

Jake

Maudie hasn't got her hair. Where's her hair gone? Dad didn't have any hair. He lost it. When he was ill. Is Maudie ill? I hope she doesn't go away. Don't worry, Maudie's right here. She's taking me on a bus to Cornwall.

I'm lucky. I can make a sandcastle. On the beach. I haven't done that for a long ago. I wasn't allowed in the sand at the playground. I'm too big. I was sad. I want to be little again. Then Dad and Mum would be here. Mum loves the seaside. She might be in Cornwall. We went there with Dad. On our before holiday. I could find Mum. I'm so clever. Derrick said that. Hello, driver!

CHAPTER 21

Maudie

We walk over to the live departure board to find where our bus is parked. I keep my head low, not that I can see any cameras at the moment. The fluorescent light from the board casts a blue strip across our faces, which adds to the surreality of the moment. Our coach is on time and leaves in ten minutes.

Jake is very excited. He waves at the driver, who's sorting the bags. The driver smiles at him. The queue to get on the coach winds around the bus station. I thought there'd be hardly anyone taking a late coach. The fewer people the better with Jake, as too many people might stress him out. Half of them should be tucked up in bed with their teeth in a glass next to them on the bedside table. Though there's a mixed group of twenty-somethings too and they have surfboards strapped to their backs. Jake will enjoy watching the serious surfers at this time of year, on Perran Sands.

At the moment, he's mesmerized by all the different types of buses swinging in and out of the station. He holds a monologue with himself.

"Jake likes that blue one best. It's a new one! Do you like that one, Jake? That one's got shiny wheels. That man's looking at him. Jake doesn't like it. It's very rude to stare. Oh! That's an open-top bus – can Jake go on that one? That's his best bus."

Lots of people are gawking at Jake talking to himself. I hate it when people do that. No one likes being looked at, and yet they just carry on staring at him. Two kids openly smirk and point at him. Jake ducks his head under his arm and their mum tells them off. I smile my thanks. I need to get Jake on the coach, safely in his seat. That's when I notice the security camera on the lamp post. Luckily, it's pointing in the opposite direction, but I still pull my collar up and cap down.

The driver shouts up the line: "Leave your bags here by the storage hatch and find your seats quickly now, please." He takes my huge rucksack and pushes it into the hold. He points at the other bag in my hand. "What about that one?"

"I need this for the journey, thanks."

"Jake's going to the seaside," he tells the driver.

"Are you, young man? Well, you're a lucky boy." He smiles at me. "Staying with relatives?"

"Um, yeah, our grandma."

"Jake's grandma—"

"Hasn't seen us in ages." I have to quickly cut in, aware Jake would've told the driver she doesn't live in Cornwall. Then I watch with horror as the driver punches Jake on the arm, but amazingly Jake laughs. I swallow my heart back down.

"You watch out for those pesky seagulls. They'll have your chips before you can say tomato ketchup."

"Jake likes lots of ketchup."

"You go and find your seat now and I'll check your ticket before we leave."

"Thank you-ou-ou-ee-oo!" Jake yodels at the top of his voice, which he thinks is very funny.

I hurry Jake in front of me onto the coach. We might as well have been centre stage at Wembley Arena for all the scrutiny we've now had. He's so chuffed with himself that he climbs up the steps – which I know he hates after his fall at school – without a single moan.

"Here, Jake – nine and ten." I point to our seats on the left. Jake sits down on the aisle seat. "Shift up, you can watch everything out the window."

"No. He can't move."

His legs are pressed up against the seat in front, his pink bag trapped behind his knees. "Jake, I can't sit down if you don't move." I can feel my forehead starting to sweat.

"Excuse me, love, but can I get through?"

"Sure." I swing round into the seat behind.

"That's my seat."

"Right." I move back into the aisle and squash up to Jake to let the lady get to her seat. "Jake, please move up."

"Come on, son, where's your manners?" a man says, who I assume is the lady's husband.

The queue is beginning to back up down the steps. I nudge Jake, who lets out a yelp of disapproval. People are starting to mutter.

"Move along, please!" the coach driver shouts through the door. "I want to get off on time."

I do the only thing possible. I climb over Jake's lap and somehow winch myself into my seat, clutching our bag. I elbow him in the face by mistake and nearly smack my head against the window.

"Get off him! You're hurting him."

"You should bloody move up, mate." A guy with a pierced eyebrow glares at Jake.

Jake points his finger at the man. "You can shut up."

"Jake!" He just had to pick the guy with the grim reaper tattooed on his forearm.

"Who are you telling to shut up?" Reaper guy pushes his sleeves up higher.

I want the ground to open up and swallow me. "Please, my brother doesn't mean anything, he doesn't understand." I can hear the wobble in my voice.

I wish I didn't always have to explain this, like I'm making excuses for Jake's behaviour – it's who he is, and he shouldn't have to apologize for being him. I admit it's more obvious when he talks and not when you look at him that he has a disability, which has always made life challenging for Jake.

But if people could stop and think before opening their mouths, and try and put themselves in his shoes, just for one minute, then it would make everyone's life easier, especially Jake's.

"Just sit down, Connor." A lady behind Reaper guy with jet-black hair nudges him forwards. He scowls at her and walks past.

Jake screws his face up. "You mustn't do that, Jake. Say sorry. He can't help it."

"No, you mustn't be rude, Jake, even if that guy was aggressive. We'll get thrown off the bus and that would be a shame."

"Sorry, girl, sorry. Jake's sorry for being rude."

"That's very sweet of you, Jake, but," I let out a deep sigh, "it's not your fault your routine is messed up and your life got turned upside down." I rest my head on his arm. "You're very special to me, Jake."

"Jake's special. He likes that word. It makes him happy." He moves his arm away so my head flops down.

"And you make me happy." I laugh.

I find Jake the cheese puffs from his supply bag. My hands are so shaky I'm struggling to open the pack. I really hope Jake can sleep after he's eaten, so I can think about when we get to Newquay. "Here, pull your table down."

"Jake can't see a table."

I lean across and unhook it. "There you are. I'll get you a drink."

He lines his crisps up in neat rows on the table and hands me the empty bag back. "When we're moving you can have your sandwich, if you'd like it?"

Jake looks at his wrist, examining his invisible watch. "It's Friday. Jake has chicken pie on Friday. He can't eat that sandwich."

"It's chicken *and* bacon, which you love, and it's all we've got. We can't cook a pie on a bus, can we?"

"No, we can't. Jake has chicken pie on Friday."

I hand him the sandwich, which he scowls at but starts unwrapping anyway.

The bus has filled up and the driver gets on. "Can I check your tickets, please?"

I hand him ours and wait while he scribbles on them.

"We'll get into Newquay about twelve-thirty, all being good. You shouldn't have to wait at Heathrow and Plymouth for the coach switch, but can get straight on. You alright, young man?"

Jake ignores him. He's too busy giving his sandwich the evils and refusing to eat it.

"Ha ha, I can see you're busy, so I'll leave you to your supper."

Jake drops the offending sandwich back in the bag and looks at me pointedly. "He needs pie."

The coach rumbles into life and leaves the station. I watch with relief as Jake's excitement at setting off distracts him enough to eat. The clenched ball inside me relaxes slightly. I stare at the pinch-faced woman opposite, who's looking fixedly at him. She looks away first.

I put Jake's strawberry trifle pot and a spoon on his little table. His face lights up.

"Jake – music or film?"

"Jake would like *Toy Story*."

I pass Jake his headphones and iPad, which he props up against the back of the seat. I let him lose himself in one of our favourite films. We've seen it so many times we both know it off by heart.

I sink back into my seat and close my eyes. How did I get to be sitting on a coach going down to Newquay, having kidnapped my own brother? Am I doing all this wrong? I want to get our family back together, but don't know if I'm up to it.

I'm so lucky that lady stopped the tattooed guy losing it. I can remember a few times Jake has reacted to people's insensitivity and yet we've been the ones blamed. Like when we went to the cinema to see *Toy Story* 4, when Dad was still alive.

"Would you like sweet or salty popcorn, Jake?" I ask him.

"He wants both."

"You eat the sweet first and I'll start on the salty, then we'll swap halfway through, yeah?"

I hand Jake the box and he immediately digs in.

Mum leans forwards. "Put your bag under your chair, Jake, or people won't be able to get past."

"He can't do that."

Mum tries to move Jake's bag. He bellows loudly in protest. Both the little girl and the mum in front turn around and stare.

"Sorry for the noise, everyone." Mum focuses her laser stare on the woman in front of Jake. She smiles weakly and faces the front. Mum turns back to Dad, who's just got back from the loo, and hisses, "Jay, try and slip his bag under his chair if you can."

"And pigs might fly," Dad grumps. "Why didn't you get tickets at the other end? Then no one would have to go past us."

"Oh, that's a good idea, then we could have disrupted the whole film when Jake needed a wee and he couldn't get past," Mum says sarcastically.

"Jake doesn't need a wee," Jake says huffily.

"Yeah, you two, he's sat right next to you," I chip in.

A dad with his young son looks expectantly at Dad from the aisle and points to the end of the row. "Can we get to our seats, please?"

"Of course."

Dad nods triumphantly at Mum and stands up. I swing my legs to the side and Mum perches on her upturned seat, but Jake refuses to budge.

"Go on, Jake, just stand up, eh? Let these two get past." Dad does his super jolly voice.

The man waits for Jake to move, unsure what to do.

"I'm afraid you're going to have to step over his feet," Mum explains.

As soon as the man manoeuvres his way past, Jake shouts, "LEAVE HIS BAG ALONE!"

It startles the little boy and he falls against his dad, who spills his extra-large Tango Ice Blast all down his front. "Shit!" he says, trying not to spill any more.

"Oooh, you mustn't say that poo word. Derrick will be cross."

"Um, what?" the man says to Jake.

"My teacher says you mustn't say rude words."

"Ah – quite right too. Sorry we got your bag caught up. Come on, Ollie, let's get to our seats."

Mum thanks him profusely then leans towards Dad. "God, why did they have to choose the bucket-size drink? I hope they don't want to go for a pee halfway through."

"They can always use the cup." Dad grins mischievously at me. I ignore him and sink further down in my seat.

"I hope this film is as good as the first three."

"Oh no, Jake's popcorn has gone all sticky. Get it off him."

A few people turn to look at us.

"Hey, I'll have that one, you have my salty popcorn instead." I hand him my box.

"What are those two looking at over there?" Dad says under his breath.

"Ignore them, Dad."

Dad shakes his head. "They're definitely pointing at Jake."

"Hey, Jake, the film starts soon. Is Buzz still your favourite?" I try and distract Jake, who's picked up that the ladies are looking at him.

Dad's foot begins jigging up and down.

My stomach clenches in a knot. I want the women to stop being so horrible.

"If those bloody women on the opposite row don't stop staring at Jake and tutting, I'm going to say something," Dad loud-whispers to Mum.

I can feel my face starting to turn red. Dad's known for having a very short fuse when it comes to Jake – not that I blame him, as people can be pretty heartless – but he can't ever hold in his anger at the injustice of people being mean to his son.

"Can we try and not make a scene, Jay? Just ignore them and they'll get bored soon enough." Mum quietly tries to smooth things over. "Jake won't even see them when it goes dark."

"You can see it's upsetting him, and I don't see why he can't be allowed to sit here and enjoy his popcorn without people judging him."

Dad looks so upset.

"Those people are staring at Jake. Make them go away."

Jake throws a handful of popcorn in the direction of the lady staring at him.

"Take it easy, Jake. It's okay." Mum keeps her voice soft and reassuring.

The lady tuts loudly. "He shouldn't be allowed to come here if he can't control himself. It's upsetting for my grandson."

The man at the end of our row stands up. "You'd think that you might show a bit of compassion. This young man was quite happy until you made him feel uncomfortable. He might not be able to control his reactions as well as some people, but he isn't causing any problems."

"Thank you." Mum beams at him gratefully and Dad nods his head at him.

"Well said," someone shouts from the auditorium. "Let him watch the film in peace!"

A few people clap and murmur reassuringly.

The lady blushes bright red, gets up from her seat and goes out the swing doors. A minute later she comes back in with a middle-aged man carrying a walkie-talkie.

Dad gets up. "What's going on?" He sounds defensive.

Mum tries to get him to sit down again.

The man puts a hand on Dad's arm. "Now, now, sir, I think you'd better calm down and go back to your seat, or you'll have to leave."

Dad throws his hand off him. "I'm perfectly calm. It's not me you should be removing but this lady here."

"This man and his son have done nothing wrong!" The man at the end of our row defends us again. "You're asking his dad to leave, for what – defending his son?"

"Thank you, sir, but I'll sort the matter out with the gentleman concerned outside."

It's all got too much for Jake. He's broken out in a sweat and is breathing rapidly.

Mum is resigned and already getting our coats. "We have to go, darling, I'm sorry."

Jake looks so confused. He picks the nail on his thumb.

He lets me take him by the arm.

"Jake hasn't had his film. He likes that Toy Story 4. He hasn't seen it before. He doesn't like this place."

"I'll watch Toy Story 3 with you at home," I promise him.

His bewildered face makes me so sad. It seems a very long walk to the front exit. Dad has already marched off down the aisle; a couple of people pat him on the arm. He smiles at them gratefully and thanks them. Someone urges us to stay.

"My brother is too upset now," I explain. "We'll come back another time, thank you."

I'm so sad for Jake but understand why Dad said something to that woman.

Jake nudges me with his elbow. "Jake likes Woody and Buzz. Reach for the sky!"

As we go through the door a young boy claps his hands excitedly when the adverts start, making Jake startle. He cries out in distress. Mum and I hold him. I pick his bag off the sticky carpet and brush it down with my sleeve.

When we get to the car everyone's subdued. Dad sits in the driver's seat just looking out the window.

Mum shifts round in her seat. "Okay, you two? We'll have a film date when we get home. Would you like to make popcorn with me, Jake? Whatever flavour you want."

"Jake likes butter salt."

"Then that's what we'll have." Mum leans over and holds my hand. "Love you, sweetie – and you, my Jake."

"Love you too, Mum."

She lets go of me and turns quickly back, so I can't see the tears in her eyes.

Dad starts to talk but I'm not sure if he's saying it to us or himself. "It kills me, you know. He's just a kid – why do people think they can treat him like that? I can't bear it. I don't know how to stop it happening and that breaks my heart."

Mum rests her hand on his knee.

He shakes his head and sniffs before starting the engine and pulling out into the road.

Jake holds his hand up high. "To 'finity...and beyond!"

I sigh at the memory. Dad was the best Dad ever, and he loved Jake to pieces – he'd do anything for him. And I'd do anything to have him on this coach with us.

I watch Jake, engrossed in his film. His little finger is bleeding around the nail where he's picked it. I know it's his way of letting the monsters out because he told me. We had a talk about self-harm in PSHE at school once and learned that people cut themselves as a way of expressing overwhelming emotional distress. Jake's habit sounds similar – that there's something awful going on inside his head and this is his way of getting it out, which makes me sad. At least his school is trying to find a better way for him to deal with his anxiety.

I rub my forehead to try and shift the low headache that's lurking there. A selfish part of me just wants to be at home, worrying about which charity shops I want to go to with Liv to find some new outfits, but then Jake laughs at something in the film on his iPad and turns and rests his hand on my head. He ruffles my hair, like Dad used to do to him; the only one allowed to. Jake laughs again, a real laugh, not one of his copycat laughs that doesn't reach his eyes, and in that laugh comes understanding. He's happy, he's with me and we're going to get Mum back. That's all that matters.

The late afternoon sun streams through the window, catching pale water streaks on the glass. The coach rumbles out of town. People hurry past like army ants on their way home. The wet pavements glint in the light. Warmth flutters through me.

The driver blasts his horn at someone and reality butts in again, as it always will, and I can't help wondering if that foster woman has told the police about Jake disappearing and if they've realized I'm a part of it yet. Aunty Eve wasn't expecting me home until late today and I haven't been speaking to her much anyway. She knows I probably wouldn't answer any calls from her either. I wonder what she'll feel about Jake having vanished…or both of us, as she'll soon find out. This'll show her what we think about putting Jake in care.

Dad wasn't having it at all when Eve brought it up that first time. I remember him and Mum arguing about it. Dad didn't want her in the house; he didn't want someone around Jake who felt that way. Mum said it wasn't that Eve didn't care about Jake, she just didn't want us all "sacrificing our lives for him" – not that any of us felt like that, and we couldn't understand how Eve could *ever* think that. How can wanting your family to stay together be sacrificing your life?

But Mum needed her sister, like I need Liv: as a shoulder to cry on, a person to sound off to and, most of all, someone to laugh with. So, Eve kept coming to the house and proved to Dad she did care and loved Jake – and it was clear he loved her too – so they agreed to disagree.

Mum and Dad would be devastated if they knew what Eve had done.

I wonder if Mum would change her mind about Eve now. She had thought she could trust her.

Movement from Jake catches my eye. He's air-boxing at his iPad. He does that when he watches *Toy Story* and sees Scud, the manic bull terrier. Jake love-hates him. The nosy lady across the aisle is staring at Jake again but looks away as soon as she sees I've caught her out. She says something to the old boy next to her, who frowns and glances over his tortoiseshell glasses at us. I give him my best smile and he smiles back.

I'm wiped out and struggling to keep my eyes open. It's only five-twenty, we've only been on the coach forty-five minutes, though it feels like much longer. I shut my eyes for a moment.

*   *   *

I jolt awake to hear Jake singing along very loudly to "You've got a Friend in Me", his favourite song in *Toy Story*. He's removed the headphones and has turned the volume up to max.

"*Jake*, shush – not so loud."

He ignores me totally. Nosy lady and her friend are fast asleep, thank god. I lean over Jake and try and turn it down, but he's not having it.

"Can you plug your headphones back in, Jake?"

In front of me a tightly-bunned head, with a very pink scalp showing through the hair, bobs from side to side past the gap in the seats, in time with Jake's singing. She turns around and pops her face through.

"Let him sing, pet, he's enjoying himself."

The lady begins to clap in time to the music and joins in singing with Jake. I love her for it. Gradually a few more people on the coach start to sing and the surfers at the back of the coach are really going for it. I think I've time-warped into a movie moment. A few people look put out, but not in a horrible way at Jake, more that they were trying to sleep. Jake is so happy he jiggles up and down and waves one hand in the air. By the end of it, nearly the whole coach bursts into laughter and applause when the song ends.

"Jake likes that. Jake sing again."

I watch Jake's face all lit up and smiley and I feel a burst of love for him.

I did the right thing.

CHAPTER 22

Jake

You've got a friend in me, you've got a friend in me, *lalalalala*... I like that song. It's in *Toy Story*. We're going to get a new coach soon. Maudie said. At the airport. I can see the aeroplanes. Dad liked watching them fly. Dad said I was his best friend. He told me in Cornwall. I helped Dad. He couldn't walk on the rocks. I held his hand. "You're so strong, Jake." Dad said that. "But I need to be strong for you." I liked being strong. We haven't been on holiday again. Dad went to hospital after Cornwall. When he came home, he stayed in his bedroom. Mum was sad. Maudie was sad. Mum cries in her bedroom. At night. I can hear her. It muddles my head up. Dad would make her better.

CHAPTER 23

Maudie

My phone pings. I scrabble for it in my pocket.

> Soz didn't text earlier cos Mum invited
> Furfaceous round for a bonding session
> with me and Seb – eugh!

I snort loudly at the name. Furfaceous is Liv's mum's new boyfriend, who has a creepy, chinstrap-style beard. Seb, Liv's ten-year-old brother invented it. I know Liv wants her mum to be happy, but she hates the thought of someone taking her dad's place – though he didn't waste any time moving in with his new girlfriend. She was terrified her dad would build a new family and fade out of their lives:

"*Our lives will grow further and further apart. Dad will remarry, then Mum; there'll be nothing left of us. How can I bear that?*"

"With me, Liv, with me," I reassured her. "I'll always be there to help you and we'll get through this together."

And we did, but having to live with someone new is even harder for her. Liv will need me again, so I have to be ready. I wish I was with her now to hug and reassure her. I sigh to myself and respond to her text.

Poor you! I'm sorry I'm not with you. Is your mum serious about Furfaceous?

> Think so
> He's SO creepy but Seb thinks he's funny
> Only to annoy me of course
> Are you OK, Maudie?

Yes, just about. What about you?

> Sort of I'll just have to get used to him
> and Mum ☹

Jake stirs, so I stroke his back to keep him asleep. He doesn't mind me touching him when he's asleep and sometimes it's fine when he's awake.

I'll look after you, Liv.

> ♡ Heard from Eve yet?

No. All good here. Changed coach at Heathrow
and managed ok in disabled loos! Changed at
Portsmouth and Jake didn't want to get off the
bus. It was SO busy and the coach is rammed.

I said Friday wasn't the best night to go

But Jake won't miss as much school and be out of
his routine too long remember. It's bad enough
he's not in his own house.

True

Jake's asleep now. Feels like we've been travelling
for ever.

The coach has slowed down and we seem to be turning
off the motorway. The driver makes an announcement
saying we'll be in Cornwall in half an hour. I feel a bit sick at
being here so far from home.

Are you nearly there?

Get into Newquay in half hour. Need to find
a taxi.

Taxi rank outside station

Have used it before
They have some black cabs – Jake will
like them

Great. Will text when at cottage. Jake waking up.
Love you. Xxx

Call me then. Love you more xxx

The coach swings into the bus station. Lots of people had dozed off and are woken by the bright lights cutting through the windows. We blink at each other, bleary-eyed. I feel the weight of the keys in my pocket; I can't wait to get to Liv's aunt's place, then we'll be safe.

Jake is rubbing his eyes. He opens his bag to check his bus pages are still there.

"Stay in your seats until I've parked up," the coach driver shouts, as people start getting their bags from overhead. Nobody listens.

"Stay there, Jake, we'll wait until everyone's gone, that way we won't get in their way."

"He doesn't know where he is. This isn't Jake's."

"We're by the sea and you'll be able to go on the beach tomorrow. Liv says there are some buckets and spades at the cottage."

"Jake likes digging. Where's his little mum? Jake can't find her."

I smile at his name for mum. She's tiny like me and Jake towers over us. "You'll see her soon, Jake." I cross my fingers.

I help Jake off the coach, pick up our bags and head outside to find a taxi. The street lights give off an opaque, orange glow. I glance at the clock on the wall; it's nearly twelve-thirty. No wonder Jake's tired and waits quietly next to me. He's really pleased when the cab is bright yellow. It has a picture of three stripy fish and some pink coral on the side, with large black lettering across it that says BLUE REEF AQUARIUM. We went there the last time we stayed here and Jake would love to go back, but it's so horrible knowing Dad will never go there with us again. Jake taps me sharply on the head.

"Gently, Jake."

"Jake wants to see some fish. There might be a shark. Be careful, Jake, it might bite you."

I snap my fingers in the air. "Ooh, be careful – he might bite your nose off!"

"Leave his nose alone," he says irritably.

We climb into the taxi.

"Ivy Cottage, Birch Lane, Pentire, please. It's right at the end overlooking the bay."

"Right you are, lovely. I know that one."

"Jake's got his seat belt on."

The driver looks over his shoulder at Jake. "That's it, you've got to stay safe, young man."

It's pitch-black outside. As we drive, an occasional car

coming towards us lights up the inside of the taxi with its headlights, then it's dark again. A shaft of moonlight appears from behind a cloud and slices across the trees, silhouetting them against the dark blue canvas of the sky. Jake's eyes have shut, so hopefully I can get him straight into bed when we get to the cottage, and he won't be too thrown.

The driver doesn't chat, which I'm pleased about, as I don't have the energy for small talk. The radio plays classical music, which helps calm me down. I couldn't face food earlier and the noises my stomach is making remind me I haven't eaten since breakfast. We bump up and down a winding road, Jake's head nodding in time with the bumps. In the distance the sea stretches out towards the horizon, cut in two by silver fingers stretching from the moon.

The road gets more uneven and I slide around on my seat. The taxi's brakes squeal as we pull to a stop, the seat belt cutting into me.

"Here we go, love."

Soft light shines out from the front of the house. Is someone there? I lower the car window to get a proper look. A blast of cold air heavy with the smell of the sea slaps my face. It's difficult to see through the tall plants that toss wildly in the wind. I recognize the old wooden gate with the white enamel nameplate that says *Ivy Cottage* in black lettering entwined with dark green leaves. I'm surprised the lights are on in the front window. My heart nearly races out of my chest because for a fleeting moment I wonder if it's

Mum, but it can't be, because she said she could never come back here again, as it was too painful. Besides, her car isn't here. Also, I've got the family keys in my bag and Liv's aunt would have told Liv's mum if my mother was here.

I open the door and lean out to get a better look through a gap in the hedge. A large woman with grey-streaked hair and a flowery shirt appears in the window.

"Oh!" I duck to the side.

I can't believe someone else is there. She looks familiar, but I can't place her. It must be a friend of Liv's family. She pulls the curtains shut and we're left in darkness. I lever myself back into the taxi and shut the door.

"This can't be the right house, it's supposed to be empty," I blurt out, unable to think of a better lie.

The taxi driver frowns. "This is the right address, it says so on the gate."

I kick myself for thinking of such a pathetic reason. My mouth goes dry.

"It...it must have been double-booked."

This can't be happening.

The driver scratches his head. "Why don't you go and check?"

I feel faint.

"No, I can't. I mean, there's no point." I glance at Jake, who's still asleep. I have to swallow hard to carry on talking. "I don't know what to do. It's so late."

The driver swivels round to look at me properly. "Can't

you ring the owner? Find out what's happened and see if they have another property?"

"They don't, they're family friends, plus they'd probably be in bed."

"Don't you know anyone here?" He looks between me and Jake.

I have to think quickly. "It was a special treat for my brother. He loves the beach...and...and..."

"Now, now – don't cry, lovely."

The darkness outside presses against the windows of the taxi, trying to force its way through the glass and swallow me up. I can't go back with Jake now. I've got to do something to get us out of this mess, otherwise I've failed before I've even started. I drag my coat sleeve across my eyes, leaving a mascara smudge. I must get a grip, for Jake's sake. I blow my nose. It comes out in a loud honk, which is mortifying.

"I'll have to find somewhere else to stay, but I don't have a lot of money. I didn't think I'd be paying for accommodation. It has to be more private than a hotel, something like an Airbnb. We need a quiet place."

The driver looks concerned. "Righto. How about a caravan site where they have those mobile homes? Everyone has their own plot. I know the owner of Perran Sands Camping Park. They take late arrivals and it's not high season Easter holidays yet, so fingers crossed he's got one you can take."

"Is it expensive?"

"Not that I know. I won't charge you for the extra bit of journey and I'm sure Brae, he's the owner, will give you a good earlier-season rate. Your brother will love it there, it's right next to the beach."

"Th-thank you."

"Tony."

"Maudie, and you know this is Jake."

I just hope Jake will be okay. He knew the cottage, but he's never been in a caravan before. The familiar tight knot of anxiety balled inside me clenches tighter. It's better than a hotel, but in a caravan park there could still be lots of people, and I bet the caravan walls will be paper thin. It could be disastrous.

We arrive at the park soon after and Tony goes to sort everything for me with the owner. I'm so relieved I want to hug him.

Jake opens his eyes. "Jake wants to go to his bed."

"Very soon, I promise." He twists and untwists the handles of his bag and talks quietly to himself.

"Jake wants his bed. This isn't Jake's bed. He doesn't like this place. Jake needs a wee. Do you, Jake? He can't see a toilet."

"You can go as soon as we get to our caravan. They're coming out now, Jake."

Tony comes back out of reception followed by a large, grey-haired man with a bushy white beard.

Jake leans forward in his seat. "It's Father Christmas!

Jake likes him. He comes down the chimney. I don't know how he does it."

Tony looks through the window. "I'll drive you down to your caravan. Brae here's got the keys and will meet us there. I explained what happened and he says you can sort the paperwork and money tomorrow."

"I don't know how to thank you."

"No need. You know, young people always get told all they think about is themselves, but from my experience as a scout leader that's rubbish. I think what you're doing for your brother is admirable."

I blush. Tony's words give me the same feeling as sitting in a warm spot out of the wind. That's before I remember that, technically speaking, I've kidnapped my own brother.

We drive down to our site. Each mobile home has its own patch and is surrounded by a hedge. In the middle of the grass is a white plastic picnic table with a sun umbrella, which is closed up and rattling in the strong wind. The light attached to the side of the caravan flickers on and off, unsettling Jake. He peers through the window of the cab. He's pulling at the hair at the side of his face. I need to get him inside asap.

This place is going to have to do, though I wish it were a bit more isolated to avoid attracting attention and giving our location away. I eye the other homes warily. The one next door has a beam of light shining through a gap in their curtain, over our hedge onto our door and reflections from television screens cavort across some of the other windows. Too close for me to be able to relax.

Tony helps me with our bags, and we wait by the side of the caravan. Jake pulls at his earlobe, turning it bright red, so I try to distract him.

"You're going to love this, Jake. We can paddle in the sea in the morning and hopefully there'll be some big rock pools."

"He doesn't want any rock pools. Jake wants a wee."

"Okay, one more minute." I rummage in my bag for money to pay Tony, but he waves it away.

"Thank you! You've been amazing."

"You're welcome, Maudie. Here's Brae now."

Jake unexpectedly rushes forwards and shakes Brae's hand. "Hello, Christmas. Jake likes presents."

Brae throws his head back and laughs.

"Nice to meet you. I hope you've been good this year, then you'll get lots of presents. Let me show you your home."

"Jake needs a wee."

"Right you are, toilet first then."

"I'll be off then. Good luck!" Tony hands me a card. "If you want a lift back to the station or anywhere else, give me a call."

I wave goodbye, feeling a bit gutted now he's gone.

The place is much nicer and way more spacious than I thought it would be. There are two bedrooms, one with a double bed and the other a single. Jake can have the bigger bed. There's a TV on the wall in the bedroom as well as in the largish living area, which is totally brilliant for Jake, a bathroom with a shower cubicle, and a small kitchen to the side with blue and white checked curtains across the window that remind me of our great-uncle's farmhouse in the Lake District.

"I'm worried I won't be able to afford this, Brae."

"We can talk about that tomorrow and what's brought you here. You look bushed, as am I, seeing as it's past one in the morning now, so I'll get going. I'll get someone to fix that flickering light tomorrow. *Nos dha*, goodnight – oh, your brother needed help on the loo. I'll leave you to it if you don't mind. Bye!"

"Ha ha, no. Night, Brae, and thanks so much."

He waves and starts to whistle as he walks away.

As soon as Brae leaves, I sort Jake on the loo. I won't worry about Brae's *"And what's brought you here"* for now.

Jake looks nervously around him. I suddenly feel furious with Mum for leaving us. If she hadn't gone, none of this would be happening. Jake would be happy and I could be at home listening to a podcast or chatting with Liv instead of in a strange caravan in the middle of nowhere feeling more alone than I've ever felt.

CHAPTER 24

Jake

I met Father Christmas. He lives in Cornwall. He's got a very large belly. It wobbled when he laughed. Ho ho ho! I can't see his reindeer. I'm in a caravan. I don't like this caravan. It's squashing me up. Where's my bedroom? Everything's different. I don't like it.

I'm glad I got my sister back. Don't leave me again, Maudie, I missed you. I was all alone.

CHAPTER 25

Maudie

My anger at Mum vanishes as quickly as it came. I'm so confused. One minute I'm angry, the next I'm devastated. Mum must have been desperate to do this, and nobody saw it. I know how isolated and lonely I can feel, but at least I have good friends. All Mum really has is Eve. When does she ever have a life outside of Jake, me, and work? And I know how much she misses Dad – they were a team, and I bet she never imagined being without him.

But Dad couldn't stop himself from dying and maybe she couldn't stop herself from leaving. I have to get Mum back, so we can help her to heal.

I can't face convincing Jake to clean his teeth, and just lead him straight to his bedroom. I feel guilty, which is something I seem to be feeling a lot recently.

We get him in his Arsenal pyjamas, which he wouldn't normally wear until Saturday but he must be too tired to care.

That seems to help settle him. He sorts himself out and tucks the duvet under his arms. His bag is in place at his side, and he looks at the TV screen, ready to watch some late-night TV to help him settle in a strange room. I forgot to bring any storybooks and I'm too tired to make one up. But I don't want to put the TV on yet, as I need to talk to Jake.

"I'm sorry Mum's not here, Jake, but I'm trying to get her back. I'm going to look after you here until she comes home to us, okay?"

Jake frowns and shakes his head. I watch as his face smooths out, then frowns again, trying to make sense of what I've said.

"Jake's mum's not here. Is she on the beach? She likes that."

"No, she isn't and I'm sorry, Jake. Mum isn't well."

As I say this to Jake, I realize how true it is – that Mum's bottled-up grief must have sent her spiralling into a very dark place. I like to think I'm sensitive and can read people's moods, so how did I not realize before? I can hear Dad's voice now with one of his favourite old-people quotes, "Pride comes before a fall, Maudie."

Jake waves his hand up and down in front of my face. "Has Jake's mum got a cold?"

"Not a cold, but inside her head isn't feeling very well. She needs some time to get better. That's why we're having a holiday and giving Mum time to rest. Then when we go home, she'll be back and you can go to sleep in your own bedroom with all your bus pictures and your own bed. Mum loves you very much."

"He knows that. Jake wants his telly."

"Okay."

I settle him down and leave him to sleep. He doesn't want me there now.

I don't know how to make this better for Jake. Maybe I can't and shouldn't assume I can. I hoped just being with me would be enough for now, but I can't take away his confusion and I know he's scared of change.

The curtains flap in the breeze from the open kitchen window. I throw myself on the little sofa, my feet propped up on the back, looking out at the night sky. If Mum was here, she'd tell me to sit up properly. All Mum needed to do was talk. Why didn't she just ask for more help? Why did she have to vanish?

I'm zombified but my brain is buzzing, so there's no point in going to bed yet. I suddenly feel so lonely and miss Liv. My mind drifts to Friday nights out with Liv, Izzy, Avni, Theo, Will and Paz. We'd be out bowling, at the cinema or at a half-price night at some club in Reading. When I go, that is. I'm happy being with Mum and Jake, it keeps everything so much less complicated. And when I do go out, I don't usually drink much – but tonight would be one of those nights I wouldn't care. I'd get completely wasted.

My mind drifts off to the best night ever, when we went to The Q for Paz's eighteenth birthday a few weeks back.

Liv grips my arm and steers me towards the bar. It's happy hour, so it's crammed with people. I'm already a bit wobbly on my feet, as we predrank before we even left her house. Her long nails dig into my skin.

"Sorry, Mauds," she shouts above the thumping music, "but you don't want to fall over before we even start."

"It's not the drink," I bellow back, "I'll need lots more before that happens – it's these shoes!" I try and lift my foot up to point at them. "I'm not used to six-inch heels. I don't know how you manage to walk in them."

"You said you wanted to be taller! You look so cool, and all the guys are looking at you."

"Rubbish, it's always you they want, not me."

Liv sighs dramatically. "You're impossible." She tugs her sixties, silver Biba miniskirt down. "God, it didn't seem this short when I tried it on in the shop."

Someone taps me on the shoulder and puts their mouth against my ear. I wobble on my heels.

"Hey you, I wondered when you'd get here."

"Paz! Happy Birthday." I fling my arms around his neck. His face breaks into a grin and he hugs me back.

He holds me at arm's length. "Wow – you look amazing. That dress! I've never seen anything like it."

"Told you." Liv smirks at me. "Mauds designed it herself, inspired by spiderwebs covered in dew." Her words are a bit slurry.

"That sounds so pretentious," I say to cover my embarrassment.

Paz shakes his head. "It's really cool." He twirls me round to get a proper look. "It's sick."

Liv rolls her eyes at me.

I'm just glad he can't see me go bright red in these lights. I'm not used to this much attention. Tonight, I must admit I'm enjoying not being quietly in the background...not being the invisible one. I can feel myself grow taller without needing the six-inch heels.

"Where is everyone?" Liv changes the subject.

"Over there. Kofi got us a VIP slot and free drinks for the first two hours, so you don't need to go to the bar. We've stocked up."

"Woo hoo! I love your brother. I love you, Kofi!" Liv shouts as she fist punches the air.

Paz drags us over to the table, where the guys all have a sharer cocktail in a treasure chest. It's so cool. I grab a straw and drink. It tastes amazing. Paz makes sure he's next to me and pushes his thigh up against mine. I couldn't move if I wanted to, we're all so squashed together.

I love Paz as a friend, but I don't want more than that. Liv doesn't get it and I can't really explain it. I just don't feel that buzz of attraction you're supposed to feel – besides which, I don't have the time. Now Dad's gone and it's just the three of us at home, I can't abandon Jake and Mum any more than I do.

Liv has squeezed in next to Theo and they immediately start kissing. Paz throws a straw at them. "Man," he shouts, "leave Liv alone and stop makin' out with her in public. You two always do this when you're trashed. Just go out with each other and get it over with!"

They totally ignore him.

"Oh my god, guys, get a freakin' room!" Izzy shrieks at them.

Liv and Theo surface for air, drunken grins twitching across their faces.

"What did you say to your mum about tonight?" I ask Izzy. Her parents are mega old-fashioned and usually want her home by ten at the latest.

"I'm revising with you and Liv and staying the night." She takes a long drink through her straw.

Her parents would be horrified if they knew where she really was – even more so if they knew she and Will were going out and that's where she's really staying tonight. It's ironic really – my mum pushes me to go out. I guess I should be grateful.

It's very dark in here, with strobe lights that illuminate everything in electric blue. People look like they're moving in slow motion. I let myself relax, don't worry about Mum or Jake and just chill with my friends.

It's such a cool club. The bar people are all dressed up in devil costumes with horns and forked tails and the barman had orange snake-eye lenses that gave me the spooks when he looked at me.

I can feel the drink rush through my veins. I'm buzzing in a happy-drunk sort of way. I take another long sip.

"Slow down," Will mouths at me. "THAT STUFF'S LETHAL."

I laugh loudly. I'm on top of the world. I'm Maudie and everyone can see me.

Flames flicker and dance on the cavernous wall behind the bar. The strobe lights bounce off the bottles lined up on the shelves. They're rigged to follow the music, so the lights blink on and off to the beat, changing colour at intervals. The giant chandeliers suspended from the ceiling spatter rainbows all over the people who dance wildly to the music. The DJ dances to the EDM she spins on her decks, totally into the sound. She's wearing yellow reflective sunglasses that cover her face and make her look like an insect.

Liv comes up for air and grabs my hand, dragging me onto the crammed dance floor. I'm squashed amongst sweaty bodies as we swing our hips to the music. I think all the bodies are holding me up on these heels. The bass amp sends vibrations through my body and makes my spine buzz. Unlike the club we're used to going to, this one doesn't smell of beer and puke, but a mix of expensive perfume and aftershave. It makes my head spin, that and the lethal mixture of spirit in the treasure-chest cocktail. It feels so good to remember I'm seventeen and, I'm me, Maudie, and no one can take that away from me.

Liv says something to me, but the music is so loud I can't hear a thing, so I just nod and laugh. We dance together for a bit more, then with everyone around us until Liv stops me and puts her mouth on my ear.

"DRINK?"

That's about all I remember from the club. The rest of it's

muddled, apart from dancing with Paz and losing my shoes somewhere. My feet were black when we left the place.

Maybe when I've found Mum, and we've talked everything through and we're all back home again as a family, I can have more nights like that. If I can find a way to fix things.

I hear a noise from Jake's bedroom and go to check on him.

He's happy watching his late-night TV, one arm snug behind his head, the other clutching his bag at his side. Just seeing him tucked up and content makes all the bad thoughts that are trying to bug me go away.

"Night, Jake, love you. Try to sleep now, it's very late."

Jake raises his hand in a salute. "Night night, bugs bite." He repeats what Dad said to him every night.

I wander back into the sitting room and look out through the window. Outside, the moonlight caps the small white waves rolling in on the tide, breaking on the beach, then ebbing away. A larger wave curls over and dissolves into foam before reaching the shore. It soothes the million bees buzzing in my head.

My phone pings. Liv's put CALL ME! in capital letters.

The buzz in my head turns back up. A feeling of dread threatens to swallow me. I just want to shut my eyes, go to sleep and wake up to find everything has gone back to normal: Mum home and nagging me about revising, Jake singing along to the radio, and Liv trying to get me to go out. I press the call button on my phone. Liv must be sitting on it because she answers straight away. All I can hear is heavy breathing.

"What's going on, Liv? I can't hear you."

"Sorry, I'm under the duvet, so I can't be heard. You know how sound carries at night. I thought you'd text me when you arrived at the cottage."

"We're not at the cottage. Someone was already in it."

"What? You've got to be kidding. You're sure? Did they see you?"

"Yes, I'm sure. I could actually see someone behind the curtains in the house. I made sure she couldn't see me through the bushes. Thank god the woman was up so late or I might have just let myself in and been found out immediately. It was some older lady, big, as in tall, with dark hair with grey bits and a massive flowery shirt. Do you know her?"

"That could be any number of my aunt's friends. I'm so, so sorry, Maudie, I don't get it, it should be empty."

"Honestly, it doesn't matter now. We're fine, thanks to the taxi driver. We're at some caravan park on Perran Sands. Just tell me what's happening, Liv."

She takes a long, deep breath. "Eve called round in a right panic. She was really freaking out, said Jake had vanished from his foster carer's house and did I know where you were, 'cause you'd been staying out late and avoiding her. Apparently she's been ringing you non-stop, and your mum, who still has her phone switched off."

"What did you say?"

"That I hadn't seen you and you'd been avoiding *everyone* recently. I'm not sure she believed me."

"Crap."

"Apparently Jake's foster carer was seriously worried, not surprisingly, and called the police. At first, they thought he'd just done one of his runners and got lost, but then when they couldn't find him straight away, they did a big search of the area. After that, they came to see me, um, about an hour ago.

"I waited to call you because Mum obviously thinks I know where you are. She kept strangely quiet and didn't go on at me to say anything to them. I think Mum's angry at Eve for shoving Jake in care when your mum had just walked out on you. It's really upset her – and that your mum didn't confide in her."

"Tell me about it. I love your mum."

"Yeah, she's pretty cool. Don't worry, I told the police the same as Eve, that I had no idea where you were. I kept it simple. They checked my phone too. Obviously, there are major alerts out round here because Jake is so vulnerable."

"Having these phones has given us at least another day, p'raps two."

"Hope so – I was so nervous I talked too much."

I feel really bad when I hear the shake in her voice. "Hey, it's not your fault, and I'm sure you were great. I'm not going to last long here, am I?"

"It depends how private it is where you are."

"We've got one of those mobile-home thingies. It's all we could get this late at night."

"Will it be difficult for Jake?"

"I don't know, hard to tell. There are a few lights on in the other caravans, so there are definitely other people around. We'll probably be found and dragged home before Mum knows we've even gone. Argh! It was a pretty wild idea in the first place."

I feel such a failure. I thought I had the perfect plan, but as usual I am anything but perfect.

"Why don't you just come home now then?"

"I don't know, Liv. Even if it is ridiculous, what else can I do to make everyone understand? Jake needs to be with me, not with some woman he doesn't know in a strange house." I sigh deeply. "But I feel so lousy that you have to lie for me and get into trouble. They'll know it's me when I don't go home tonight, and then they'll be back to interrogate you. I'm so sorry, Liv."

"Forget it, even if you do come home sooner than we thought, your mum's bound to hear about it, and it'll hopefully shock her into coming back. Surely she's going to message Eve again, and when she does she'll see all the calls and texts from her. Hang on, I can hear something – I'm going to poke my head out... I'm just on YouTube, Mum. Yeah, I know what time it is. Sorry. I didn't mean to wake you... That was Mum. Gotta go. Love you."

"Love you more."

The phone cuts off.

Liv's the best friend you could have, and I've just dumped all my problems onto her. My angst grows until I can't stand it. What if Mum doesn't contact Eve again? What if she can't? I stop my brain thinking the word that's hovering there trying to scare me. Mum's not Dad. I'm letting my thoughts spiral. She's not…dead. I'm angry I said the word, even in my head. "You're doing this all wrong," I say to myself.

I go outside, closing the door quietly behind me, and look over the fence to the beach below. I want to watch the waves crash against the rocks, so I can fling my anxiety out to become part of them and break my pain up into pieces.

The moon is hiding behind the clouds now and the night is dark. The water looks black but for the tiny green lights from a cruise ship moving slowly across the horizon. Sea sprays on my face and I taste salt in my mouth. I slip between the other caravans and stand on the precipice, leaning over the fence.

The moon emerges from the backs of the looming clouds and lights up where I am with an unearthly light, making blue shadows move across the grass. On my left, dark caverns yawn in the rocks, gulping down the water and spewing it back out in a plume of white foam. The sea swells and retreats. Stars prick the sky where the clouds have parted. I watch a lone figure, her hair caught by the wind, hunched over, hands in pockets, walking along the edge of the water. She doesn't seem to notice when a bigger wave comes in and splashes up to her knees, she just keeps on walking.

The woman reminds me how sad and lonely I feel. I want to be cuddled up next to Mum on the sofa or sewing one of my designs with her and her telling me how to check the different thread types. Already everything is going wrong and I'm scared of what might happen to me when I'm found – have I made things worse for Jake potentially? He could end up in care permanently and I might never see him again.

"What else could I do?" I shout out, my words tiny against the roar of the sea. My tears blow across my face. I cry until there's nothing left. All I want is for Mum to come home. I just want her to hug me and tell me everything is going to be okay.

CHAPTER 26

Jake

There's a telly in my room. I want one of those in my home bedroom. Mum said no. Not until I'm bigger. I'm very big already. I can touch the ceiling. I can hear a noise. I think it's a ghost. Maudie said it was the wind. I don't like wind. It howls in your head.

Tomorrow I can build a sandcastle. Mum makes the best castles. Mum has a box of glass rocks and stripy shells. On her window shelf. I will find her some. Has Mum come to Cornwall? I don't know. She's not in my caravan. I will look for her. I can hear tapping. On my window. Uh-oh, uh-oh. The monster is here. Where's my sister?

CHAPTER 27

Maudie

I open the curtains and morning light bursts through the window. Seagulls circle above a fishing trawler heading back into the harbour, their faint squawking cries carrying on the wind. I dare to believe it's going to be alright here with Jake. It's funny how everything always seems so much better in the morning.

No one else is around, not surprisingly since it's only six-thirty on a Saturday morning. I'm lucky if I've even had three hours' sleep. Jake got up in the night; I think he was spooked being in yet another bedroom. He said a monster was tapping on his window. He often mentions monsters, but we don't know what form they take. I tried to help him draw them out, but we couldn't find the words to make the picture. I showed him the tapping was from a bit of cable, but it took for ever to convince him, even after I went outside and hooked it out the way. Then we had to sort his bus leaflets into colours. By the time we banished the monster, I was wide awake. At least it isn't summer, because then Jake gets up with the birds. He seems to have this internal clock in tune with nature, because Dad put up blackout blinds and yet he still wakes up at four. Dad used to say he loved hearing the dawn chorus, but once I heard him moaning to Mum that he'd like to shoot every one of the "chirruping little fuckers".

The mobile home in front of us looks empty, but I can see a shadow moving behind the poppy-patterned curtains in the one on our left. My heart sinks.

I'm going to have to help Jake shower, and I'm dreading it because he hates it so much. He says the water hurts him – not because it's too hot or anything, but his skin is really sensitive, so perhaps it feels like needles or something. He hates baths too, though, and showers are quicker. It upsets me to see him so distraught. I wish I knew what the worst part of it is for him and how it feels, so we could work out a way to avoid distressing him. I consider just forgetting about the shower for today, but we both need one after our long journey yesterday and he has that typical teenage boy, locker-room smell about him.

I can hear Jake talking to himself, the walls are so thin.

Then he shouts, "The big bad wolf is going to get him!" I can hear the fear in his voice and run to help him, like in the night.

Jake is sitting on his bed, his blonde hair sticking up in

the middle like a bog brush but dark at the sides where it's wet with sweat. His leg is jigging up and down.

"I'm here, Jake, I'm here."

I sit on the bed next to him and he rests his hand on my knee. It's hot and sweaty.

"That wolf was going to eat Jake up."

"I won't let him. I'll kick his butt for you."

Jake laughs. "She said butt."

"Butt, butt, bottom…BUM!"

Jake roars with laughter – he's such a typical boy. Dad used to shout things like, "bog roll" if Jake was getting fed up on a long car journey, to cheer him up, but he would be in hysterics himself.

I miss Dad more than ever now.

"Jake needs breakfast. He has egg in shells on Saturday. With Marmite soldiers. At-ten-tion!" He salutes me.

"We don't have eggs yet, so it has to be Frosties. Shower first."

"Jake doesn't want a shower."

"Well, Jake has smelly armpits, so Jake has to have a shower."

Dad was better at jollying Jake through it. Jake gets up and moves over to the window. I know he's trying to ignore me.

"Look at that ship." He points out the window.

I peer through it. There's a tiny speck on the horizon.

"How can you see what it is? Your eyesight is incredible. You must be Superman."

"He is."

"Well, even Superman has to wash, so let's do it!"

"Jake wants breakfast."

"After your shower."

He looks mutinous, which doesn't bode well.

I run the water, which at first refuses to be anything but boiling hot or sub-zero. I'm getting stressed out and Jake's not even in the shower yet. How can I possibly help to wash him when the cubicle is so small? In the end I get a chair and place it in the doorway. Then I make sure all the windows are shut, as people hearing the noise and coming to bang on our door will only upset Jake more.

I help Jake undress and somehow get him under the shower. It's been some time since I last did this, as I've just let Mum do it. I'm shocked at how much he's grown up. He's not a little boy any more.

It seems there's a lot I've not been noticing lately. I feel small and bad about myself; an uncomfortable ball sits heavily in the pit of my stomach. I wish Mum was here so I could tell her.

"Ow! Don't put those pins in him."

"I'm so sorry, Jake. I know, I know. I wish it didn't hurt you."

I feel terrible and hate that I have to put him through this. Mum and Dad tried everything to make it better for him – flannel, baths, tried to get him to do it, but nothing worked. I speed up, deciding it's best to get it over and done with as fast as possible, for both of us. Water is getting everywhere, and the floor of the caravan is turning into a lake.

"He doesn't like it."

Jake tries to push the shower gel away and his elbow catches my eye.

"Argh! I can't see properly. Put your arm down, please."

"Go away."

"Hold this flannel over your eyes, Jake."

I grit my teeth and squirt shampoo on his head. That's when things get loud.

"STOP HURTING HIM! GET OFF HIM. OW OW OW, SHE'S KILLING HIM!"

I move fast. "No one's hurting you, Jake, really I'm not. Oh god, I'm so sorry. I have to wash you. It'll be quicker if you just let me do it." I wobble on the chair and cling to the shower door for support. "Don't push me, Jake!"

"She's shouting at him."

"No, she isn't. I can't leave soap in your hair. Sorry, sorry, sorry."

I angle the shower onto his head.

"SHE'S KILLING JAKE." He lets out a piercing shriek that I swear nearly bursts my eardrums. "AAAAAAH!"

I topple off the chair and end up winded on the floor, sat in a pool of water.

BANG!

The caravan door flies open, and a figure half stumbles, half falls through the door.

I scream.

Jake screams.

A young guy, only a few years older than me, barks, "What the fuck's going on in here?"

"Get out!" I shout at the guy. "Who the hell are you?"

His bewildered face looks from me to Jake, who's now standing butt naked next to me, gripping his pink bag that he grabbed from the floor outside the shower and flapping his arms up and down, waving the bag like a flag. He does this when he's very stressed and can no longer speak. This guy is scaring Jake, and I need to get rid of him – *fast*.

First, I pull his bag down to cover his privates, but Jake flaps his arms again. I stand in front of him to protect him.

"Are you hurt? Someone said they were being *killed*." There are beads of sweat on the guy's nose. His eyes flit round the caravan. He barges past us into the bedrooms.

"Ow! He hit Jake."

I make him look at me. "It's alright, Jake, he's not going to hurt you. He heard you shouting."

We hear a strangled, "Oof! There's water everywhere!" then, "Is it just you two here?" he asks, coming back to us.

"Yes."

Jake starts to rock. "He's going to hurt him. Take him away."

The guy frowns. "I won't hurt you. I thought someone was being murdered."

"It's not what it sounded like. My brother has multiple

learning disabilities and doesn't like the shower."

"I'm not sure what it sounded like, except fucking weird."

"He said fuck. You mustn't swear. Derrick won't like that." Jake tells him off.

"Who the hell's Derrick?" The guy's face shows his bewilderment.

"One of his teachers at school," I reply. "Can you not shout, please? It's upsetting you, isn't it, Jake?"

He nods.

"*I'm* upsetting him? You've obviously freaked *him* out and you've freaked out half the campsite." He looks at his watch. "It's not even seven-thirty in the morning yet. Is he okay?"

"Maybe try asking Jake for yourself instead of speaking over him. Who are you anyway?"

"I...I...Jee-zus!" He takes a deep breath to calm himself down. "I thought I was putting my life on the line for you here."

"I'm sorry about that, but as you can see, we're fine."

He frowns suddenly, half turning away while pointing in the direction of Jake's naked body. "Don't you think you ought to cover him up? You should too." He's trying not to look at me.

"Oh god." I yank my white T-shirt down, mortified that the water has made it see-through. I take Jake's arm and steer him into the bedroom and push the door to. He's shivering and whispering under his breath, "He's okay, he's okay, he's okay."

"Hey, it's alright, there's nothing to worry about. No more man. No more shouting and no more shower. There, there. Shush now. He won't hurt you; he was just checking we were okay. You're going to have to stop screaming and accusing me of murder, or the police will come next time."

"Jake doesn't want that policeman here."

"Neither do I."

I wrap a towel around him, tuck it in at the waist and slip his hoody over his head. "Sit on the bed and I'll help you get properly dressed in a minute. I'm going to sort this guy out. You get your bag."

Jake screws his face up and sways from foot to foot, so I gently manoeuvre him onto the bed and push the wet hair off his face and kiss his forehead.

"Ah that's nice," Jake says.

He places the handles of his bag over his knee while I switch the TV on for him.

He waves at the screen. "Ooh – Jake likes that cooking."

I grab his other sweatshirt with a picture of Kevin, Stuart and Bob – Jake's favourite Minions – on the front, and pull it on over my top. Luckily it goes down to my knees.

"Alright now, Jake? I'll be back in a minute."

He's already engrossed, which is a huge relief, as it will give me time to sort everything out.

I walk back out to find the young guy sitting on the edge of the table, grinning at me from beneath his fringe, which keeps falling over his eyes. He's tall, over six foot, slim but not too skinny, with dark, almost black, curly hair and gorgeous deep-blue eyes. I'm irritated that my heart does a little skip.

"Cute top." He winks at me. God I hate that. Does he think he's being sexy? It's just weird. Almost as though he can read my thoughts, he stops smiling and looks serious. "Look, sorry, but you might not be able to stay here – I'll talk to my uncle. If he freaks out like that a lot, you'll clear the site."

Something in me snaps. "His name's *Jake* and he only does that if something frightens him. What would you do? Lock him away?"

"*Whoa!*" The guy holds his hands up. "That's not what I was saying at all! How the hell did we get from, 'he can't stay', to 'locking him away'?"

"You can cut the snarky, patronizing comments." I practically spit at him, my emotions boiling over.

"There's no need to get hysterical."

"I. Am. *Not*. Hysterical." Except I can feel myself losing it after everything that's happened, and I can't seem to stop. "It's not *my* fault the place I was supposed to go to was double-booked and I had to come to this…this tin box on wheels! I need somewhere to be safe with Jake, and Brae said I could stay here with him. I had n-no choice and now you're, you're *throwing* us out on the street."

"Throwing you out on the street? Are we living in alternative universes?"

I ignore him. "I don't know where else I can go. This is

discrimination! I can report you for this, you know?"

He stares at me for a moment before throwing his head back and laughing out loud, which makes me burst into tears. I want to be furious at him for laughing at something so important, but all the stress is coming out instead.

"Oh crap, I'm sorry – I didn't mean to be a patronizing dick." He gets up and pats my shoulder awkwardly. "Look, um, shall we start again? Why don't you sit down? Er…tea?"

"Tea?" I'm completely thrown by the change of direction. He pulls his sleeves up and puts the kettle on. I sit down at the table and let him take over, because I'm not capable of doing anything other than snivel.

"I really am sorry, I didn't mean to laugh. Nervous reaction." He glances up at me from beneath his fringe. He's blushing. He puts two mugs on the counter.

"You'll need four mugs. Jake has two and he has his tea with half hot water, then topped up with c…cold water and m…milk." I hiccup.

"He drinks tea?"

"No, Jake drinks fermented yak's milk from Outer Mongolia."

The guy laughs awkwardly.

"I was being sarcastic."

He stops laughing. "I know. Embarrassed reaction this time." He gets another two mugs from the cupboard. "I'm Gerren, by the way."

"Maudie and—"

"Jake." He finishes for me.

"Oh, no! I've just left him sitting half-naked watching the TV."

I run into the bedroom, mortified I let this guy take over and forgot Jake was by himself.

"Sorry, Jake, I got distracted and shouldn't have."

"Jake was learning how to cook brownies. He likes those. He wants to make those with his mum."

A wave of sadness sweeps over me. "Yeah, you and Mum love that, don't you? When Mum gets home you can make brownies with her, or we can do that, if you like."

"Jake does like," he says very seriously.

I help dress him properly before bringing him out to the kitchen and sitting him down for breakfast.

"Jake, this is Gerren, and Gerren, as you know, this is Jake."

Gerren puts his hand out and so does Jake, but as soon as Gerren holds Jake's he whines, "Don't touch him," which makes Gerren go even redder than he did before, and he's left looking at his hand.

"You did put your hand out too, Jake," I remind him. "Right, let's get some breakfast," I say to cause a distraction.

I pour a large bowl of cereal for Jake, which he starts shovelling in, he's so hungry. He doesn't look up when Gerren tentatively puts his mugs next to him then steps back as though Jake's going to bite. We're used to this reaction, but it still makes me frown.

"Did you top the tea up with cold water?"

Gerren nods, looking slightly puzzled.

"Thank you."

Jake reaches out his empty hand, picks up his teas one by one and knocks them back.

"Wow – that's impressive. I get the cold water now. He, er, I mean, Jake, you should come to the yard of ale contest at The Tinners Arms."

"Maybe not, since he's only thirteen."

"I wouldn't have known!"

"Don't worry, his height and build always make people assume Jake's much older. He takes after my dad."

Gerren passes me my tea and sits next to me.

I rest my head on my arms for a moment. "What am I going to do? If I can't stay here, I think I might have to go home, but I can't go home yet, I *can't*. Do you have any mobile homes on their own somewhere?"

I can hear the desperation in my voice, and I can feel Gerren scrutinizing me.

"Why can't you go home?"

Crap. I think fast.

"Mum needed a break and she asked me to bring Jake here for a treat."

"What about your dad? Sorry, that's none of my business. Aren't you a bit young to be a carer to him?" He nods in Jake's direction.

"His name is JAKE," I say, exasperation making me snap.

"That's twice you've talked as though he isn't here, and for your information, I'm not his carer, I'm his sister and I'm very happy to be on holiday with him."

Gerren holds his hands up and smiles, not bothered by my spikiness. "For sure, I didn't mean to offend you both. Give me a chance, please?" He does this cheeky grin. "Pretty please?" His face becomes more serious. "Look, I'm sorry if I'm doing this all wrong but I'd like to help if I can."

Butterflies explode in my stomach, which really annoys me since I'm cross he's making Jake invisible. But we do need help. I don't know what to say. My eyes fill with tears. I take a long, slow breath to stop them.

"Honestly, I wasn't having a go at you," he says. "Are you still at school then?"

I'm grateful Gerren's taken the attention away from my beetroot face and that I've managed to avoid answering the dad question. I'm not ready to open up about him. I think I'd fall apart having to deal with any more emotion right now, so I answer without thinking.

"Yes, sixth form."

Gerren frowns. "It's not the Easter holidays yet or we'd be full here. Shouldn't you both be *at* school?"

Uh-oh. Clearly he's not buying into my story. How do I get out of this one?

CHAPTER 28

Jake

Pinch pinch pinch! Water has pins in it. It makes my skin crackle and burn. I don't want to shower.

I got a shock. There was a big bang. I screamed. I don't know that boy. Get him out of here. Maudie was cross with him. He frightened me. I don't like shouting. It makes my ears bubble. I like bubbles in the air. I can get some later. For outside.

I'm hungry. Mum said I had a big appetite. She said I love my food. I do. I want some toast. Maudie isn't talking to me. She's talking to that boy. That boy can't see me. Maudie keeps smiling at him. Talk to me! Go away, boy.

CHAPTER 29

Maudie

"Knock, knock – can I come in?"

Brae pops his head through the open doorway. I am so relieved to see him, as it means I don't have to answer Gerren's question about school or Dad.

"Mornin', lass, morning, young man – how are you doing?" He nods at Jake.

His bushy white beard kind of moves up and down as he speaks, which makes me think of the giant light-up, mechanical Santa Claus on the roof of Tesco last Christmas. Brae has a red checked shirt on today with black wellies, which makes him even more like Santa.

Jake jumps up in excitement. "Father Christmas's back!"

Gerren laughs and this time looks at Jake when he says, "That's what I used to call him when I was little."

"Ho ho ho!" Brae booms and hands Jake a small brown paper bag, "That's from me," and then places a large wicker basket on the table and starts pulling things out to show us. "Not from me but my cousin Beth who runs the site shop. When I told her you were here, she wanted to give you this. She thought you might need a few supplies, so there's some eggs, bread, bacon, fruit, cheese and milk – full cream, none of that skinny muck, mind."

"Oh, that's so kind of her and you to—"

Brae holds his hand up to stop me talking. "It's a pleasure. No need to thank me or Beth."

Jake holds the brown bag up in the air. "Jake's got a present. Look."

He thrusts it towards me.

"Open it then."

We all watch while he rips the bag open. Inside is a die-cast model of a blue and white open-top bus. Jake's so pleased he squeals.

"Look what Jake's got! That's his best bus!"

"That's brilliant, Jake, I love it. Thanks, Brae, they're his favourite. How did you know?"

"Jake told him last night when he was having a crap," Jake says, with a wicked grin on his face. "Oh no, Jake said a bad word."

I don't know whether to laugh or cringe with embarrassment, but can't help joining in with everyone else laughing. "I'm so sorry. Jake, thank Brae."

"He was going to!" he informs me huffily. "Thank you, Christmas. Jake's got a new bus."

Brae pumps Jake's hand and Jake doesn't object at all – must be the magic of Santa Claus. "Look after it, young man. Perhaps you can put it in your special bag. My nephew Evan, Beth's son, had Down syndrome. Lovely lad he was. He liked things just so too – had a backpack he always wore, full of his stuff."

"Jake can't put it in his bag. It's full up."

"It looks empty to me," Gerren says, clearly puzzled.

"I think Jake means he's got everything in it that he wants. Isn't that right, Jake?" Brae explains.

It's so great to find someone who understands Jake and makes me feel less alone.

Jake is too busy shunting the bus backwards and forwards across the tabletop to answer Brae.

Brae sits down on one of the stools and pulls it up a bit closer to Jake. "Now I hear from Mrs Andrews in the next-door mobile home that you've been causing a spot of bother, young lad. She just popped up to see me in reception."

Jake shakes his head. "Jake hasn't got a spot."

"I'm so sorry, I'll apologize to her," I butt in, terrified he's going to tell us we'll have to leave. "Jake hates baths and showers, don't you?"

"They're dis-gusting," Jake tells Brae.

"I know it's scary hearing someone shout out that they're being murdered when they're not." I can almost hear Liv's voice telling me to get a grip, but I'm on a roll. "But Jake never used to say that until he started watching CSI. Mum blames Jamie Manson at his school for getting him into it—"

"Jake likes the fighting." He karate-chops his bus.

"Mum wasn't happy. And we didn't mean to upset all your campers, but please, please is there anywhere else on site we could move to, on our own, so it doesn't matter if there's a few screams? You see, I can't go home yet – Mum… Mum needs a break." I finish my words in a rush.

Both Brae and Gerren look slightly stunned. Jake shoves his empty cereal bowl at Brae, oblivious to my desperate plea.

"Jake can't eat any more."

"That's probably because you've eaten it all." Brae winks at him, puts the bowl in the sink and says to me, "Look, there's no need to worry, Maudie. You've obviously taken time off work to be here with your brother before the Easter invasion."

He thinks I'm older than I am. I plead with my eyes for Gerren not to say anything. He opens his mouth then shuts it again, a slight frown on his face.

Brae continues speaking, oblivious to our silent communication. "I understand the challenges for you here and I've an idea if you're happy with it. We've our family mobile holiday home on the outskirts of the site, nearer to the beach, tucked away in a secluded spot. It's empty until the Easter weekend, so plenty of time for you to use it. It has a nice bit of decking that looks out over the sea and a secluded garden with a barbecue you can use.

"Jake, you can scream bloody murder if you want to, without disturbing anyone. I remember Evan had a pair of lungs on him. What d'you think?"

His face is lit up with good intention, as he looks from me to Jake.

Jake salutes Brae and I'm speechless, so throw my arms around Brae instead and kiss him on the cheek, something I'd never normally do. His beard tickles my nose. "Thank you, thank you, thank you!"

"I'll take that as a yes then." He grins.

"Don't kiss that Father Christmas," Jake tells me off.

His comment brings me back to reality and cuts my elation dead. "Except...I-I don't know if I can afford..." My voice trails off.

Brae thinks for a minute. "I don't rent our own home out normally, but if you just cover a few costs, then we'll call it quits. How does that sound?"

"Too good to be true?"

The morning is bright with sun, though I'm chilled by the cold wind whistling through my denim jacket. I can hear the sound of the pebbles shifting when the water pulls them back out to sea.

I can't believe my hysterical rant earlier at Gerren and Brae – though why am I worrying what Gerren thinks about me? Except he didn't dump me in it when his uncle assumed

I was older than I am, which was pretty cool. I do feel terrible about deceiving Brae over why I'm down here though. He's been our guardian angel.

Along the edge of the dunes, silvery marram grasses bend, straighten and bend again. Next to me the steady thwack of Jake's spade scooping up sand carries on the breeze. It's nearly empty at this end of the beach. In the distance I hear the twanging sound of boat cables vibrating against their masts, from the fishing boats moored around the cove. A few seagulls squawk and cry, as they let themselves be carried on the air currents that draw them towards the horizon.

I keep imagining Mum in her car, randomly driving away from us in the rain, staring out of the window as the windscreen wipers slide back and forth across the glass, leaning over the steering wheel, not knowing which direction to go in. I wish I knew what she was feeling. I think back to her goodbye note, which is now under my pillow at the mobile home. It doesn't tell me anything, except that she had to go. But it's the last thing she touched before she left.

I think we all became very good at hiding our emotions after Dad died, because we had to get on with things. I don't know what to do with all the feelings that are churned up inside me now. I check my phone for about the hundredth time this morning, but still nothing from Liv since our morning texts. I'm on edge until I know what's happening with the police. Will they find us and bring us home today? I wonder if Eve has tracked Mum down. I hope Mum at least knows we've gone.

Everything must have felt hopeless to Mum, if she had to run away. She used to talk to me, tell me things that were going on in her head – worries over paying the bills, something Eve said that upset her, concerns over some new anxiety Jake or I had developed – not that I was ever much help in sorting them out. But I guess it made her feel better to have offloaded them.

I used to lie awake at night, trying to work out what I could do to help her. I do the same now, wondering how I can help give Mum time and space to work through her emotions about Dad, when she's back with us. I could do more stuff with Jake during the summer holiday. And I could focus on getting a place at the nearer art colleges next year, which would mean I could carry on living at home and be there when she needs me. Why didn't I talk to Mum more about Dad dying, instead of letting her bottle up her grief? All this might not have happened.

Something cold and damp lands on my foot. Jake's covering it in sand.

He's focused on what he's doing but he still talks to himself constantly, as though he's another Jake, looking for reassurance.

"It's alright, Jake. You can do that. It doesn't go there. You're not in trouble. Jake doesn't like sand on his hand.

It tickles. It's alright, you can wipe it off. Jake has cheesy meat pasta on Saturday. That's his favourite. Jake can cook it for us. He likes mixing the cheese up."

"I hadn't thought about Saturday dinner, but we could make it together. I'm sure we can buy the ingredients at the campsite store."

Jake shakes his head. "Maudie can go to Lidl's – 'big on quality, Lidl on price'."

He scoops up more sand with his spade and adds it to the mountainous pile on my foot, which won't stay on because I'm laughing so much.

"Stop laughing, girl! Can you help me?"

"Of course I can. Pass me that other spade. Do you want to build a big castle with a moat? I can get you some water to put in it and some shells and pebbles to decorate it. If you're lucky we might find a feather to stick in the top like a flag. What d'you think?"

"Yes, he'd like that. He doesn't know what that moat is."

"It's like a big pond that the castle sits in the middle of. Oh, I know – remember when we went to Hever Castle with Mum last year and we saw all those knights fighting on horseback?"

Jake stares into the distance. "Yes, he does. That horse did a poo."

"Trust you to remember that. Well, the castle was surrounded by water, and we went over the drawbridge. The water underneath it is a moat."

"Jake knows that."

I raise my eyebrows at him. Jake flicks a bit of seaweed at me, which I bat away with the back of my hand. He keeps doing it for a bit, as it makes him laugh.

The wind drops and I feel the sun, warm on my bare ankles and wrists. I watch Jake then look away, his joy folding in on me, wrenching at my heart. Most teenagers wouldn't dig sandcastles, even if they'd secretly enjoy it. Jake just goes for it.

His curls shine gold in the sunlight, with copper glints, just like mine do when they're not dyed brown. His long straight lashes cast shadows on his cheek. Cow-lashes – that's what Dad used to call them. That annoyed Mum. He glances up at me, as though he senses I'm thinking about him. His green eyes watch me, trusting, and it makes me smile.

"Help me fill the bucket with sand," I say, grabbing my spade.

Jake digs energetically, flinging up sprays of sand into the wind. He winces when some lands in his hair. "Get it off him!"

"Silly," I say, brushing the sand out.

"Don't do that!" Jake swipes his hand at me.

"Careful – no hitting, remember. How can I get the sand out if I can't brush it off?"

Jake is still throwing sand around. "Dig a bit more gently and then that won't happen, see? Now squash it down and we'll turn it out. Go on, turn it upside down."

"Jake doesn't know up-down."

I wonder if Jake finds it hard to process all the information I sometimes shower him with. I make a mental note to try not to do that.

Jake thwacks the top and then does it several times, getting more aggressive with each thwack.

"Jake's Dwayne 'The Rock' Johnson. He likes that wrestling."

"Yeah, and Mum hated you and Dad watching it. Okay, that's enough." We both giggle at his overenthusiastic thumps. "Right!" I lift the bucket up.

"Whoa – way to go! Cool castle."

Jake and I both spring back. "Jeeze, Gerren, do you make a habit of scaring the shit out of people?"

"Don't swear, Derrick won't like it," Gerren teases.

"No, Derrick doesn't like shit," Jake says approvingly.

"Who does, mate?" Gerren puts his hand up to high-five Jake, who screws his face up and gives a grunt of dislike. Gerren doesn't know what to do with his hand and sticks it in his pocket. "Sorry, didn't mean to upset him...you... Jake."

He goes to sit on the rock next to me, but Jake picks up a large piece of wet seaweed and plonks it on the rock, then goes back to stabbing his spade into the sand.

"What are you doing, Jake?" Gerren asks him.

"Jake's digging a tunnel." He empties the sand onto Gerren's trainer.

Gerren stands there with it on his foot, uncertain whether to shake it off.

"Is everything okay? I thought you were working." I shield my eyes from the sun as I look up at him.

He slides his foot back, carefully dislodging the sand. I fling the seaweed down the beach and pat the rock next to me, feeling slightly sorry for him. Gerren smiles, relieved.

"It's lunch and I thought I might find you here. I brought some sandwiches, to kind of make up for this morning."

Jake stops digging instantly. "Jake wants a sandwich."

"Great, I'm glad I bought them then." Gerren looks pleased with himself.

"It's fine about this morning – it's not your fault. I didn't mean to cry all over you. It's just there's been a lot going on recently."

Gerren tilts his head to the side. I can almost see his brain cogs grinding as he prepares to ask another awkward question about what we're really doing down here and why I didn't want him revealing my real age. I've got to think before I open my mouth.

"Jake wants a sandwich," Jake says a bit louder, with perfect timing.

"Right, yes, of course." Gerren removes his backpack and unzips it. He reads the label as he holds each one up. "Chicken and avocado, BLT or pick of the day – falafel with mango chutney and shredded lettuce in a wholemeal pitta bread."

I can't help laughing. "You sound like an advert for Pret or something."

"I help in the cafe here, as well as doing lots of other jobs on site. What would Jake like?" he asks me.

"Ask Jake."

"Jeeze, I keep putting my great big foot in it." Gerren grimaces.

"Ha ha, Bigfoot." Jake chuckles to himself.

Gerren and Jake grin at each other.

"It's okay. How would you know the best way to be around him?" I say, realizing, as I say this that perhaps I can be a bit unfair on people. It would be great if Jake could just be treated like everyone else and not talked over, but sometimes he does need a little extra understanding, and that usually only comes with getting to know him. I don't ever remember seeing someone like Jake in a book or on TV – it's as though people with learning disabilities don't exist in public. The sadness of that overwhelms me. Jake's been blanked out of life.

Jake pats the sandwich he wants. He's gone for the chicken.

"It's got avocado in it though, Jake."

"Get it out!" Jake looks horrified. "He wants that chicken."

"You'll have to take out the avocado, unless you want an international incident, Gerren."

"Why? What's wrong with avocado?"

"It's green," Jake tells him.

Gerren frowns. "But your bag is green."

Jake holds it up in the air. "Jake likes this one."

"He's not going to *eat* his bag – are you, Jake?" I tease him.

"That girl's being 'diculous."

"I am! You don't like green food, do you, Jake? Peas are the worst, aren't they?"

"True, I've never liked them, either." Gerren nods. He unfolds a blanket from his rucksack and spreads it on the sand. "Jake, I got you some apple juice as I noticed some in the caravan earlier. Is that okay?"

I can't deny I'm impressed. Jake doesn't look at Gerren, but he puts his hand out to take it.

"What d'you say, Jake?" Jake ignores me, which he's very good at. "*Thank* you." I shrug my shoulders at Gerren and turn to Jake. "Once you're focused on food, that's it, we've lost you, haven't we?" Jake shows his agreement by handing me the empty carton.

Gerren passes me Jake's sandwich and I pick the avocado out and hand it to Jake, who takes a big bite.

"God, I'm starving." Gerren plonks himself next to me on the blanket and takes his trainers off, placing them on the damp sand next to mine. The toes point in different directions. Jake leans forwards and repositions them so they look like they could walk off together.

"Do you live down here, then?" I always feel I have to fill in any gaps in a conversation.

"I start uni in the autumn, at Exeter, studying Marine

Biology, so I've been working a gap year with Brae to earn some money. But I've worked down here every holiday over the past few years too. Brae is my uncle, Dad's brother, and we've always been really close. He's much older than Dad and always looked after him too."

"Did you know his nephew then? Evan, wasn't it?"

"Yep – I met him once, a long time ago, but he was a different side of the family. Brae often talked about him though."

"Brae's the nicest guy, isn't he, Jake?"

"Yes, he is."

Gerren nods in agreement. "He's brilliant. He helped me through a rough patch and now he's determined to make sure I never have to worry about supporting myself through uni. Not that my dad isn't too."

"That's amazing! I'm going to have to get a job if I want to go to art college in London. If I decide to move away from Mum and Jake. It's SO expensive there. Why d'you want to do Marine Biology? It sounds really cool."

"I'd love to be a reef restoration project manager someday." His eyes light up and match the sparkles on the sea where the sun catches the tops of the waves. "Oceans and reefs have been doing fine all by themselves for millions of years and then we come along and wipe them out like that." He clicks his fingers. "I can't stand that. I've been coming down to Cornwall all my life and spent half of that on the sea, surfing. Now I spend any spare time *under* the sea, diving. It cuts me up to see the amount of plastic and human waste just dumped in the water. People don't think about it being a death sentence for marine life."

"My best friend Liv follows a designer on Insta who turns recycled plastic from the sea into pictures."

"That's cool. But I can go on and on about it. We should totally go out diving together – this part of Cornwall has a lot of wreck-diving. The boat wrecks provide a diverse ecosystem that becomes home to some amazing local marine life – even grey seals." His face is animated until he stops and frowns. "Oh. I guess it's not possible for you to come. Um – hey, would you like to see a giant lobster and some sharks, Jake?"

His head shoots up. "Jake wants to see one."

"Great, maybe we could visit the aquarium in Newquay and see all the sea life, where it's safe. I hate them being in a tank, but it's good that it makes it possible for some people to be able to see them."

"Jake knows that lobster. His mum loves that lobster." He gets up, ready to go to the aquarium right now. "Jake see his mum. Let's get her now."

"Not right now, Jake, very soon, okay?"

He sits back down on a rock and talks quietly. "Mum might be there. Jake find her."

"Very, very soon, Jake, I promise."

"I'm glad he likes the idea so much." Gerren looks pleased.

I'm so grateful for Gerren including Jake like that, especially when he barely knows us. Gerren focuses his blue eyes on me. I can't believe he's already realized what's important to me and that it's okay my life's not straightforward. Liv is the only person who's ever really understood that about me before. I miss her terribly, so even though I've only just met Gerren, I feel a bit of my guard come down. He's seen some of the real me and not just the outline of me.

Jake shoves a razor-clam shell in my face. "Jake's mum has a shell like this. In Jake's house. In the bathroom. Jake's mum's not there. Jake doesn't know where she is. Jake's mum has gone. Jake needs to find her."

Gerren looks at me strangely, a puzzled frown on his face at Jake's words. My senses are on hyper alert and my mind races. I just stare at Gerren, unable now to think of a thing to say.

When he speaks, his voice is hesitant. "Why don't you tell me the real reason you're down here, Maudie?"

CHAPTER 30

Jake

Maudie was getting me shells. For my sandcastle. She forgot.
I don't want to dig by myself. He's here again. That boy.
He's not sharing Maudie. He's drawn on his arm. It's called
a ta-too. Mum doesn't like them. She said Maudie can't have a
ta-too. Maudie has one on her neck. A blue bird. It hides under
her hair. It's our secret. Jake likes having a secret with Maudie.

   Maudie's laughing. What's she laughing at? I don't know.
That boy wasn't funny. He said he can take me to see a lobster.
Dad took us to see them. On our before holiday. Mum got
excited when she saw a big lobster in the tunnel. It was made
of glass. I want to find her now. I don't have time to eat my
sandwich. I'll get rid of it.

CHAPTER 31

Maudie

Jake's busy burying something in the sand. I know Gerren is waiting for me to tell him why we're really here, but I don't know what to say.

He feels like someone I can talk to, someone safe…but can I really tell a stranger everything that's been going on in my life?

"Hey, you don't have to tell me anything if you don't want to." Gerren smiles at me. "I thought it might help – you know, a problem shared—"

"—is a problem halved," I finish for him. One of my dad's expressions.

"I'm good at listening, Ma4udie."

I glance at Jake to make sure he's okay. He seems happy digging by himself.

"Maudie?"

I feel Gerren's eyes watching me and when I look across

I see the encouragement in them, as he waits quietly. His fingers brush against my arm, the intimacy confusing me, but at the same time drawing me to him. To tell him everything feels like it would stop the loneliness that has swamped me since Mum left.

Gerren presses his knee against my thigh. My heart starts to pound. It's so loud I'm certain he can hear it above the sound of the sea.

Jake screws his eyes up and mutters under his breath. "He mustn't touch her. Don't touch that girl. Leave her alone."

Gerren immediately moves away from me. "Sorry, Jake."

He sounds genuinely apologetic. That decides me – and the fact he used one of Dad's favourite expressions. It feels like a sign. I'm going to tell him about Mum, but as I open my mouth Jake taps my knee.

"Jake wants his music."

"Oh, okay." I find Radio One for him, as Jake loves that, and help him put the headphones on. He drapes the handle of his bag over his knee and stares out over the beach, lost in a song. Gerren waits until he sees that Jake is completely happy before he speaks.

"Sure it's alright for me to stay? I realize I'm intruding on your time. I'm sorry."

"Jake's fine for the moment, he adores music and is oblivious to anything else. He'll let us know when he's had enough."

Gerren takes Jake in, as though he wants to really understand him. He bites his bottom lip. I lift my face up to the sun and feel it warming my skin, aware of the distance between us now, somehow wanting to connect again. Gerren does it for me.

"You know, whatever you say will stay with me – I'm not about to go and shout my mouth off to anyone, if that's what's stopping you," Gerren reassures me.

"I think I know that. I wanted to thank you for not giving away to Brae that I'm still at school."

"I'm not sure why I didn't – it just felt right not to. I wanted to find out why though." He looks at me intently for a moment, then turns away.

I clench my hands in my lap. I notice that Gerren is doing the same and not looking at me still, to give me space to decide. Shall I, shan't I, battles in my head before I take a deep breath and go for it.

"Jake and me, we're not on holiday. Well, not really. I took Jake from his foster carer to try and get my mum to come back. God, that sounds ludicrous."

Gerren shakes his head. "Don't say that – tell me more, so I can understand."

He smiles at me and for a moment my heart doesn't ache and there's nothing in it except that smile.

"Why was Jake in care? Sorry, d'you mind me asking that?"

"I don't. It's complicated. Mum is on her own…"

"Divorce?"

"N...no." I'm not sure I want to say it out loud. That Dad's dead. It opens up the wound.

Gerren shifts closer, so our elbows are touching. "You don't have to say."

"I know."

Jake nods his head up and down and punches his hand at the sky. "Who, who, who, who, don't forget to breathe, don't forget to breathe. Who, who, who, who."

Gerren looks at Jake with respect. "Is Jake rapping?"

"Sounds like Stormzy." I smile weakly. "Hopefully it's only one song because it can make him quite hyper."

Gerren looks at me intensely. I was about to tell him about Dad, but I'm relieved Jake caused a distraction. I look at Jake to compose myself. He's taken his headphones off and is watching a small golden-haired dog barking at the seagulls and calls out to him. "Hello, dog!"

We all watch the dog for a bit. He's super cute with teddy-bear eyes. He's lost interest in the gulls and is snapping at the waves that keep washing over his paws.

Gerren checks his watch.

"Do you have to go?" I surprise myself at how disappointed I feel.

"Not quite yet, Brae's cool."

"Girl help Jake put his ears on."

I stick his headphones back on, making sure they're comfortable.

Jake nods his head. Gerren tilts his head on one side and whispers to me.

"What happened that made you run away with Jake?"

I hesitate, but the look of concern on Gerren's face is genuine. "A few weeks ago, Mum hit rock bottom. She just couldn't cope, not after everything that happened with my dad." My voice breaks.

"Hey, I didn't mean to upset you." Gerren rests his hand on mine. "You don't have to tell me anything else." He squeezes my hand and then lets it go.

"I even had to put Mum to bed that night. Then the next morning I got downstairs and my aunt was with Jake. Mum had gone and had left a note saying she needed some space. We have no idea where she is or when she's coming back, only that she's alive." I have to stop talking again because the ache in my throat is too strong.

Gerren is staring out to sea. The muscle at the side of his cheek twitches and his Adam's apple scoots up and down. He's trying to control himself but I'm not sure why. Before I get a chance to check that he's okay he sits up, puts his arm round my shoulders and gives me a quick hug before Jake notices. It feels so right I forget about saying anything and instead let a tiny crack in my protective shell split open to let in a speck of light. A sort of calmness drifts over me.

I tell Gerren what happened after Mum left, and about Eve putting Jake in a foster home. Gerren wraps his arms around his legs, resting his chin on his knees. I tell him how my whole world crashed all over again.

"Was his foster carer trained to look after people like Jake properly – she must be, yeah?"

I lean back against the rock, which is warm through my jacket. The sun flicks on and off between the shifting clouds.

"Supposedly, but Jake was taken from everything he knew, and he hates change. It was a nightmare, and they wouldn't even let me see him."

"You're kidding!" Gerren sits up straight, shock in his voice.

"So, I decided to kidnap him." I glance at Gerren, anxious about how he might react. "It was the only way I could think of to try to get Mum to come home. Then we can help her."

Gerren's voice is hoarse when he speaks. "So you still don't know where your mum is?"

"No. I wish she hadn't just run away."

"No."

Gerren's face is rigid. I'm probably imagining it, but his eyes are wide and full of hurt. That can't be for me, can it? We don't even know each other and yet I can almost *feel* his sympathy, it's so strong.

"I don't get her walking away, especially when Jake must really need her," he says.

"We really need her – but she must have been desperate to do that, so I've been trying not to be angry."

Gerren won't look at me and the silence builds. He finally speaks.

"I understand why you did what you did."

His body language is stiff and awkward, having been so chilled. As though he can sense me scrutinizing him, he looks at me and smiles with all his teeth, but his eyes don't match.

I don't understand what's going on with him. There's something he's not saying. I shift my position, as Gerren is obscuring Jake and I'm suddenly aware I've been ignoring him.

I look around. I feel as though I've been hurled into ice-cold water.

The beach is empty.

CHAPTER 32

Jake

Maudie isn't moving. We can't find Mum yet. I saw a dog. He got all wet when the sea chased him. Hehe. I don't like seagulls. They have sharp beaks. A seagull took Dad's chips. On this beach. It hurt his finger. There was blood. I don't like blood. It makes my head go round and round.

I can't see Maudie's face. That boy's hiding her. He's got writing on his back. On his jacket. I can't read it. I wish Mum was here. She'd help me make a pond. Mum? Jake can see her. That's my mum! Walking on the sand. My mum is on holiday. She came back. Oh no! She's going the wrong way. I have to catch her. Run, Jake, run!

CHAPTER 33

Maudie

Me and Gerren desperately scan the beach. I can't believe I've lost him. Jake was right next to me. Why wasn't I paying attention? I have visions of Jake being swept out to sea or tripping over a rock and splitting his head open. I want to throw up. I run up and down, stopping and starting, scouring every inch of the beach, my eyes straining to catch a glimpse of Jake's blond head.

"He can't be far." Gerren tries to reassure me. "He must have gone in that direction," he points to the right where the bay stretches around the corner, "or back up the steps to your caravan."

"He wouldn't do the steps by himself, he hates stairs. He's left his bag. Jake never leaves his bag. Why would he do that?" My voice rises in panic.

Gerren grabs my hand. "Let's head up to the busy part. He must be there."

"This beach is huge, he could be miles away!"

"He can't have been gone for more than a couple of minutes."

I'm out of breath keeping up with Gerren. "Wh…what if we…don't find him?"

"We will. There's plenty of people at that end of the beach, they'll help him."

"What if he…he gets h…hurt?"

A grey cloud covers the sun; the darkness presses down on me. How could I be so stupid? The sand sucks at the soles of my feet, pulling and sinking away from under me, slowing me down. When it surges back the sea spray stings my eyes, making it hard to focus. Something sharp pierces my heel, but I keep running.

"Maudie! Over there, that crowd."

I follow the direction of Gerren's finger, where a group of people crowd around something on the sand. Some of them are waving their arms about, others yell. A man with a pushchair is trying to pull people away. I can't hear what he's shouting. Above it all, I hear Jake scream. My stomach churns violently. Jake screams again and the sound propels me and Gerren forwards.

"Move back – give him some space!" the guy with the toddler orders people. "Can't you see he's scared?"

"Who's with this kid?" An angry-looking man with a wild ginger beard and bushy eyebrows glares at the crowd. I don't look at him.

We push our way through the bodies and find Jake curled up in a foetal ball, his arms wrapped around his head, rocking from side to side, a low moaning sound coming from his mouth.

"Is he with you?" A grey-haired woman asks. "You should take better care of him, poor love."

I push past her to get to Jake. My face burns, especially remembering how horrible I was about Jake's carer not looking after him properly. Tears prick my eyes.

Gerren takes charge of the crowd. "Get back, give him some space! You're making it ten times worse." He moves everyone backwards.

I kneel in the sand beside Jake, half a metre back, my breath coming out in short, ragged gasps. I try to get closer and hold him, but he's too upset. The long, low moan of anguish coming from his mouth rolls over everything. I steady my voice and talk to him. Eventually Jake's arms stop flailing about and I can get nearer to him. He starts to chant. "Hurt Jake hurt Jake hurt Jake hurt Jake."

"No one's going to hurt you, Jake, it's Maudie." I move in a bit closer still. "You're safe. I'm here now. I'm here." I do what Mum does and keep talking softly, my voice low and consistent, and slowly it starts to soothe him. It's hard keeping my voice steady.

"Hurt me. He kicked that ball. Hurt Jake." A dry sob comes from Jake's mouth.

"Who kicked a ball at you? Christ, who'd do that?" Gerren

confronts the crowd. Most people look away or down at the ground.

I focus on Jake. "Shush, Maudie's here. The ball's gone. You're safe with me."

He lowers his arms. His eyes are screwed tight shut. His mouth is set in a fear grimace.

"You should have him on a lead." The ginger-haired guy holding a rugby ball says this under his breath, but loud enough for me and Jake to hear.

"Is that the ball?" I challenge the guy, shooting daggers at him.

"What are you saying? He messed up our game – ran right through it. It's not my fault the ball hit him."

Jake shoots back into his foetal position and wraps his arms around his head.

"What's he doing out on his own?" The ginger-haired man waves one flabby arm at me.

I lean over Jake to protect him. "He's not on his own," I say between clenched teeth, aware this is all my fault.

Gerren flicks the guy's arm away. "Back off, you can see he's scared." Gerren crosses his arms and digs his feet in the sand.

Just as the red-haired guy is about to square up to Gerren, the man with the baby in a buggy marches over, stands next to Gerren and folds his arms, challenging the red-haired guy too. "What's wrong with yous? Do something useful and go home. Let the girl help him. That goes for all of yous," he challenges the gawping crowd. The feet around me shuffle and some turn the other way and start to walk.

Gradually the crowd disperses.

Gerren comes over to help me sit Jake up, which is hard because he's a dead weight. "Let's get you up, Jake. That's it. We've got you."

Jake lets Gerren help him. He looks white and shocked, and I feel even worse.

Gerren puts his hand out to the guy who helped us. "Hey, mate, thanks for your help."

"Yes, thank you, you were brilliant." I smile up at him gratefully.

"No problem, aright?" He drags the buggy backwards over the sand, leaving deep tramlines. His little girl is still fast asleep.

Beads of sweat roll down the side of Jake's face. He wipes it away with his fingers. "Uh-oh. Jake's all wet."

I hand him a tissue from my jacket pocket. He screws it into a ball and wipes across his nose and chucks it on the sand. I pick it back up and dab it on his forehead. He turns his face away.

"What happened, Jake? Why did you run away?"

"People shout. That man shouted. His ball hit him."

Gerren squats down beside us. "Did he hurt you, Jake?"

"Uh-oh, uh-oh, Jake hasn't got his bag! It's all gone away." He struggles to stand up but is clumsy in his bag-panic.

"Careful, take it easy. It's back where you left it on the rock, Jake. No one is going to take it. We can get it now." Jake heads off at a gallop with me panting beside him, steering him in the right direction.

I realize how badly my legs are shaking, worse than after an hour of circuit training for the netball team. My heel is throbbing, but it's not too bad, thank goodness. I'm more worried that it's only my first full day with Jake and we've already blown our cover, though I think screaming blue murder in the shower earlier on made a good start to that. I'm guessing half of Cornwall will have heard about the beach episode by the end of the day.

It doesn't seem to matter how hard I try, I can't get anything right.

Jake picks up speed when he spots the green square of his bag. When he picks it up, his face loses its frown, and his eyes focus on a world I can't see. Gerren and I gather the blanket, shake the sand out on the wind and wearily head up the steps to the caravan.

"One at a time, one at a time." I steer Jake up the steps. He arrives at the top puffing and panting.

"Jake doesn't want those stairs here."

"It's the only way home, Jake."

"That's not Jake's home."

"Just-for-now home, our holiday home. You okay, Jake?"

He doesn't answer but rocks from foot to foot.

"Jake needs the loo."

His hands are shaky and dark sweat patches have formed under his arms.

"Okay, let's take you in. Then we'll do some art."

"Jake likes art."

I settle Jake in the bathroom and pop back out, half expecting Gerren to have gone.

"You need to get back to work," I call out to him.

He's sat on the fence with his back to the sea, which is racing into shore behind him. In the distance I can hear merry-go-round music that has caught on the breeze.

"I don't know how to thank you for sticking up for Jake like that, you were amazing."

He looks a little embarrassed. "Any time. Some people's attitudes stink. D'you get a lot of that?"

I sigh. "It's got better the last couple of years but, yeah, it's been pretty rough at times. There are a lot of really great people too though."

Gerren nods. "That man who helped us was brilliant. The look on Jake's face when that bastard was shouting at him really got to me." He shakes his head.

"It breaks my heart every time."

Gerren takes his iPhone out of his pocket. "I'll send you my number in case you need anything."

I pull out my phone.

"What's that?" He laughs loudly at it. "My dad had one of those when I was in playgroup!" He snorts.

I can't help grinning myself. "The phone's just for here,

so no one could trace us."

"Ah, I get it. A burner. Your number?" He hands me his phone.

I don't know my number, so he gives me his instead. His phone pings with a message.

"Crap! I forgot I'm with Tegen this afternoon. I need to go."

I really want to ask him who this girl is, but don't want to look silly.

"I have a stint at the cafe. I help all around, reception, the cafe, the farm shop, on site, accounts, as Brae hates doing that. I'm a general dogsbody."

"Thanks again. I can't believe I lost Jake – I'm so glad you were there."

"It wasn't your fault. I shouldn't have distracted you. Bye, see you again."

He sprints across the garden, hurdles the gate and vanishes behind the line of palm trees. Does he really mean he'll see me again or was it just a goodbye?

Why do I feel as though a shadow has passed across the sun? My heart somersaults crazily when I think about him on the beach, taking charge and squaring up to that horrible guy.

Jake calls out from the mobile home. "Jake can't wipe his bottom. Can Maudie help him, please?"

Reality brings me back to earth with a bump. "Coming!" I put my shoulders back and head inside. Once Jake is done and we've battled with the hand washing, we go and sit outside at the garden table, taking some paper and pens with us that I brought with me. Jake takes the caps off all the pens and puts them on the opposite end, ready to use. He lines the pens in a row and folds the paper in half. I used to make Mum and Dad's birthday cards with him and now he always wants to make them.

"Get that water off the table! It's too wet!"

I wipe the drop of water off the table with my sleeve. "Would you like me to draw something for you?"

"Yes, please. That dog on the beach. He was excited."

I hand him his picture and start one for myself. I could draw all day.

I check my phone for Liv. It's gone three in the afternoon. What's going on? The police must have seen her again by now, and I'm a hundred per cent sure it'll be out on local news that a teenager with a developmental disability has been kidnapped by his sister.

"Uh-oh! Girl's broken it."

I've made a hole in my picture where I've gone over and over the same spot with the pencil.

"It was a rubbish picture anyway, Jake. Yours is brilliant."

"Jake likes this dog. Can he keep him?"

"Of course you can. I love his pink, dotty tail. We'll cut him out and then we can stick him in your scrapbook when we get back to Shiplake."

"Jake likes his bed. He likes his armchair. Do you, Jake? Yes, he does."

"You like it here though, Jake, don't you? By the beach, our own little home on wheels. We can barbecue later – what d'you think?"

"Jake likes barbecue. Jake can have it instead of cheesy meat pasta on Saturdays."

"Exactly. Poo to that when you can have sausages!"

"Ha ha ha. She said poo."

"Poo poo poo, lovely poo."

Jake nearly explodes at that. It's so good to hear him laugh. He repeats "poo" quietly to himself for a bit. I'm relieved, though I can't pretend he wants to be here like I do. I'm worried I've been selfish bringing Jake down to Pentire and that it was totally unrealistic to think we could hide out long enough to get Mum's attention.

I don't want to think about Gerren, but I can't help it. I've never had a proper boyfriend, partly because I've always wanted to concentrate on getting to a good art school and being around for Mum and Jake, partly because I've never met anyone who makes my heart do wild somersaults in my chest before. Liv's been hanging around with Theo for nearly two years and despite their protests they are so obviously an item and she's really happy. Then I remember: I got distracted by Gerren earlier and look what happened.

I'm tempted to text Liv after all, but she told me not to, so I won't, even if it's nearly killing me not knowing what's happening. Are the police on their way? Can you be arrested for kidnapping your own brother? An invisible woodpecker drums its beak on my brain.

I watch Jake's head bent over the paper he's covering in odd squiggles and dots. He doesn't often seem able to concentrate for very long on anything except his colouring and painting. I wish things were easier for Jake. I sometimes wonder what his life would be like if he didn't have learning disabilities. But that's so wrong of me – maybe Jake doesn't think his life is hard – how would I really know? And Jake has a great life in so many ways. Dad would tell me off for even thinking about it. I can hear him now.

Oh, Dad, why did you have to die?

My gloomy thoughts sit inside me like stinking sediment at the bottom of a pond, tarnishing everything, extinguishing the bright afternoon sun and the silver-specked sea sparkling across the bay.

This isn't fair on Jake. I came here to be with Jake, as well as trying to get Mum to come home.

"Pass me the blue crayon, Jake, and I'll colour his eyes for you. Thank you. Shall I help you with his fur?"

"Jake can do that. He wants orange. He hasn't got that colour."

"I'll show you how to make it. Pass me the red and yellow. Now colour the yellow first, that's it, then put the red on top. See – orange."

Jake's eyes go wide. "Maudie did magic."

"I did! I'll teach you some more. Would you like me to draw you something else, as you've finished that?"

"Jake help Maudie make a dress."

"Oh – okay. What would you like to design this time? A party dress, something for the beach or what?"

"A party dress." He passes me the purple pen.

"Does it have a short skirt or longer?"

"A big skirt. That goes round and round. When you do dancing. Like on telly."

"Great idea!"

I sketch out the shape. Jake starts to colour it in, dotting it with silver.

"Jake?"

"Jake's putting sparkles on."

"I know, they look great, but can you remember why you ran away this morning on the beach?"

Jake stops what he's doing and stares across the sand, locked in his thoughts. I'm not expecting him to answer, but I always try and figure out what triggers the things he does. Finally, he says quietly, "That Mum."

"Mum? What about her?"

"Jake saw his mum."

"You saw Mum? I don't think so, Jake. On the beach?"

"Jake can't see her." He looks out across the sand, frowning.

"No, not *now*, but did you run after Mum this morning? Oh my god – is that why you left your bag? To catch Mum? You'd never leave your bag unless it was something major. No, it couldn't be. I'm jumping to conclusions. It must have just been someone who looked like Mum."

His face lights up. "Jake saw her."

I can't help the way my heart leaps. What if it's true? *Has Mum come down to Cornwall to hide?*

"Jake saw Mum in her green jacket. Jake couldn't catch her."

"Lots of people have green jackets," I tell him, still unable to believe it could be Mum.

"Jake saw Mum's 'fari jacket."

"Her safari jacket?"

"That's what Jake said. Jake wants some gold stars on his dress. Derrick gives him gold stars at school."

I take the pen from the pencil case and hand it to him. What if Jake really did see Mum on the beach?

CHAPTER 34

Jake

I like painting. It stops the bees in my head. It stopped me seeing that big man in my head who knocked me over. On the beach. He threw that ball at me. I saw him do it. I saw his teeth. They were very yellow. I didn't hurt anyone. I was scared. I wanted my mum. I couldn't reach her. All the people got in my way. I wanted all the people to go. I saw Mum climb over the sand hill. She got very small. She vanished. I was on my own. I made a ball with my body. So I couldn't see anyone. That man couldn't hurt me any more. Maudie rescued me. And that boy helped me. Thank you, boy! We need to find Mum. She will look after me and Maudie. We will look after her.

CHAPTER 35

Maudie

The stone wall in front of me is covered in moss that's warming in the afternoon sunshine. I watch a line of ants make their way around the dips in the stone, where it's started to break away. They're picking up the crumbs from Jake's cake and carrying it back to their nest.

Just when I think I can't cope any longer, my phone rings. I snatch it up.

"Liv! Jake thought he saw Mum here on the beach. D'you think that's possible?"

"Hang on, slow down, Maudie. I don't know – Jake can't have seen her, can he? It's very unlikely. Don't you want to know about the police?"

"Of course, but if Mum's down here, they're irrelevant, 'cause I can find her and then we can all be together again and we can tell the police everything's fine."

"Yee-es, but why d'you think your mum is there? That's unlikely isn't it, because—"

I cut Liv off. "I know Mum said she'd never go back to Cornwall after Dad died, but Jake said he saw her on the beach. He even described her jacket. Argh! I just don't know. Jake wouldn't make up something like that, and he has extraordinary eyesight. He can recognize someone from miles away."

My brain hurts from all the thoughts churning round in my head. The longer I'd sat drawing with Jake, the more convinced I'd become it must have been my mum.

"You haven't said anything, Liv."

"I was listening, Mauds. Did *you* see your mum?"

"No."

"If your mum was down there, surely she'd have stayed at my aunt's cottage?"

"Someone else was there, remember."

"Exactly!"

"I guess no one your end has heard from Mum?"

"No, nothing."

That hurts me so much. It feels like I've been cut off from her love. Her silence has eroded my confidence. I feel somehow...inadequate.

"You think I'm being ridiculous believing Jake saw Mum?"

"Oh, Maudie, did I say that? I'm trying to help you."

"Sorry, Liv, I'm just wobbly. We were on the beach earlier and I didn't notice Jake do one of his runners. We belted after him after I saw he'd gone and—"

"We?"

I feel completely deflated now, so I'm not about to talk about Gerren. "I'll explain that later…and forget about Mum, it can't have been her. A part of me was hoping it was, so I got excited." I take a deep breath and try to get my thoughts back in order. "What did the police say?"

"They came to the house and I had to answer lots of questions, with Mum. Obviously, the police are taking it seriously, considering Jake's needs, although to be fair Mum did say you were more than capable of looking after your brother, and that Jake adored you."

"That's so cool of your mum."

"You know she thinks you're the best. The police were sniffy about it and pointed out Jake was still a minor and a vulnerable one at that. I stuck to my story and said I didn't know where you were, but I could tell they were suspicious, me being your best friend. They said that 'withholding information was a serious offence', blah, blah, blah."

"Oh god, I didn't think of that. Shit."

"Me neither, not really, but we can't do anything about it now."

"Me and Jake could come home." I don't really want to, but I hate the thought of getting Liv into trouble.

"No, it's fine, I can cope with it – it's too important not to. They kept asking me where I thought you might have gone, places you liked and where you'd been on holiday to. They asked about your mum too. They're trying to track her down to piece everything together, though because she's left messages saying she's fine, she isn't classified as missing or anything. If they find her first, that'll achieve your goal, won't it? Surely she'll have to come home?"

"At least that's something positive in all this."

"I told them a few places to distract them, like Brighton for the open-top buses for Jake, Lyme Regis where you became obsessed with fossil-hunting, the Lake District, where your dad was born. I didn't mention Cornwall and luckily Mum was distracted by Seb disturbing her about his football kit, so she didn't notice."

"You're completely amazing! Thank you, that could buy us a little bit more time. Of course, Eve knows we went to Cornwall with Dad, but she also knows that Mum swore she couldn't ever go back there."

"Mum said the police have spoken to Eve and she didn't have much information to give them either."

"He needs help." Jake shoves his picture under my nose.

"What colour do you want to use for the shoes?"

"Jake likes blue."

I hand him the pen.

"How's he doing, Mauds? Was he upset after everything today?"

I turn away and lower my voice. "He's okay now, very upset when it happened but he's doing some dress designing with me now and loving it. I'm going to base one of my ball gowns on it. What else did the police say?"

"Jake's disappearance is only going to be on the local news for now. Mum said Eve has put out some social media post about you and Jake missing on Twitter and Facebook and there's some Thames Valley Police site too; you've got to be pretty sad to look at that."

"They must have about five followers!"

Liv laughs. "I'm not sure exactly what happens after that but thank goodness you dyed your hair and changed your clothes, as they're bound to have asked Eve for a picture. Mum said the picture she used on Facebook was from ages ago and you both look younger and very blonde, so let's hope she gives them the same one. D'you know, the police even mentioned that I'd just passed my driving test and hinted that maybe I drove you somewhere."

"How the hell did they know about your driving test?"

"They know everything about us, Maudie. It's not difficult nowadays, is it? There are CCTV cameras everywhere, which is why I parked in a side street and not the bus station. Anyway, I denied driving you, said I'm too nervous to go far in my car yet."

"What if someone saw us in your car going up to the bus station? We kept stopping in the rush hour traffic."

"Possibly, but you look so different they probably wouldn't make the connection. Just keep a low profile."

I don't say anything, which Liv picks up on straight away.

"You might as well tell me now, because you know I'll get it out of you eventually."

I tell her about the shower incident, but that at least we got a very private mobile home out of it, and how the beach episode ended in disaster with a crowd of people all focused on us.

"So if you'd stood there with a vuvuzela in the middle of the beach, you'd probably have attracted the same amount of attention?"

"Yeah, yeah, I know," I say gloomily. "I should have the word disaster tattooed across my forehead."

"Here you go again, Maudie-bashing. Honestly, Maudie, it's not your fault some vile guy on the beach was horrible to Jake. I wish I'd been there to say something!"

Jake shakes his hand in front of me. "Get it off him!"

I knock a tiny black fly off that was crawling up his finger.

"So, Mum hasn't contacted Eve?"

"I'm so sorry, Maudie, Eve spoke to my mum and there's been nothing, not even another text." She sighs. "I'm going to have to go back soon, Mum's on my case big time. I've probably got about ten minutes before she sends out a search party."

"Or worse, sends Furfaceous out to find you. How embarrassing would that be?" I say jokily, trying to show Liv I'm okay, even if I'm not.

"Mortifying."

"Where are you?"

"Just walking around, so we could talk easily. I told Mum I needed some fruit for a smoothie, so I mustn't go back without it. She's turned into the phone police and made me leave my mobile with her. She doesn't believe I don't know where you are and she's worried about you, so she's doing my head in. I can't talk or message anyone, even Theo, without her butting in."

"How long do you think I've got until they find me? Do you think this could make things worse for Jake? God, you don't think I'll get put into foster care too, do you?"

"No, that won't happen."

"How do you know?"

"You can leave home at sixteen without your parent's consent, so you can live by yourself in your home, I guess."

"It's all so complicated, Liv! What if they ban me from seeing Jake at all?"

"You're really happy being with Jake and him with you. You're doing all this so you can be together. Don't fret about what might not happen. Perhaps this might make Eve take Jake back. She's pretty cut up, you know. Mum said she was crying her eyes out and wished she'd tried harder to keep him at home."

"I'm...I'm not sure I can believe that, Liv. I want to, but I can still see her face when I begged her to let me see Jake. She could see how desperate I was, how much I was hurting, but she wouldn't budge. I felt completely abandoned and worthless.

"We could've talked it through. I keep going over and over it in my head, but I still can't make any sense of what

Eve did." I blink the tears out of my eyes. "But it's true Jake is happy right now, so I want to keep him with me as long as possible, then I'm happy too. Coming back would feel worse and I'm not sure what we'd be letting ourselves in for."

"True," Liv agrees. "I'd enjoy your freedom while you can."

"Jake's fine. Yes, he is. He's de-signing." He holds his picture up for Liv to see.

"He's showing you his amazing party dress especially for dancing in, with lots of glitter." I hand my brother the phone. "Here, Jake, say hi to Liv."

"Jake covered it in stars. It's very shiny." He hands the phone back.

"I miss you both." I know Liv is chewing her lip.

"We miss you too."

"I'll let you know everything that's happening this end when I can, Mauds."

"Great, and don't forget to let me know about the big date tomorrow night! Bye, Liv."

Jake chimes in. "Bye, Liv. Bye, Jake."

"Jake said goodbye too. Love you."

"Love you more." She ends the call.

It pings again almost immediately.

Who's 'we'?!! Don't think you're worming your way out of that one!

For some reason I don't want to tell her; I'm still not ready to share Gerren yet. So I text back:

Really nothing to tell. He's the campsite owner's nephew. Brae knew we didn't have much food, so he sent him with some sandwiches. He was there when Jake ran off. Call you later xxx

I've lied to Liv. It's only a silly lie, not terrible in the scheme of things, but we've always told each other everything as soon as it happens. My emotions are on a roller coaster already, without me adding to it. The lie darkens my mood again.

Jake pushes a piece of paper under my nose. "Jake did writing."

I pick up the bit of paper and peer at the confusion of wiggles and random dots.

"That's great writing, Jake. What does it say?"

He puts his finger on the paper and taps it randomly. "Jake...Maudie...love."

I burst into tears. There's no way I'm going to let them separate us. We need each other.

CHAPTER 36

Jake

Maudie cried when I made some writing. Maudie said they were happy tears. I don't understand. Tears aren't happy. Mum cried when Dad went away. She was sad. I have a picture of my dad. I hide it in my bag. In a secret place. I look after him. I got frightened when Aunty Eve took my bag for shopping. She took my dad away. I have to keep him safe. At night he watches me. In my pyjama pocket. I want Dad to come out my picture. I haven't got a picture of Mum. I need one. I want her back. I don't want that lady in the big house to be my mum.

"Maudie. Jake needs to find his mum. Jake saw her."

"You're right, Jake. We can't just sit and do nothing, not if you saw her. We need to take control."

"Take control."

I'm going to help my sister.

CHAPTER 37

Maudie

I sit Jake at the corner table in the cafe garden, where it's sheltered and he can watch all the people coming and going but without being too visible himself. It's about half four and lots of people have got cream teas. Jake watches every mouthful they take. He's safe there because this end of the garden has a hedge all around it, so unless he decides to high-jump it, he won't be doing any runners. I figure with my brown hair and cap hiding my face, I'm not obviously me, so I think I can relax for the time being out here. I can't keep Jake locked away and, truthfully, I want to try and talk to Gerren. I need his help with an idea that's been ticking over in my mind, thanks to something Jake said.

"Hey, Jake – you want some ice cream?"

"Yes, he does. He doesn't want a cone. He doesn't like eating cardboard."

"Ha! Me neither. I won't be long."

He looks up at me and holds his hand up in the air in his salute. I salute back.

I weave my way round the other tables and make my way over to the counter, where a teenage girl is refilling a plate with some very large cookies. Her fitted white tee has the campsite logo on it, and she is wearing black jeans. Her hair is done up in a long blonde ponytail and she has incredible dark-brown eyes. As I approach, Gerren comes through the door behind her and leans over her shoulder, grabbing one of the biscuits and shoving it in his mouth. The girl slaps his arm playfully, smiling up at him. Weirdly I feel a bit sick. She obviously likes Gerren, as she's flirting with him big time. If I hadn't promised Jake a Coke, something he's not normally allowed to have, I would have turned around and gone back out. Then Gerren spots me and his face lights up.

I snatch my cap off and run my fingers through my hair.

"Hey, Maudie! Come and meet Tegen. Me and her brother Dewi go diving together."

"Hi, T-Tegen," I stammer in a dorky squeak.

"Hey – nice to meet you." She smiles.

Not for the first time I wish I had my blonde hair back and my own clothes.

She puts the glass dome back over the cookies and moves closer to Gerren, so obviously comfortable with him. "I'll help you lock up later. You coming to the house tonight? Dewi's got some beers in."

"Cool – thanks, Tegen. I'll let you know. D'you want to sort those tables outside?"

"Sure," she says, picking up a cloth and heading out.

Gerren leans across the counter towards me. "Where's Jake?"

"Corner table in the garden, so I'd better not be long."

Gerren shakes his head firmly. "Not after this morning – that was tough. What can I getcha?"

"A large Diet Coke, no ice, please, two mint-choc-chip ice creams in a bowl, not a cone. We both think cones are like cardboard," I twitter at him. What's wrong with me?

"Fair enough, can't argue with that." Gerren laughs. "I'll bring it all out."

"You don't have to," I smile, "I can wait if it helps you."

Gerren raises one eyebrow. "Er, it's okay, it's what we do – table service."

"Right!" I squeak, feeling the biggest loser ever and wishing somebody would shoot me. I start to gabble again. "We're thinking of doing a barbecue this evening. I, we wondered if you'd like to come? I mean, don't worry if you're going to see your friend…" My voice tails off. Could I sound any more pathetic?

Gerren stands up straight and pushes back the fringe that's flopped over his face. "Sure, I'd love to, but I'll have to check a couple of things first."

I wonder what those things are.

"Brilliant. If you can come, bring Brae too, if he isn't busy."

Why did I mention Brae? I have a chance to spend what could be my last evening here with a really cute guy and I invite a responsible adult along too. Mind you, it's the least I can do in the way of a thank you to Brae, and for Jake, who will love him coming.

"Cool, I'm sure Brae would love to come, if he can." Do I detect a hint of disappointment in Gerren's voice?

"And I'm wondering if you might be able to help me with something? It's about my mum. Maybe we could talk about it tonight?"

"Sure! You don't mind if Brae's there then?"

"Oh – I thought we might talk after Brae's gone?"

He doesn't get a chance to answer, as a tray laden with cups is put down on the counter between us. Gerren smiles at Tegen. I head back out to Jake.

Gerren comes out a few minutes later, balancing the tray with our order on one hand as he weaves his way around the tables. As he heads towards us, I notice his T-shirt has risen up from holding the tray high, showing his tanned stomach.

"Hey, Jake."

Jake turns his head away. Gerren looks dejected. My brother hasn't taken to Gerren quite like he did to Brae, but I really want him to like Gerren – though I'm not sure why, since we'll never see him again once we're home.

"This is yours, Jake." He puts Jake's drink in front of him. By the time Gerren's put his ice cream down the Coke has gone.

Jake looks at me cheekily, puts his head back and lets rip with one of his velociraptor burps, the loudest I've ever heard. It rolls around the tables and seems like it ricochets off the walls of the cafe.

A dad with twins cheers, pumping his fist in the air, and two older ladies stare at Jake with their mouths open. Gerren and a boy of about nine near us both crack up.

Gerren tries to keep a straight face. "That was unbelievable!"

I want to curl up into a ball and bury myself. Yet again we've managed to attract all the attention.

"Man, that burp would get you in *The Guinness Book of Records*. The guys at the pub would be mega impressed."

"Jake likes the pub."

"When you're eighteen, you can come to The Tinner's Arms with me."

Jake leans forward and shoves his face in mine to make sure I hear him. "Jake's going to the pub."

"Maybe not today, but definitely one day." I raise my eyebrows at Gerren. "You don't know what you've started. He'll ask every day now until we go. You love sitting in a pub garden with a bag of crisps, don't you?"

"He does. His dad took him."

"I know one out in the country that has a quiet garden," Gerren says.

"Thanks, not many people would include Jake." I say it quietly, so Jake doesn't hear.

"I remember the time our road held a summer street party and we weren't invited. We only knew about it when we looked out the window. Mum cried."

"That sucks." He pushes his sleeves up and I can see on his wrist he has a small intricate tattoo of an octopus. One tentacle wraps around his wrist.

"That's beautiful."

I reach out without thinking and start to trace my finger over the design, before pulling back abruptly.

Gerren touches where I touched. "I love octopuses – I'm in awe of them. They're so intelligent, almost human."

"Gerren! Can you come and help, please?" Tegen calls across the grass. "There's a queue at the counter."

"Sure! Coming!" He turns back as he heads off. "What time tonight, if I sort stuff?"

"Is seven too early?

"Cool, seven is fine. I finish my stint here at six-thirty. I'll let you know for sure though. I'm always starving after work."

"Jake's starving too."

"Totally with you there, Jake." Gerren nods seriously as he walks away.

Tegen is heading towards us with a loaded tray. It can't be for us, but she comes straight over to Jake, smiling at him. "Here you go, one plate of chips, a chocolate chip cookie and a pint of Coca-Cola."

"I think you've got the wrong table?"

She looks confused. "No, I don't think so – this was your order, wasn't it?" She checks with Jake.

"Yes, it was." Jake answers with complete confidence, as he knocks back his full-sugar Coke.

I'm too stunned to stop him.

CHAPTER 38

Jake

Maudie said I was on the ceiling. Because I drank lots of Coke. That's very silly. My feet are on the floor. I'm going to the pub. That boy said. I want to do Ka-ree-o-kee. I'm a great singer. I can't sing at the moment. I have to find Mum first.

I saw Father Christmas tonight. He ate all the dinner sausages. He asked me what I want for a present. I said my mum. Maudie said Mum was having a rest. At home. Mum's not at our house. I know that. Mum wouldn't send me away.

Father Christmas has a name. He's called Brae. He said we could do something together. He could take me in his sleigh. To find Mum. I think his sleigh might take me to heaven. Then I can find Dad too.

CHAPTER 39

Maudie

A tiny blue flame bursts into life on the barbecue then fades away again.

"Are you sure that's okay?" I watch Gerren anxiously. I'm not sure he's completely on board with my idea. I was so pleased when he came along with Brae tonight, I thought it would be easy to get him to help me out.

"Of course. Before he went just now, Brae said I should take a day off, didn't he? And I've worked non-stop since I got down here three weeks ago." He sighs. "But my car needs new brake pads, so I can't use it at the moment."

He starts to speak, stops, then decides to say, "You do realize it's unlikely we'll find your mum. And are you sure you really want to find someone who ditched you?" He sounds quite angry.

"I don't see it that way! I might have felt a bit angry about it before, but now I've had time to think about it, I see she didn't have any choice – I think it was like she couldn't function any more. That devastates me."

"I'm sorry, I didn't mean to upset you." He runs his fingers through his fringe, making it stand up. His voice is calmer when he speaks again. "She could've been on a day trip to the beach and is miles away now or not here at all. I mean, Jake probably got it wrong."

"What, because he has learning disabilities? He has as much chance as anyone of being right or wrong."

"Woah – I didn't mean it like that! I meant she was likely too far away for him to see properly." Then he adds, almost to himself, "I'm making a real mess of this."

I can't tell if he did mean that or if he's covering up quickly.

"You don't have to come then. I know it's pretty pointless, but I have to try."

I wasn't going to look for Mum, but it's been nagging at me since Jake said he saw her. I tried to tell myself he was wrong, but I can't let it go, not after him mentioning her jacket. I pretend I'm looking at a cruise ship sounding its horn as it drifts across the water, lit up by hundreds of tiny lights.

Gerren places both hands on my shoulders and turns me around so he can look right at me. "I said I would, and I'm happy to. I just don't want you to be disappointed. Sometimes…sometimes people don't want to be found. Sorry, but that's the way it is, Maudie." He drops his hands and looks away.

Liv's voice saying the same thing echoes in my head.

"She has to come home, then Jake can move back too and we can help her get better. Mum'll be as upset as me about Jake being fostered. Eve betrayed what Dad wanted. Mum would never do that."

Thinking of Dad stops me going on. Gerren picks up on it immediately.

"You never told me about your dad, Maudie. You don't have to, of course, but would it help?"

Gerren's trying so hard now to help me and his expression is so kind that it makes me want to be totally open with him. I dive in.

"Dad died two years ago. I was so heartbroken I couldn't think straight. We all were. And now Mum's gone I feel the same, like I'm grieving all over again – but for both of them."

Gerren waits patiently while I sort what I want to say.

"This…this roller coaster of emotions that I'm going through feels like it never really stopped, because I haven't even got over Dad yet. I'll never come to terms with him dying, there'll always be an empty space where he should fit."

"It must be awful to lose your dad at such a young age." A look of pain flashes across his face.

I nod, not trusting myself to speak. Gerren gently squeezes my hand.

"Sometimes it seems as though I'm watching life through cloudy water. I feel cut off from the rest of the world, and my heart hurts so much that I can't understand why it doesn't give out. Dad was our everything, especially for Jake. Dad would do anything for him, to help make his life amazing." I have to stop talking to regain control of myself.

"Jeeze, that must have made everything so hard for you and your mum, coping with your grief." He looks at me with wide eyes, full of concern. "How d'you explain *that* one to Jake?"

"It was awful. I don't know what he thinks happened or if he truly understands death, but he never talks about Dad. Both Mum and I talked with him about it but didn't feel we'd done a good job. I was worried I'd confused him more. I think he dreams things that have happened or thinks about Dad at night though, when all the noise of the day has gone away and he can hear himself think, because he shouts out things about him in his sleep. What must Jake be feeling about Mum now?"

Gerren gazes off into the distance at the red light flashing on and off across the bay. "What you said just now – you were right, your mum obviously needs a bit of space to work things out."

I nod. "I wish she hadn't just left though."

"Too true." Gerren bows his head and studies his shoes.

I decide to check on Jake, confused by Gerren's withdrawal. Jake's already gone to sleep, which amazes me after his sugar burst made him super hyperactive.

I look at Jake properly in the slant of light from the door.

He's growing a soft fuzz on his face. How could I not have noticed that before? I can see Dad more clearly in him – the family nose with a slight bump at the top, the strong, thick eyebrows and the squarish chin. Jake's tall and well built, but in my head he's still my baby brother. Perhaps I need to let him grow up more. Perhaps we all do.

I tiptoe over, kiss him on his forehead and push the damp hair back from his face, making the most of being able to hug him. He's peaceful. I wonder how long that will last before the nightmares begin and he starts to shout. As if Jake can read my thoughts, the faintest of frowns creases his forehead. I gently smooth the lines away until I'm sure he's relaxed. I pull the door to as I leave.

I head through the kitchen area, grabbing our drinks from the fridge.

We sit in comfortable silence. I watch Gerren's face as the candlelight from the miner's lamp flickers across his skin and highlights his cheekbones. His blue eyes reflect the nearly full moon. I surprise myself by wanting to trace my finger along his jaw where dark stubble is starting to show through. We're sitting so close I can feel the warmth from his body on mine. The coals on the barbecue glow softly red and a small breeze picks up tiny bits of grey ash and spins them up into the sky. There are millions of stars in the clear blue-black night. I feel so small and yet so big, my heart beating with the rhythm of the waves that crash onto the shore.

Our knees touch and I feel this spark of energy fizzling through us. Gerren is watching the sea, his eyes half closed. He shivers. Does he sense it too? For a moment, I feel alive – more than I have in a long time. It feels like the cold waves have washed through me, sweeping away the debris from my mind and leaving it clear.

Gerren takes my hand and twists the silver moonstone ring on my little finger that Dad bought for me when I was eight years old.

"Your hands are cold." Gerren holds them between his own to warm them up.

His touch makes my skin shiver. I'm sure he can feel my heart racing faster, beating in the palm of my hand, beating in rhythm with the little blue-green vein on his temple. I wish we could stay like this for ever. He twists a curl of my hair around his finger.

"You're blonde really, aren't you?"

I nod. "How do you know that?"

"There are blonde hairs on your temple."

"You can see in the dark then?" I tease.

"I noticed them earlier on the beach."

That makes me smile. "Most guys wouldn't notice that, not unless you gave them a magnifying glass and directions."

"That's a bit sexist! I've always noticed stuff. I was a quiet, introverted kid. Shy. So I got used to observing everything and taking it all in. I guess I never got out of the habit."

I rest my hand on his knee; I can feel it trembling.

He starts to speak, but laughter from the beach below breaks the spell. A group of teenagers chase each other across the sand, shadowy figures racing into the dark.

I watch enviously as they kick water at each other, oblivious to anything else. "God, it would be brilliant to be down there on the beach. We could swim."

"You've got to be kidding! I'd end up with nuts the size of raisins."

We both crease up.

I pick up my bag and find the picture of me and Liv in London. "The real me."

Gerren studies it closely. "I prefer you blonde, but you're just as cute like this."

"Thank you," I giggle, all pleased.

He squints at the photo. "Are you both in fancy dress?"

"Er, no, that's what we wear," I say, brought back down off my pleased cloud. "We, um, like vintage clothes or make our own. I design a lot of my stuff. Mum taught me to use the sewing machine properly when I was ten. She used to help me sew, but since Dad died she's been too busy." I tap the photo. "Those dresses have a fifties vibe." My voice tails off as I worry he thinks we look weird.

"That's so cool – it's brilliant," he says, as though he read my mind. "I'd never have the guts to do anything different."

"They're tame – you should see our sixties look!"

He tucks up next to me. "I hope I do."

I'm amazed at how relaxed I'm starting to feel with

Gerren. It's bizarre since I've only known him a day, though it seems longer than that.

"Tell me about Liv, was it?"

Hearing her name makes me want to see her so badly. I realize how nice it is having someone to talk to, as she's not here. There's a part of me missing without her.

"Yes, Liv, Olivia or Livvy, but only her mum calls her that. Liv's amazing, as well as super cool. She's always there for me and she's funny and clever and Jake loves her, which says it all really. I wouldn't have got down here without her help; she'd do anything for me and me for her. She's very together, everything I'm not, and she's an amazing artist. She does these three-dimensional pieces that transform a whole space, and you feel like you're completely...I don't know... *immersed* in it. You'd have loved her shoal of fish made from waste plastics and recycled objects."

"It sounds awesome. Are you into art too?"

I almost feel myself grow taller when he says that. "I want to be a fashion designer. I saw this amazing Dutch designer on YouTube, Iris Van Herpen, a couple of years ago. Her work is so innovative. She kind of meshes technology, marine ecology, science and architecture together and uses 3D imaging to create works of art that you wear. She made this top that was inspired by the transition of water when it crystallizes. It blew me away, it was so beautiful! I knew then that it's what I want to do. Now Liv and I want to get a place at Central Saint Martins in London, one of the top art schools for fashion design."

"Wow! It's like you switched a light on inside you when you were talking then. I'm useless at anything arty."

"Well, I'm not sure I could dive – I'd panic underwater."

"I'll take you one day and once you've done it, you'll catch the diving bug. It's so peaceful below the waves. All you can hear is the sound of your own breathing, and you feel a part of the marine world. It's magic, the nearest thing to flying. The corals and rock formations are surreal."

"You're giving me some great ideas for my portfolio," I say excitedly. "If I could overcome my fear of going that deep!"

Gerren's looking at me very seriously. I stare back into his eyes. He leans forwards and I think he's going to kiss me when a ship's horn booms out across the water in two mournful blasts.

Gerren nearly falls backwards off the bench. "Woah! That cargo ship's timing is perfect."

From inside the caravan Jake shouts out, "The monster's here!"

The ship's horn must have scared him. I run inside to find Jake sitting up in bed, his eyes wild, his hair wilder. His knuckles are white where he clutches the handles of his bag. He shivers violently, but is covered in sweat, making his forehead shine. He looks at me, but I can tell he can't see me.

"The monster's outside," he whispers. "He's shouting. He has a tall hat."

I don't touch Jake, but I start to sing to him, as it's the best thing to do when he has night terrors and he's not really awake. It's like he's locked in a world he can't get out of.

Jake screams again and starts to rock violently. The whole room shakes, and the coaster on the bedside table moves across the surface and plops to the floor. I keep singing, as I know it will work eventually, but it could take a long time.

I sense Gerren behind me. His face is shadowed when I turn around. He hops nervously from foot to foot. He starts to come towards me, stops and steps back. "Can I help?" he mouths, looking anxiously from me to Jake.

I shake my head. "You go," I mouth back and carry on singing.

I don't hear him leave.

Jake stops rocking. "Jake can see Mum. She's running on the path. The monster is chasing her. It's too high. Jake doesn't like it."

"It's okay, Jake. It's a dream. It will go away. You're safe with Maudie. Shush, now, Maudie's here."

As my singing soothes him, Jake starts to calm down, but then his body spasms as though a bolt of lightning has zapped through him and I have to hold his arms to his side, to stop him from hurting himself. It takes all my effort, as he's so strong. I finally sit back down but as soon as I do Jake flings his duvet off, stumbles out of bed and stands up on tiptoes and shouts at some invisible thing only he can see. He flails his arms around, punching at the air in front of him.

I duck down. I'm desperate to get him back into bed, where he'll be safer, but I'll have to wait until he's less agitated. I hold my arm in front of my face, lick my lips and start to sing again. His arm swings out blindly, and he nearly falls over. I'm terrified he'll hurt himself.

"Stop chasing him!" Fear is etched into the lines on his face. "Go away! Leave him alone. Don't do that to him. Don't do that."

I flinch. I wish Mum was here. I start to sing again, repeating the same line over and over again until it has a hypnotic effect. Jake's arms flop to his sides, he starts to tremble and then he gasps with short intakes of breath. A single tear rolls down his face and drops onto my arm. I sit him on the bed and swing his legs over as best I can without disturbing him. He lies back onto the pillow and shuts his eyes. I put the handle of his bag in his hand. He grips it tight.

His face is as blank as an empty piece of paper, waiting for the next pencil mark to determine what it will show.

I sit on the chair next to Jake's bed and stay with him to make sure he's deeply asleep again. I'm overwhelmed with sadness. I hate not being able to help Jake more, and I can't bear the way his mind tortures him like this at night.

I'm shaking. Tentatively, I stroke his arm and watch his chest rise and fall. This is only my second night of looking after Jake and I'm shattered. Mum gets up with him every night, often more than once. When did she last sleep properly?

A small moth flutters past my face and lands on Jake's pillow. It opens and shuts its wings. It calms me down. I carefully brush the moth away, not wanting to disturb Jake. It leaves a smudge of gold powder by his ear and dust particles float through the air. I gently take my hand away and start to tiptoe out of the room when Jake turns his head towards me, his eyes wide open.

"Mum's dead."

CHAPTER 40

Jake

I saw a bad man. In my night head. I was frightened. He had a beak-nose. And a big hat with flowers. He put a fishing net over my head. "I smell children." That bad man said that. I saw him on the TV a long time ago with Dad. Maudie said it was a dream. Like Dad. They said the man isn't real. I SAW him. I couldn't stop him. It was too dark.

My mum looks after me at night. She lies next to me and tickles my back. I don't mind at night. It makes me sleepy. She can't do that 'cause she's for ever gone. Maybe the bad man took her. Maybe he took Dad. He's for ever gone. I hope he doesn't take Maudie.

CHAPTER 41

Maudie

I'm exhausted but I can't sleep. The dark night sky folds over me, blackening my thoughts even more. Is Jake right about Mum?

He can't be…but if something has happened to her, perhaps he sensed it?

It was a dream, just a silly dream. I'd sense it too if Mum was dead; I'd feel the empty space of her having gone. I stop my thoughts growing into a swarming panic. I mustn't think it. I mustn't say it out loud. I did before and it wasn't true. Dreams only seem real at night.

My head aches with the weight of the idea that something has happened to Mum. The tiny red dot of light in the distance still winks on and off out at sea. A warning signal?

Mum once said: "Never run from anything. There's always a way through – we have each other, we have love, and that's the most important thing in the world."

But you did run, Mum, so does that mean you couldn't find a way through?

I don't think I could cope if Mum was dead. I've not really coped with losing Dad. Not a single day passes that I don't think about him. I never asked Mum if it was the same for her. We rarely talk about him, only on those days where we can't avoid it, such as his birthday, Father's Day and Christmas. Dad loved Christmas so much, and his excitement was infectious. He spent weeks sneaking around the house hiding presents and it took him two days to prepare Christmas lunch with Jake, while Mum and I decorated the house. Choosing the right Christmas tree could take hours, as Dad insisted it had to be exactly the right shape, "like a well-fed robin" as he put it.

The cavernous loneliness of how my life would be, just myself and Jake, stretches out in front of me. I'm scared of failing him.

The cold sea wind seeps through my bones, chilling me. I need to talk to someone but it's nearly one o'clock in the morning. Liv tried to call me several times while I was with Jake. She left two messages. I've listened to her voicemails three times already, just to hear her voice. I sent her a text, but she didn't reply, so I don't want to wake her now, even though I know she wouldn't mind; I don't want to risk her getting caught if anyone hears her. I stare at Gerren's number on my phone. I can't ring a boy I barely know at one in the morning. Can I?

I listen to Liv's message for the hundredth time.

"Hey, Maudie, am guessing you're with Jake. I'm in the bathroom with the shower on if this is a bit hard to hear. You were on the local news tonight. They gave your and Jake's descriptions and asked anyone with any informationto call the number they put up on the screen. You should be fine with anyone that saw you on the coach going down to Cornwall, as they won't get our news down there yet, but who knows who might have seen you both at Reading coach station.

"They showed that photo of you with Jake when you went to Longleat, over a year ago. I'm surprised Eve didn't give them a more recent picture, but, as I said before, it's good because you and Jake look younger and very blonde, so it might help. It was so weird seeing you on the telly. Mum was at karate with Sam, or she'd have started on at me again. Are you okay, Mauds? I worry about you dealing with all this alone. I should have come with you, we could have got a train together or something and it would have been fine about my date with Theo because it's cancelled now anyway – which is what we both chose to do, so don't start feeling guilty."

The message cuts off here, so I go onto the next one.

"Where was I? Oh yeah, Theo knew I'd be too upset about you to enjoy our first proper date and he was right, so we're going to rearrange it when you're safe home. I haven't told him I know where you are, as it's less risky and it's not fair to ask him to lie to anyone.

"Listen, I feel bad I was so negative earlier on. I didn't mean to hurt you. Hang on... Stop thumping the door, Seb! You'll have to wait, I'm in the shower. Cross your legs! I don't know when. If you do that on my bed, I'll make you eat it and I'll stick a video of it up on TikTok! Tell Mum then, I don't care.

"Hey, Mauds. I've probably got thirty seconds before Mum bangs on the door. Let me know you're okay, yeah? I just have a feeling you're not okay, I mean, more not-okay than you would be under the circumstances. Call me any time you want, yeah? Mum! There's no need to break the door down. He's lying, I did NOT say I'd force-feed him with his own—"

The message clicks off. I can't help but smile. It helps give me a sense of perspective. Mum's not dead. I'm overthinking because I'm on my own and it's night.

I put the phone down on the table and slide it away from me. I lean across and pick it up again, put it back down and then up again and press call. I really need to talk to someone. It rings three times before I realize how full on it is ringing Gerren at this time.

Just as I'm about to click it off a voice says, "Hello? Who's this?"

I end the call. It was a girl's voice and I recognize it from earlier. That was Tegen and I could hear music and laughter in the background.

Gerren obviously couldn't wait to go around to his friend's house after here and have some real fun! And be with Tegen. I feel such a loser. I nearly let him kiss me. After one day.

No one's tried to call me back, so I text Gerren.

Don't worry about tomorrow, it's silly thinking we
could find my mum. She might not even be here.
Thnx for offering to help.

I press send then switch my phone off. This mess is all
my own fault for putting some boy before Liv, before Jake,
before everything else. I should have rung *her*. I have no
idea how I'm going to look for Mum now either. I might just
as well go home.

But part of me wants to stay here. I want to be free and
irresponsible, like those guys at the party tonight. I'd like to
meet Gerren, under different circumstances…except he
ran from here straight over to Tegen.

But I kidnapped Jake and brought him down here, and
now I'm wishing him away.

I decide to check on him, anything to stop me checking
my phone. He's deeply asleep, not even talking to himself.
I should make the most of it and go to bed, but I know I'm
too hyper to sleep. So I grab my jacket and head down the
steps to the beach.

I rip my trainers off and feel the cold sand seeping
between my toes. I run towards the sea, wanting the icy
water on my skin, to be like those teenagers earlier.

At the shoreline I kick the water, enjoying the feel of the
sea on my legs and grab handfuls of swirling seaweed. I spin
them around my head and fling them out as far as I can into
the churning waves. My feet slap through the wet. The wind

picks up the spray and hurls it back in my face. My skin stings and my eyes burn from the salt, but it stops the monster in my head shooting blackness through me, telling me that I'm useless and will never be the perfect daughter, the perfect sister, perfect friend. Or perfect anything.

"I'm not listening!" I shout, spinning around on the sand until I'm too tired to do it any more. It feels great.

I sit at the water's edge, not caring that I'm soaked through and that my lips feel blue. I watch a tiny crab in the gloom, being pulled backwards and forwards by the current, fighting to get ashore. I feel just like that crab. I grab it as it surges towards me and put it further up. I wish Mum would come and scoop me up. I shiver. I don't know what the time is or how long I've been here. I struggle to my feet. I shouldn't have left Jake alone for so long.

I stagger up the beach, the weight of water in my clothes pulling me back. My eyes are fixed on our mobile home. Something moves. I can see a dull red square, a dark silhouette circled by the light from the mobile home. It's Jake. My heart punches my chest. Jake's shape vanishes. Then it's up again.

His cry carries out to me on the wind, which shrieks over my head and booms against the rocks. He can see me. He's heading across the garden towards the low cliff edge.

I look up and shout at him to stop.

He keeps coming.

CHAPTER 42

Jake

I need a wee. I don't know where the loo is. I can't remember. I mustn't forget my bag. Where's my sister? She can take me there. "Maudie! Jake needs a wee." She's not answering. I'll have to find it myself. That's Maudie's bed. It's empty. Uh-oh. Here's the loo. I must put my bag on the handle. Don't splash the floor! Oh no, my foot's wet. Maudie's not in the kitchen. The child-catcher might have taken her. I must rescue her. Mind those steps. I don't like stairs. I fell down them at school. My leg was broken up. My eyes can see better now. Maudie's on the beach. "Come back, girl!" I can't see the bad man. I must hurry before he gets her. I'm coming, Maudie.

"Jake's come to rescue you."

CHAPTER 43

Maudie

I have to stop him.

"STOP, JAKE! I'm coming up!" I yell.

He keeps walking, then he stumbles. I can't see him – I think he's hurt himself. I run up the steps as fast as I can, my heart beating erratically as I race around the corner and fling myself at my brother, knocking him into the picnic table with a crash.

"Ow! Don't push him! Jake banged his knee." He levers himself up, moaning loudly as he does it.

I go to help him but Jake steps back from me, his face showing the confusion he feels.

"I had to grab you. You'd have gone over the edge. See – you mustn't run towards that little fence. It's a b-big drop to the beach."

"Big drop. Uh-oh. Ow! Jake's got a bruise." He pulls his pyjama leg up for me to see.

In the door light I can see a deep-red mark. He'll have a bruise tomorrow; it's already started to darken in the middle.

"Let's...go in and sort it."

"Leave it alone – Jake doesn't want you touching it!"

I bend over double, clutching the stitch in my side. "That scared me."

"Jake was scared too. He couldn't find his sister. Jake was worried about Maudie. "

"I'm so sorry, Jake. I was thoughtless, but it won't happen again," I gasp.

My legs are very unsteady as I guide him to his bedroom. I make as if to help him in when Jake says, "Jake can do it." He climbs into bed, huffing and puffing about his knee, and pulls his duvet over him. He checks his bag is flat against the side of the bed, pulls the cover up under his chin and shuts his eyes. "Bugs bite."

"You want me to look at your knee?"

He doesn't answer, just turns on his side.

"Night night."

I lurch into the bathroom and wade through wet. I'm standing in a pool of yellowy liquid. I don't know whether to laugh or cry. Jake sorted himself out, going for a wee by himself. I realize I could let him do this more – he's sure to eventually get it in the bowl!

As I'm hosing my feet down with the shower head, the shock of Jake nearly tumbling over onto the rocks hits me and I start to shake violently. I must be more responsible.

I'd never have forgiven myself and neither would Mum. Mum, who's alive. Not dead. I need to get a grip on my emotions. Jake didn't ask to come here, so I need to focus on keeping him safe and happy.

It's two fifteen in the morning. I hobble my way into my bedroom, fall onto the bed face-down and stay there. The dull tick of the wall clock eventually sends me to sleep.

Tap, tap…tap-tap-tap!

"Just shut up!" I bury my head under my covers and stick my fingers in my ears. When I get so hot I can't breathe, I throw the duvet off and lie on my back, looking up at the damp patch on the ceiling, any chance of sleep gone. I used to think the branches tapping on my bedroom window were witch's fingers. Now it reminds me of the time ticking away that Dad has left to live.

A car's headlights swing around the walls and zigzag across my cover. The low bass beat coming from its stereo thumps through my already aching head.

Tap, tap, tap-tap-tap-tap.

How long have we got? I wish I could block it all out with a sleeping tablet, like Liv's mum, but I'm scared then I'd miss the moment Dad… No, I can't go there.

A bedroom door opens across the landing. Someone groans and shuffles across the carpet to the bathroom. I hear the murmur of voices. The door clicks shut, but I can still hear my dad vomiting in the loo, Mum's soft voice comforting him. I know she'll hold a cool flannel against his face when he's finished, and stroke the baby hair that's grown through after the chemo. I bury my face in my pillow and sob quietly.

A cool hand touches my shoulder and Mum curls up next to me on the bed and pulls me round, into her body. She smells sweet and soapy. I can feel her heart beating on my hand.

She gently trails her fingertips across my eyelids. "I'll always be there for you, Maudie."

"Don't go."

I don't want to be alone.

Jake shouts Mum's name. She kisses me on the forehead and goes to help him. "I'll be back."

Tap-tap-tap-tap-tap.

I wake with a start, the tick-tock of the clock confused with the tapping of the branches in my dream. It takes me a few seconds to remember I'm not at home in Shiplake, back with Mum. But I can still smell her.

Mum told me she'd always be there for me.

I wish she was here now.

I sit up and swing my legs out of bed. I feel like I've been rolled over by a truck, both physically and mentally. There's no sound from Jake and it's gone eight o'clock. I peep round his door and am staggered to see he's still deeply asleep. I wish I was.

I can see his injured knee where his leg is resting on top

of the duvet. The bruise is bigger already. Mum would have rubbed some Arnica cream in to soothe it. I didn't think to bring anything like that. I'm beginning to wonder if I've done any thinking at all. A rush of guilt puts me through agonies, but I try not to let it; feeling guilty won't help now, so I'll keep it as a reminder not to get distracted again.

I tiptoe back to the kitchen.

A winter-grey sky hangs over the beach, a bank of dark clouds pressing down on the water. The sea is choppy and has thrown up all sorts of things onto the sand. Clumps of seaweed and twisted driftwood form a bank just above the water's edge. A small wooden boat, its bow pointing towards the sky, bumps across the waves, heading out towards the horizon. It reminds me of an old poster I saw of *Moby Dick*. I almost expect a giant whale to rear up from beneath the waves and swallow the boat whole in its gaping red mouth.

I find my phone and switch it on. I make tea while it charges up, then I wrap myself in a red tartan picnic blanket from the arm of the sofa and go and sit outside. I take the photo of me and Liv with me and prop it up against Gerren's empty beer bottle from last night. My phone screen lights up. I manage a weak smile when I see Liv's message. I have a lot to fill her in on.

> Get your lazy butt up and give me a call
> Mum's driving the snitch to his football
> match and she won't be long

Let me know you're alright
Hope you got my garbled voice
messages last night
Nothing on the news this morning Xxx

She must be sitting on the phone because she answers it immediately.

"Hey, Mauds." Liv's voice is serious. "Did you get my voicemail?"

"Yes. I guess nothing's changed this morning?"

"No, your picture is out there, but it was on local news only. Are you okay? Don't know why I'm asking, I know you aren't."

I sigh. "I had a crappy night, but it's all my fault. And Jake had night terrors. It was awful, but after a long time I got him back to sleep, then just as I was leaving him, he sat up straight in bed and said Mum was dead. Just like that. You... you don't think it's true, do you?"

"No, of course it isn't, and if you really thought that you wouldn't be sitting in your caravan doing nothing. It was Jake's subconscious brain working things out. Dreams are just that, aren't they – like you dream you fail an exam because of all the pressure. For Jake – your dad was there and then he wasn't, now your mum has vanished overnight, so perhaps his mind was trying to make a link. It's so easy to make assumptions because of what we think though."

"Yes, yes, you're right. I know that really."

"Anyway, Jake thought he saw her on the beach yesterday, didn't he, so that must have churned up some major feelings in him."

"Last night it felt like a premonition, Liv. I keep thinking, what if Mum is...dead."

"Stop it! Stop thinking like that. Why didn't you call me last night? I could've helped."

"By the time I could it was gone one in the morning, and I didn't want to wake you or risk you getting caught talking to me. We had a barbecue and then there was the thing with Jake—"

"Who's this 'we' again? You and Jake?"

"Yes, and the campsite owner Brae and his nephew, Gerren."

"Sandwich guy?"

"Yes."

Liv gets straight to the point. "You like this guy, don't you?"

"Oh!" How does she know? Am I that transparent? Of course she knows – it's Liv. "I do – did. But then when I was looking after Jake, Gerren left and went round to his friend's house."

"He just left you?"

"I told him to leave, I didn't know how long it would take to calm Jake down, but a part of me hoped he'd still be there when I got outside."

"He's a boy, Mauds. You tell him to go, he'll go – he's not going to read between the lines."

"This girl was there who clearly has the hots for Gerren, and she's so pretty. They work at the site cafe together, so I don't stand a chance."

"They work together, it doesn't mean he's going out with her. Does he seem like a player to you?"

"No, though I hardly know him. I wouldn't have anything to do with him if he was."

"Right, but didn't he bring you a picnic yesterday? And help you when Jake was upset? And come around last night to see you?"

"Ye-es."

"Jeez, Maudie, what d'you want him to do? Charge towards you on a white horse brandishing his heart on a stick."

"It's all irrelevant, Liv, and I've only known him for a day! I'm not here to find a boyfriend, I'm here to stop our family falling apart for good, and because I got majorly distracted yesterday, Jake nearly fell over the fence onto the beach."

"Oh my god, what happened?" Liv exclaims.

As I explain, the enormity of it hits me again. "You sh-should've seen his face. Jake was so worried. And after Mum vanishing, what must he have thought? He must hate me," I say dramatically.

"As if. Jake could never hate you. Anyway, he'll have forgotten it by now—"

"You know that's not true," I wail. "He has the memory of an elephant, like Mum!"

"He'll have *forgiven* you then. Stop beating yourself up all the time. You're a human being, not a robot. We all make mistakes – remember Seb had nightmares for weeks when I forgot he was with me and left him alone in the torture chamber at the London Dungeons? You couldn't love Jake more than you do or be a better sister."

"Not yesterday." I sniff.

"So what? Mauds, you have to stop this 'being perfect' rubbish. It's exhausting just watching you try."

"I have to be, Liv. Mum and Dad couldn't have coped with me being a difficult teenager."

"Only you put that on yourself. Did your mum or dad ever say you had to be faultless?"

"Well…no."

"Exactly." Liv sighs. "By the way, loads of our friends and even people we don't hang out with have asked if I know if you're okay. So many people care. You must be awesome to get that amount of attention, even though you keep yourself to yourself. So stop putting yourself down. What are you going to do today? Where's Jake now?"

I can almost see the determined look on Liv's face as she deliberately changes the subject, her chin tilted upwards.

"In bed still, dead to the world, which is unheard of for him."

"Great. You can have a shower and put some make-up on. Forget what's happening on the news—"

"Is there more?"

239

"No, I would've said. Maudie, just have some fun while you can with Jake. Go to the Blue Reef Aquarium in Newquay. My aunt used to take us there every time we stayed in her cottage. Didn't Jake love it last time you were there?" She doesn't wait for my answer, as she's in full fix-it mode. "Then go to the beach cafe for the best fish and chips in Cornwall and admire the fit surfer boys while you eat."

"I thought we'd do a bus tour."

"That's a bit risky."

"No riskier than going to a crowded aquarium!"

"True." I can hear her scratching away at the varnish on her old school desk, a noise that sets my teeth on edge.

"Stop doing that – pleeeease." The scratching goes silent. "It's probably our last day, so I figured it didn't matter what I did. Much."

Why haven't I told Liv about looking for Mum? It feels like another small betrayal to her, and I hate it. I know she wouldn't think I was childish if I told her…but. But what?

I don't want to feel any more of a failure than I already do.

"You could have two more days, if you're careful." Liv's tapping the porcelain ink well from her desk against the wood. She's anxious about me and Jake. I hear a loud clunk as she puts the inkpot back into its hole. "I've got about ten minutes before Mum gets back, so tell me, what's this Gerren like? I want details. How hot is he on a scale of one to ten?"

"Ha!" Liv always knows how to cheer me up. "I guess a nine."

"Nine! Tell me more."

"He's tall, slim not skinny, nice muscles."

"He works out? God, I hope he's not one of those gym-obsessed macho guys with a pin head."

I crack up with laughter, as Liv meant me to. "He has amazing blue eyes, almost-black curly hair and he has this incredible tattoo on his wrist of an octopus. It's so beautiful, you'd love it. He wants to be a marine conservationist."

"Wow! I think I'd like to go out with him. That's so cool."

"I told him about your amazing artwork."

"I hope you said I was amazing too!"

"Course I did." I realize, as I'm talking, that I really do like Gerren.

But Jake comes first. I go and check on him. He's sat on the end of the bed, his hair sticking up on end, sorting through his magazine pages, which he's spread out on the bed. I watch him from the doorway, engrossed in the pictures. He's totally happy now.

"Jake's up, Liv, so I have to go soon."

"Let me say hi."

I pass the phone to Jake. "Say hello to Liv."

"Jake's got a BIG bruise on his knee. It's purple. Jake likes purple. He's got his red bag today. Look."

He holds his red bag up to show Liv. I can hear her speaking to him.

"Yes. He wants to go and see the lobsters. Eight legs? He doesn't have eight legs. He'd like to see an octo-puss. He needs to see the lobsters first."

Jake shakes his head. "Sharks have sharp teeth. They might bite his fingers. Okay, Jake will."

He hands the phone back.

"I told Jake to look after you today."

"I think you should be saying that to *me* after yesterday."

"It's good for Jake to know that you need looking after too and you're a team."

"Jake looks after *me* a lot!"

"True. Mum's back. I can hear her car on the gravel. We'll talk later. I'm doing some sorting with Mum this morning then after lunch I'm going to Theo's. I'll put my phone inside my art folder, so text if you need me."

"Thanks, Liv. Love you."

"Love you more – now go and eat your own body weight in Cornish ice cream!"

Jake is very happy sorting through his pictures. He's laid them out on the floor. I get a piece of paper and a pen and sit next to him in case he wants me to help him choose and so that he can help me. Mum seems so far away to me right now and I want to do something positive to stop feeling out of control.

"Okay, Jake, you're the one with the good memory. We need to make a list of all the places Mum loved when we came down here with Dad. Okay?"

He nods his head seriously. "Okay. Mum likes coffee with oats. Mum can't funk-shun without her morning fix." He repeats what Mum always says.

"Ha ha – no, she can't. There were two cafes she really loved, weren't there? God, I can't remember."

"One had lots of pictures. Jake said they were boring."

"So did Dad – he said there were too many paintings of 'sunsets on the beach'."

"Mum likes sunsets." Jake puts his pictures in his red bag, then takes them out again.

"The other cafe was very old-fashioned."

"The Teapot. Mum teased him. She said Jake had to eat a hot dog. He didn't want to eat a dog!"

"Ha ha – that was so funny. Do you remember how we all loved the rock-pooling at Treyarnon Beach? Mum found a hermit crab."

"Jake put it in his bucket."

"We put him back in the sea before we went home but—"

"Jake wanted to keep him. Dad—"

"Said he'd get all smelly!" I sigh at the memory, wishing we were all hunting for hermit crabs now, instead of me making this pathetic list.

There's no chance of finding her, it's like looking for a needle in a haystack. I don't have time to scour Cornwall. The most I can hope for is luck, but that won't happen twice, not after the beach sighting yesterday. If that even was Mum. *Argh!*

243

I screw the list up into a ball and throw it in the bin in the corner.

"Oh no, his sister squashed it up."

"Yeah, we don't need it after all, Jake."

"Mum liked the 'quarium. She called that lobster Ti-tan."

"She did!"

"Let's get Mum."

"We'll go to the aquarium straight after breakfast."

Jake plonks the two bags he's discarded on my lap, keeping the pink one for today. I put the pencil down and take a deep breath to get my head together.

"Maudie?" Gerren shouts through the doorway. "I didn't see your message till this morning. What's going on? Can I come in?"

He doesn't wait for me to say yes but walks through the caravan and stands outside the open bedroom door.

Jake looks up at Gerren, pulls his trouser leg up and points to the bruise on his knee.

"Maudie left him. By himself."

CHAPTER 44

Jake

I'm going to find Mum. With Maudie. We can do it together. That boy is here again. I told him I had an accident. My bruise is very pretty. We need to go to the aquarium. That boy said he'd take me and Maudie. Hurry up, boy! Can't you hear me?

Last time we were in Cornwall Mum went shopping. With Maudie. Dad took me to the sea. Where the boats are. We caught lots of crabs on a piece of string. Near the Aquarium. Dad said if anyone got lost, we could meet there. Mum is lost now. I need to go back there with Maudie. We will find Mum again. With Titan and all the fishes.

CHAPTER 45

Maudie

I feel like I'm drowning in the silence that follows what Jake just said. Gerren will never understand like Liv – she knows Jake, but Gerren has only just met him.

"Jake was in bed, so...so I went down to the beach, to clear my head." My voice is croaky.

"Jake nearly fell over the cliff."

Gerren doesn't say anything. He just looks confused. "Um – what happened?" Gerren points to Jake's bruise.

"I stupidly went for a late walk on the beach, leaving Jake on his own, and he came out to look for me. He ran towards the fence, but I managed to stop him in time – except I crashed into him, sending him onto the picnic table. He took a hell of a thwack."

"Jake's got a bad knee." He points to his purpling bruise, that has spread quite dramatically.

"That's nasty." Gerren's eyebrows shoot upwards. "Does it need a bandage?"

"Jake doesn't want a bandage. It irritates him."

I plead with my eyes for Gerren to understand. "I had to stop you tumbling over the rocks – didn't I, Jake?" It feels like I'm defending myself too much and making it worse.

Gerren runs his hand through his hair and puffs air out in a short, explosive burst.

Jake looks at him, a puzzled expression on his face. I want to cry.

"Maudie sit next to him." Jake pats the bed beside him.

I sit down. Jake rests his hand on my head. "Maudie alright?" he says, a worry frown creasing his forehead.

I can't speak for the moment, I'm so touched by him doing this, but I manage a watery smile.

Gerren reaches out and lightly touches my arm, but Jake gives him the evils, so Gerren folds his hands under his armpits and moves slightly away again. "It's fine, Maudie. I get it, really. I know you'd never let anything hurt your brother."

"Maudie didn't mean it. Jake didn't look where his feet were."

No matter what mistakes you might make with him, Jake is totally forgiving and won't ever hold it against you. He's the best, as Liv reminded me earlier.

"Course she didn't, Jake, I know that – it just threw me, that's all." He looks at me now. "What more could you do?"

"Not leave him on his own in the first place?"

"There is that." Gerren grins at me and I feel the tension in the room sliding out of the door. "It's obvious he adores you."

We both smile at Jake, but Gerren hovers between us, not sure what to do with himself. After an awkward silence, where neither of us know what to say, he blurts out, "Why did you cancel today?"

"It suddenly seemed silly to look for Mum, and I thought you'd want to be with Tegen." I can't believe how childish that sounds now.

"Tegen? No, why would I want to be with her if I said I'd be with you today?"

"Well, I thought perhaps…" My voice fades away.

"That we're going out?"

I nod.

He pulls a face. "I've known her since I was three, when she was born. I think I nearly drowned her in the paddling pool once. It would be like going out with my kid sister."

"Jake wants breakfast."

Relieved to change the subject and have an excuse to hide the smile that wants to burst onto my face, I head for the kitchen area.

Gerren moves over to the kettle. "I'll make us a drink."

"Here, you want to sit down, Jake? You'd never get Liv's brother to make tea, he sits back and waits for it all to come to him. Mind you, he is only ten."

Gerren shrugs. "No one had time to wait on me, even at that age. I'd have starved if I hadn't helped myself."

I get a sudden picture in my head of Gerren when he was small, unable to reach the cupboards without standing on a chair; sitting at the table, or a breakfast bar, by himself.

Behind that shrug is a sad little boy.

"Hey, daydreamer, you still want me to help today?" Gerren waves a spoon in front of my face and looks at me quizzically.

I jolt out of my thoughts. I hope Gerren doesn't notice me going slightly pink at what I was thinking about, but I also like to think that it's something he can share with me at some point, if we have time. For now, I change the subject and focus on my brother. "Would you like to go to Newquay on the bus today, Jake?"

"Ooh he likes that! Jake wants to go on that bus." He's out his seat, ready to go.

"After breakfast, okay, or you'll be hungry."

Jake sits back down. "It's alright, Jake. You can get the bus," he reassures himself.

"And we'll definitely go see all the different types of fish, like we decided. Yeah?"

"Yes," Jake grins, "with chips, please."

We all laugh out loud.

"Jake made a joke."

"A brilliant one, Jake!" Gerren says before looking concerned. "Won't doing all this be a bit chancy, Maudie – you know, if you're trying to stay hidden?"

"I figured I might as well do some fun stuff with Jake while we can, and I can keep an eye out for Mum, though really she could be anywhere in the country. I know it's laughable to think we'll see her here."

"Jake saw his mum."

"Exactly, Jake, you did." His words spur me on.

"Couldn't you just text her to find out where she is?" Gerren pushes.

"Me and Aunty Eve tried and tried to call Mum on her phone before I came here, but it's always switched off."

He frowns. "I can't believe she'd block you. You know, it would be better if three of us went out today, as they'll be looking for just two people."

Gerren looks so vulnerable, like that small boy desperately hoping his wish will be granted. Three would be better than two, yes, but I haven't had a chance to check with Jake. "Jake, would you like Gerren to come with us? Or just you and me today?"

He ignores me, as he's rearranging his bus picture in his bag.

"Jake? I know you heard me, what d'you think?"

His answer is prompt.

"That boy said he'd take Jake to see the bloody lobster." He sounds exasperated with me.

"Of course he did!" I laugh out loud.

Gerren laughs too, raising his eyebrows at me. "Right, who's for scrambled eggs? I'm starving."

"Jake has full English on Sundays. With mushrooms."

* * *

I've made an effort today and have put a flick of black eyeliner on and loads of mascara with some rose-tinted lip gloss. I'm wearing my favourite black retro 501 Levi's, which I just had to sneak into my bag. They fit me perfectly and I love them. I wish I'd bought my black calf lace-up boots, as they make my legs look longer, but the trainers will have to do. Jake's excited we're going out of the campsite and on a bus.

Gerren looks really cool in his faded denims, black Timberland boots and his black leather jacket over a midnight blue T-shirt that makes his eyes the colour of a summer Cornish sea. I catch him looking at me. He breaks into a big smile when he sees me. My heart beats faster and I smile back at him with this goofy grin. I wish I could control my face.

We huddle together against the wind while we wait for the tour bus that stops outside the caravan park. For a moment we're just a group of friends on holiday. If only. The open-top sightseer bus appears round the corner and Jake nearly explodes with excitement.

As soon as the door opens, Jake boards the bus and bellows, "Morning, driver!" at a very bored looking woman behind the wheel, who takes no notice of him. Jake heads upstairs.

It's the only time you'll get Jake up stairs without him getting too upset. He heads straight for the front seats, which are free, thank goodness, or otherwise I might not have got him to sit down. He wraps his bag handles over his knees and holds his arms up as though he's gripping a steering wheel.

"*Bing bing!* Jake's driving the bus. Mind that car, Jake."

I slide in next to Jake and Gerren sits in the row opposite. He glances at Jake and away again. I wonder what he's thinking.

"*Broom broom!*"

The wind picks my hair up and blows it about my face. I huddle down lower to keep warm. At least it isn't raining. I gaze through the front window. There's only grey sky and grey water as far as the eye can see. I watch the waves slapping against the shadowy cliffs. The coastline looks barren in this light, the only colour the muted moss-green hills rolling off into the distance.

"*Beep beep.* Out the way, van."

Jake drives us along the road into town.

As soon as we get to Newquay, I sit up straight and look for anyone like my mum. We pass a boating lake where a little girl runs around the edge of the water after a small sailboat that is motoring along, its white sail billowing in the breeze. We turn right past a golf course, where an older couple zoom past in a bright-green golf cart. The lady holds onto her cap with one hand. We pass the sign for Fistral Beach. Dad had a surfing lesson with me there when we came on our final holiday. He was useless, but we had such a laugh. Later on, I heard him say to Mum that he just couldn't find the energy after all the chemo earlier in the year, but he didn't want to let me down. I cried myself to sleep that night.

We pass Harbour Beach and the quayside. Patches of blue sky have opened up in the grey, and gulls scream, beating their huge wings as they dart down to pick up the fish the trawlermen are throwing back into the water. The sunlight catches the silver scales of the mackerel, making them shimmer. The moored boats rock up and down, their masts seeming to pierce the sky before plunging back down again, pulled by a fierce undercurrent that churns up the fields of copper seaweed clouding the water.

"*Beep beep!* Put the brakes on, Jake." Jake waves at the seagull that swoops past him. "He's got a big beak."

"That's a whopper seagull, isn't it, Jake? I always forget how big they are."

"Go away, seagull," Jake shouts after it.

I refocus on spotting Mum's favourite gallery from our holiday, as we pass along Fore Street. Despite the grey day the town is quite buzzy.

"What are you looking at?" Gerren peers out the window trying to see.

"Trying to spot Mum's favourite places from when we were here. A couple of cafes she loved. She—" It suddenly feels pointless. "She has to have her caffeine fix each day, so I figured she might be in town." My voice gets quieter as

I speak. Gerren's face is weirdly blank. I suddenly wish Liv was here – I know everything she's thinking when I look at her.

"Jake wants his coffee. He has a doughnut on Fridays. Do you want jam, Jake? No thank you. You're very polite, Jake. Jake wants a doughnut with a hole."

Gerren sits up straight. "Doughnuts! Great idea, I could eat a whole box of them."

"But you've only just had breakfast, both of you!"

"That was *ages* ago, wasn't it, Jake?"

"Yes, it was." Jake stops turning his invisible steering wheel and looks at his bare wrist.

Gerren frowns. "You got something on your arm, Jake?"

"Jake's checking the time on his watch. It's ten thirty, Jake's coffee time." He shoves his arm under my nose to emphasize his point.

Gerren checks his own watch and looks up, mouth open in surprise. "That's amazing, Jake, it's exactly ten thirty."

"He just told you that," Jake says disdainfully.

Gerren perseveres. "Would you like to see my watch? It's special and took me ages to save up to buy it." Gerren slips his watch off his wrist. It's large with a blue face and stainless-steel case. "Try it on." He leans across me. "It's a Seastar 1000 diving watch, which means you can go under the sea with it or wear it in the bath."

"That's very silly," Jake says.

"Totally," I agree, teasing Gerren.

Jake takes the watch and tries to put it on. "He can't do it."

Gerren leans across me again to help him and tries to pull it over Jake's wrist, but he yanks his arm back.

"Ow! He doesn't want it!" Jake shouts.

Gerren shoots backwards. "Whoa! Sorry." He checks over his shoulder, looks embarrassed and sinks down slightly in his seat.

I pass the watch back to Gerren. "Thanks for trying." I turn back to Jake. "Sorry, Jake, we thought you wanted to try it on, as you took it."

"It pinched his skin. Ow!"

Gerren sits up straight. "Oh crap, I'm so sorry, mate. It's one of those stretchy linked straps that can catch your skin." Gerren puffs his cheeks out. He lowers his voice. "Sorry, Maudie, I didn't mean to react like that. You must always be on edge wondering if something might upset him."

I whisper back. "You get used to what works for him and what doesn't. New things can sometimes be hard though. But how would he know what he likes and doesn't if he never gets to try? Also, I know him so well it's easier to understand when something will upset him. I should've thought about it, even though he took it from you."

Gerren looks despondent. "Yeah, you're right. I just need to get to know him more." He smiles at me hesitantly. "This is our stop." Gerren gets up. He still looks a bit forlorn.

I stand on tiptoe and impulsively kiss him on the cheek.

"Thank you for coming with us. I couldn't be more grateful for you being here. There are so few people who bother to make any effort to get to know my brother, let alone try and make friends."

He smiles, all pleased at what I've said.

Jake pulls at my elbow. "No kissing. Derrick said Hannah mustn't kiss all the boys."

Gerren snorts. "This Derrick sounds like a right party pooper to me."

"Ha ha ha! Boy said pooper."

We traipse off the bus.

It all seems familiar but there are new shops and cafes that weren't here when we were on holiday two years ago. We stop outside a typical seaside shop with brightly coloured buckets and spades stacked high on the pavement, blow-up beach balls in a metal dustbin and patterned boogie boards strung to the yellow and white awning. Jake stoops down and picks up a green frog-shaped bucket with big eyes, and a red spade with a long wooden handle.

"He likes that. Jake loves frogs."

"Let me get this." Gerren takes his wallet out and heads into the shop before I can say anything.

"Look what Jake's got!" Jake shouts out loud, making me jump and the poor woman beside him. She moves to the other side of the shopfront. Jake's clutching a postcard in his free hand, looking very pleased with himself.

"He likes that one."

"Show me."

"It's a puppy dog. Poor dog. She's got funny eyes."

"They're pretend, googly eyes, Jake. See, if you shake it her eyes move. Let's go and pay for it together. You can give the man the money."

"No, he can't." He shakes the card forcefully, mesmerized by the moving eyes.

"If you can order yourself food and drink at the cafe, you can pay for this. Come on." I realize that I don't let him do things like this and perhaps I should, especially since Jake's proved he can. We go inside.

Gerren is at the counter and turns around just as we get there. "Here, I'll do it." He reaches out for the card.

"Jake can do it, thank you."

I hand him the exact money and he stands at the counter to pay. He turns to check I'm still here, then puts his hand out, with the card in it. He leans towards the man and shakes the card up and down. "Her eyes have gone funny."

"She's gone cross-eyed." The shopkeeper crosses his own eyes at Jake. Jake doesn't react, not even a smile, which flusters the man. "O-kay, that's thirty-five pence, please." Jake gives the money to the man. "Would you like a small bag to put your card in?"

"No thank you." Jake walks away with the card. "Jake paid the man," he informs Gerren, taking the bucket and spade from him and putting the postcard in the bucket. He holds that in one hand and his bag in the other.

"What do you say to Gerren, Jake?" I'm surprised he hasn't, since he thanked the shopkeeper.

Jake looks past me out the door of the shop.

"That policeman's coming to see Jake."

CHAPTER 46

Jake

I don't know why that policeman's here. I hope he goes away. Policemen put you in prison. It's coffee time. I need my doughnuts. Then I can find Mum. I won't find Dad there. Derrick said Dad is in heaven. I don't know where that is. Derrick said you can't get a train or bus there. He said you go there on a cloud. Derrick can be very silly.

This policeman is grumpy. He pushed past me. That's rude! When I find Mum, she can live with us in our caravan. I'm going to give her my new dog. On my postcard. She can keep it for ever.

CHAPTER 47

Maudie

I think my heart's stopped. Gerren grabs my hand and squeezes it tight. What if someone's recognized us from the news and reported us? There's no way out of the shop except past the policeman, so we're blocked in. He seems to fill the doorway. He takes his peaked cap off and rotates it in his hands.

Not now, please not now. Just give us another day, so that we might get Mum back.

Jake hovers awkwardly in front of the policeman. I can't see his face, but from the frown on the policeman's I'm guessing he's thinking we're the runaways.

"Could you move to one side, please, young man? Wait over there." His voice is stern. Jake doesn't budge.

"Move over here and let the policeman get past you." I don't say my brother's name.

"Can I come through?" The policeman barks at Jake,

stepping round him and knocking the postcard stand, which wobbles on its pedestal. He grabs it. "Is this the young man you called about, Terry?" he says irritably.

It's over. I'm not going to cry. Not here.

"Hi, John. No, I didn't manage to keep him in the shop – I think he cottoned on I'd seen something. I'm not the only one who's had trouble with him round here."

"Can you give me a description?"

Gerren and I exchange looks. We let the policeman take his notebook out and go up to the counter before we walk slowly out of the shop, so as not to look any more guilty than we already do. As soon as we're all outside we head as fast as we can across the road towards the nearest cafe.

"Jeeze!" Gerren lets out a long breath. "That was worse than when I got hauled up in front of assembly for getting caught smoking in the bottom field."

"Oh my god, I nearly vommed on the shop floor! I really thought he'd recognized me and Jake."

"They can't have heard about you down here yet if he didn't say anything. But still, would you rather go back to the campsite, Maudie?"

I shake my head. "No – yes. Should I? I don't know." Seeing that policeman was a warning to me to stay alert. I make up my mind. "The police obviously haven't tracked us down yet and we're all happy. Let's just go for it and try and keep out of trouble."

Gerren laughs and playfully punches me on the arm.

"That's a joke – you seem to attract disaster. I can't believe it's still only eleven o'clock! It feels like mid-afternoon."

He peers through the window of a cafe, his breath misting up the glass. "I haven't tried this place before, it replaced one that had been here for ages. Fancy it? Hmmm – it's called Peace and Plants."

I press my nose against the glass. I think this used to be one of the places Mum liked before it changed, because she said it reminded her of holidays with her mum and dad when she was a little girl – all chintz tablecloths and tiered cake stands with fresh cream eclairs you could peel the chocolate off in one strip.

"It looks cool and it's great that it has vegan options."

I go through the door before Gerren has time to object.

Jake checks his wrist. "Jake can't see his doughnut."

Gerren frowns as he notices the sign with the vegan quote *Our food is grown, not born*. "Let's hope they have a normal doughnut here."

We find a table at the rear, in the corner, to be less visible. Jake refuses to sit on a bench, so I grab a chair from the next table and sit Jake on the end. He starts reading the menu upside down. He's still clasping his frog bucket in his other hand.

"What would you like with your Friday doughnut, Jake? Milkshake? Apple juice?"

"Jake wants brown milkshake and a doughnut with a hole."

"Same for me," Gerren declares. "Assuming brown means normal chocolate and not some cacao-nib, almond-milk creation."

"That's exactly what I was hoping it was," I say, absolutely meaning it.

I think it looks great in here, all wood floors and white-painted brick walls with vintage kitchen equipment on the shelves. Liv would love it here. I'd love it if *she* was here.

"I'll order then I'll go to the loo afterwards. I won't be long. Will you be okay?" I say to Gerren.

"No probs." He looks wary but sticks his thumb up. "I'll be fine. Not much can happen in a few minutes."

I'm going to tell him that actually there's an awful lot that can happen, but I *must* pee.

After I've ordered I head to the ladies. I notice Jake has cleared the vase of flowers off the table, taking over one half with his bag and bucket and lining the sauce bottles up in the other half. Gerren is sat as far back as he can go on the bench, obviously not allowed to touch anything.

I head into the loo, glancing at myself in the mirror. I'm too pale, with dark shadows under my eyes, not helped by the dim lighting. I look strained. At least my hair hasn't turned into a bird's nest in the damp air and wind. I tuck the front strands behind my ears, revealing two crystal studs in each ear and two turquoise bead earrings that get covered by my hair. When I get back, I'm going to get my top bit of cartilage done, though Liv said it's painful.

I let out a big sigh. Normal life seems far, far away at the moment.

As I pee, someone bangs the outer door, charges into the loo next to me and slams that door, ramming the lock across. It seems like she's crying but doesn't want anyone to know, as I can hear her muffled sobs. She sounds so unhappy I have to ask her, "Are you okay in there?" Immediately the crying stops. "Hello, are you alright?"

There's complete silence; she must be holding her breath. Then I hear her bolt shoot back and her door bang against the wall, making it shudder. I pull the chain and open my door quickly, wanting to help.

Disappearing through the exit is my mum. I *think* it's my mum – her hair's the same from behind, dark blonde curls, khaki safari jacket, buckled black wellies.

The shock shuts down my legs and I lose a few seconds until I belt out the door after her.

There's no one going out the exit onto the main street, but I push past a delivery man coming through with a tray of seeded rolls.

"Hey! Watch out!" he shouts at me as he rebalances the tray.

I ignore him and head up the street towards the town centre. Nothing. I run back the other way, glancing in shops and all around. She's vanished. I go back inside the cafe and look frantically around the room. There's another door to the garden, opposite the loo. I go up to the counter, pushing in front of an old man in a waxed jacket, who complains loudly about my rudeness. "Sorry, sir, excuse me, is there a way out through the garden?"

"Yes." The girl behind the counter glares at me and apologizes to the gentleman as well.

I charge out into the garden, ignoring Gerren's anxious voice asking me what's up and where am I going. The garden's empty, but the back gate bangs open and shut in the wind blowing across from the quay. I go out onto Fore Street and turn a full circle trying to see Mum. I run up and down the street, which is lined with uneven buildings. It's no good. She's nowhere to be seen. I slump against the stone wall.

A sky as grey as a January day hangs over the quay. A pale sea mist hovers over the harbour. It feels like it's rolled over me, blotting out the boats, the water, the people milling past me. I call Mum's name in the hope of…I don't know what, because she won't answer me. A small boy tugs at his mum's coat. "That girl's lost her mummy." The mother glances my way and keeps walking.

Mum's gone. Thinking it doesn't make me accept it. I call out her name one more time. When she doesn't answer, my stomach aches and the ache spreads throughout my body, extinguishing everything that felt good.

I can't cope. Mum must have seen Jake or else why would she have run into the loo crying? She heard my voice, but she ran away.

But it *can't* have been Mum. She wouldn't do that to us. I'm hallucinating – my anxiety about Mum has made me see things.

My phone vibrates in my pocket and I pull it out quickly, desperate to see what Liv says.

Love you xxx

It's as though she has some sixth sense about me.

The faint smile on my face fades as I realize: I know what my own mum looks like. Can I really question whether it was her? Which means she's just run away from us for the second time. She's wiped us out like the sea mist that's coiled around the harbour.

A deep black hole opens in my chest. There's no point in looking for somebody who doesn't want to be found.

It hits me; even if Mum sees that I kidnapped Jake on the news, she won't care. She doesn't want to be with us any more. That's it.

So now what?

What will happen to me and Jake?

I shiver. I can barely pick my feet up they feel so heavy. Someone touches my shoulder. It's Gerren.

"Hey, the waitress is keeping an eye on Jake. What's going on? You just left." He sounds really fed up.

"Is J-Jake okay with th-that?" I struggle to get my words out.

Gerren stops me tugging at the thread on the end of my sleeve. He peers anxiously into my face. "For sure. She was just herself with him, unlike I was first of all. What's up, are you okay?"

"N-no." My teeth chatter. "B-better not leave them too long."

It's surreal, I can hear myself answering Gerren and my body is there but my mind has flown far from here.

"Let's go back inside. You can explain there." Gerren tugs at my hand and pulls me along. "Your hand is *frozen*. Jake's finished his food and drink already."

His calm, controlled voice brings me back into myself. I take a gulp of cold air. I can't have a meltdown. Jake needs me. Now. I have to pull myself together and take charge. I can think later. I've put Jake through enough. I need to be the adult.

But first I must check something. "Gerren, did you see that lady in the green jacket with blonde curly hair, who ran out the loo?"

"No, I was facing away from the loos. Why? What's up?" He looks apprehensive, his top teeth tugging at his bottom lip.

"I think it was my mum – the lady who ran out. She was in the loo next to me, and she was crying. I called out to see if she was okay. I didn't know it was her then and I think she must have recognized my voice. She ran out of the loo quickly, so I couldn't get to her in time, but I saw her. She didn't stop. She must have known it was me, but she didn't stop. She vanished up the road." Pain cramps my stomach, making me reject the idea again. "Maybe it wasn't her. It couldn't have been, could it?"

Gerren flinches and looks anywhere but at me. When he does, it seems as though it's a huge effort for him to speak and his voice is strained. "Wouldn't surprise me if it was."

"So you think it *was* my mum?" I didn't expect him to say that.

His face is completely white. "Yeah."

"No. There's no way she'd ignore Jake. She would have come over to him, wouldn't she?" I pull back so I can see his face clearly. I don't want any bullshit.

"I don't know, Maudie, I don't know your mum. But let's face it, you do and you'd know her if you saw her. Look, Jake needs us to go back, he'll be getting scared that you've gone."

"Yes, yes we must." I guiltily remember last night. "It's Jake who's important."

"You are too, Maudie." Gerren says that so bitterly it makes me uneasy. He doesn't make an effort to smile when I look at him, but he gently tucks a strand of my hair behind my ear. "You're just as important." His voice is subdued.

"But Jake's vulnerable, Gerren – I'm not," I say gently, not wanting to crush what he said. "Sometimes he can protect himself, but sometimes he can't and then it's up to me to do that for him." My voice sounds calmer now, even if I don't feel it inside. I've switched into a different gear. "I'm not letting him down again."

I put Mum in a mental box and seal the lid, just like I imagine Jake did with Dad.

Then I walk back through the gate into the cafe. How can I face Jake, knowing what I do?

I'm more than relieved to find Jake isn't missing me. He's colouring in a place mat with one of the waitresses, who is sitting next to him showing him what to do.

"Thanks, Jiera. This is Maudie." Gerren looks slightly embarrassed as he introduces me, and I feel myself blushing. *Meet the weirdo who just ran out of the cafe, abandoning her brother.*

Jiera is super cool with purple-streaked jet-black hair and a thin silver chain that goes from her nose stud to her ear. She glances at me quickly, gives a tiny smile and then looks away again, focusing on the colouring that she's doing. I have to swallow very hard to get rid of the lump in my throat, my emotions threatening to overwhelm me. "Th-thank you," I stutter. "I'm so sorry. I thought I saw someone I hadn't seen for a long time."

"Luckily I get Jake and his need for structure and alignment. I don't like surprises either."

She says this very matter-of-factly, as though she's known Jake for years. I stand there with my mouth open, lost for words.

"Don't worry," she says, still focusing on the paper. "Me and Jake were having a great time, weren't we?"

The silver chain trembles as she talks.

Jake holds up a picture of a fish covered in yellow crayon. "Jake wrote his name." He points with his finger at some black curly shapes over the fish's tail. "J, A, K, E, spells Jake. He's very clever."

"That's wonderful, Jake, really wonderful. Dad would be so proud of you."

He looks me straight in the eye. "Yes, he would. Jake is proud of Jake."

I can't help but laugh at that – a bit too loudly after all the upset. Jiera looks at me with her eyebrows raised.

"I better get back." Jiera stands up but leans over and finishes the fin she was colouring in before she goes. "I can't leave things unfinished, or it'll bug me for the rest of the day. It used to really wind my mum up until she understood I wasn't doing it to annoy her and just needed to do it. None of my teachers got it until I was a Year Four and had Mr Williams, who let me stay in at break time to finish something." She sighs. "I irritated a lot of people as a kid."

"People can be SO intolerant," I agree. "Jake gets that a lot."

"For sure." She nods and puts the crayon back in the pack and stands up straight.

Jiera's much taller than she looked sitting down and has legs that go on for ever, most of which you can see in her shorts dungarees. I catch Gerren checking them out. Jiera doesn't notice him looking. She waves another piece of paper at Jake.

"Next time you come in, Jake, we could colour in the monkey and draw some jungle foliage around him."

My heart sinks. There might not be another time for me and Jake here.

"That's a good idea. Jake likes that monkey." He suddenly sings his favourite song from *The Jungle Book*, from when he was a little boy. It makes the elastic band around my heart let go a little bit.

"Thanks again. You've loved it, haven't you, Jake?"

"Yes, he has. Thank you, girl. Jake has a dis-ability," he tells Jiera proudly.

She claps her hands, clearly elated at what he's just said. "That's right, me too!"

Gerren frowns, clearly confused by Jiera's reaction.

"Disability isn't a bad thing – it's what makes us, us." She says this looking straight at Gerren.

Gerren looks at her, mortified, then down at the floor, as though she's read his mind.

She sighs. "I'm neurodivergent and I hate the assumptions made about me. It isn't something bad or something that I suffer from, it's just who I am. I'm me, not some stereotype. I'm not brilliant at anything, I can't remember all the names of the kings and queens back to Medieval times, or work out complex maths equations in my head – and I *don't* want to pretend to be like everyone else, when being me is way better."

"I totally get that," I say.

"I never thought of it like that," Gerren admits.

"Then you should start now," Jiera tells him before turning to Jake. "I had a great time – thank you, Jake."

"Jake wrote his name. Thank you, girl."

"Jiera, I need your help, please!" the owner of the cafe shouts over.

"Better go. Bye, Jake, Maudie, Gerren."

"Jake likes her."

"And you're pretty cool too," she replies.

Gerren checks his watch. "Shall we go to the aquarium, as it's literally around the corner. I've already paid here, so we can just go."

"You paid for Jake's bucket and spade!"

"I'm earning, don't worry about it."

"Thank you."

I'm not convinced Gerren seems happy. He probably wants to move on quickly and get the day over with. I gulp my tea down, grateful for the bit of warmth left in it. I square my shoulders and head towards the exit. I. Won't. Break. Down.

"Let's go and see the stingrays. They were Dad's favourite – do you remember, Jake?"

"Dad said they were pancakes. Jake likes pancakes. With syrup. Those fish were big. Jake has to find Titan."

"Definitely."

Jake looks happy as he clutches his bucket, spade, fish picture and his bag. Getting around with that lot isn't going to be easy, but it's worth it seeing how pleased he is.

How could Mum not want to see him?

CHAPTER 48

Jake

There are lots and lots of fishes. I can't see the lobster. Is he hiding in that rock? I looked all down the tunnel to find him. I looked all down the tunnel to find Mum. They're not here. A little boy said Titan was dead. Oh no. I won't find Mum if he's not here. I don't know where to look for her. I'm sad. "Don't be sad," that little boy said. He gave me a purple shell. With brown spots. It's a cow shell. I put it in my bag. The little boy's called Ben. He said the lobster is in heaven. Like my dad. Titan can see my dad. They can look after each other! I want to see them. My dad. My mum. How can I get to heaven?

CHAPTER 49

Maudie

The aquarium is brilliant, and Jake's loving it. He's found a friend – a little boy who's as excited as him at seeing all the different species of fish – which is just as well, as I'm so distracted with my own thoughts about Mum. I have a few moments to myself while Gerren gets us some water. I think back to her sobbing in the toilets at the cafe, running out the door – and somehow vanishing. Then I have one of those light-bulb moments, which completely switches what you're thinking. Perhaps the fact she was crying showed Mum *does* care and that maybe she feels bad about what she's done? Suddenly I feel more hopeful again – I bet Mum was just totally shocked at seeing us, but once she's over that she might try and find us now. Will she come home?

Gerren sits next to me and hands me my water. "Jake's mesmerized – he's got his face and hands pressed up against the glass." He looks thoughtful. "Please don't take this the wrong way, but do you think maybe you're a bit over-protective of Jake sometimes? I'm sure I'd be the same if he was my brother, but he's having a blast here and, actually, he was fine in the cafe with Jiera."

I'm about to react but stop myself. I'd thought that myself earlier when he paid for his postcard. Perhaps me and Mum should let him be a bit more independent.

"I think you have a point, Gerren," I say as I watch my brother.

We can hear the little boy talking to Jake.

"Jake! Jake! Look at the stripy octopus. Can you see him – he's crawling out of that pot? He has one, two, five, six – eight legs." He wiggles his fingers at Jake.

"That's a lot of legs," Jake says, waving at the octopus.

The little boy waves at him too. "Mum, Mum, the octopus said hello to me!"

"That's wonderful, Ben," his mother calls over from the bench where's she's feeding his baby brother or sister.

"Here comes the shark!" Ben squeals.

Just as Jake peers at the glass, a small shark thumps into it, making him shoot back clasping his nose.

"It bit Jake's nose!"

Ben nearly wets himself laughing. Jake keeps pretending the shark has got him, until Gerren, Ben's mother and I are laughing too. It's lovely seeing Jake making a friend. He doesn't have people he sees outside of school unless it's on an outing. Mum asked Hannah round to tea once and Jake got upset and said she couldn't come in. Derrick told Mum it's only us who get sad about this – he thinks Jake's quite happy keeping the different parts of his life separate.

Jake and Ben go to the other side of the tunnel. His mother joins them with her baby, now strapped to her front.

Gerren's knee is jigging up and down, sending vibrations through the seat.

"You okay?" I'm puzzled he seems so agitated.

Gerren gives a sigh that makes his cheeks puff out. "Can I tell you something?"

He's nervous, which makes me wonder what he's going to say, but then he launches into it.

"I should have told you before, but it was way too soon – we barely knew each other. I mean, we barely know each other now! One minute I was breaking your caravan door down because I thought someone was being murdered, the next I find out you've kidnapped your brother *and* that your mum's disappeared. I wanted to walk away, but I don't know, I just had to see you again."

I don't know how to respond, but he doesn't give me an opportunity anyway.

"Normally I reject people long before they can reject me." He swallows hard. "The thing is, I know some of what you're dealing with. You see," he leaves a big, fat pause that seems to go on for ever, "my mother abandoned me when I was five years old, and it's taken a couple of years of therapy for me to understand that it wasn't my fault."

I'm speechless at first. I never guessed that what he was holding back would be anything like this, but it explains what didn't add up when I told him everything that had happened to me. His blue eyes watch me and I feel his grief slice through me.

"I'm so, so sorry, Gerren. I can't believe you were only five, that's terrible."

"I watched her go. I didn't understand what was happening. She came downstairs with her coat on and her suitcase in her hand. She didn't say anything to me. She didn't even look at me. I told myself later that was because she couldn't bear to. Dad was pleading with her to stay. She walked out the door. She didn't shut it, so I ran out into the front garden. She slammed the gate in my face.

"I watched her through the railings, pulling her bag behind her. It had a squeaky wheel. I thought she'd look back at me, but she didn't. Not once, Maudie. I kept thinking she'd turn around and wave, then everything would be alright, but she just kept going until she was so small I could balance her on my hand. Then she vanished round the corner."

I'm devastated for him. No wonder he acted strangely when I said my mum had dumped me and Jake, and, of course, that's why he got so disturbed at the cafe when I said Mum had vanished up the road. His face looked haunted, and bewildered, as though he couldn't make sense of what I was saying. Now I know it was reflecting what he felt as that abandoned little boy.

I cup my hand around his face, trying to give him some sort of comfort. He holds it there with his own, before grasping it back around his water bottle, his face a picture of misery.

"See, Maudie, all the times you've blamed yourself since you've been here, I could have told you it definitely wasn't your fault – because you can't find someone who doesn't want to be found. The important difference between you and me is, from what you've said, it seems like your mother loves you – she just needs time to get over losing your dad and sort her head out."

His words come out in a rush, as though he doesn't want to forget what he'd planned to say. He finishes his water and wipes his mouth on the back of his hand.

"I spent my childhood feeling guilty, wondering if I was so horrible it drove my mum away. It took me a long time to accept it wasn't my fault. And when I wasn't feeling guilty, I took it on myself to make my dad feel better. But it wasn't my responsibility to do that. It should've been the other way around.

"I thought if I was perfect it would help, and that Dad would love me so much it would blank out my mother for good. Of course, it doesn't work that way. I was set up to never feel good about myself."

"That's exactly how I feel now – like no matter what I do I'll always fail, always let people down."

He looks at me intently. "But you don't, Maudie."

I hesitate, wanting Gerren to know how much it means that he just opened up to me. "I know how much it took to say what you just did out loud, and it must be unbearable to think your mum didn't love you."

"It's thirteen years ago, almost to the day, that Mum left." He stops for a moment, as though he's seeing it replay in his head. "I've accepted it, but I'll never get used to it...if you get what I mean."

"I do." I take his free hand in mine. "Have you seen her again? You don't have to tell me if it's too much."

"Yes, I saw her. I think it would have been better if I hadn't, though, then all the fantasies I'd created in my head wouldn't have been smashed to pieces." His voice breaks. I hold his hand tighter. "We hadn't had contact or spoken in years. I wasn't even sure where she was, and Dad refused to talk about her. She was alive but might as well have been dead. I almost wish she was, then I could bury her and put an end to this. That sounds really shitty but it's a...a living grief that never goes away."

I wrap my arms around him as tight as I can, holding his pain with him, the same as he has for me. He clears his throat before continuing to talk.

"I was sixteen, just done my GCSEs and got way better results than predicted. I thought if my mum knew then she might be proud of me, want to have me back in her life." His face looks grim. "I managed to track her down and she agreed to see me.

"When I got there, she couldn't care less about my results, all she wanted to know was if my dad could help her out with some money, as he was doing alright for himself. I hated her in that moment. I haven't seen her since. Not fucking once has she tried to see me again." Gerren clings onto me. When he lets me go, he says, "My mother never loved me in the first place."

The thought is sad enough to make him close his eyes. I wish I could take some of the pain carved into his features. His blue eyes open. He looks so sad I want to cry, but I keep my voice strong, for him. "But you're going to be alright, and you have Brae, your dad, your aunty – great friends."

He nods. "And you're so lucky to have Jake and him you. I wish I could've told you all this before, Maudie; I just couldn't. It's way too hard sharing my feelings. I bottle everything up."

I smile sadly. "And you're scared to show your true feelings in case you get rejected again?"

"Yes. Do you sometimes feel like you're always on the outside—"

"Looking in at what everyone else is doing." I finish the sentence for him.

He nods his head. "Yeah, that's it exactly!"

Gerren pinches the bit between his eyes with his finger and thumb. When he looks up his eyes are haunted. "You never stop grieving, do you? It just hides behind your face, as time goes on."

I nod, holding back the tears forming in my eyes.

He gives a sad smile and looks away.

We're going to have to stop, as I can see Jake is coming over with Ben, but I just want to say something to Gerren before he reaches me.

"It must be really hard for you to be helping me after what you just told me. Thank you."

Now that he's opened up, now that I understand him better, I feel even closer to him. I hope Gerren feels the same.

"Jake saw a puffing fish."

Ben hops from foot to foot. "It blew up!" He blows his cheeks out as large as he can.

"I wish I could've seen that!" I join in.

"Jake thought it would pop."

His face is bright with happiness. It gives me a warm feeling.

"Ben, we have to go." His mum takes his hand. "Thank you for keeping him company," she says to Jake.

"Jake made that boy laugh."

"You did – it was brilliant. Say goodbye now, Ben." She smiles at us.

"Bye bye, Jake!"

They head towards the gift shop.

"You want some lunch?" Gerren says hopefully.

I shake my head in disbelief, but Jake's up for it. Of course. We head for the cafe, where I order fish and chips. The tables are covered in blue and white check tablecloths, held in place by metal clips, which Jake immediately removes and he smooths the cloth out. An old plum tomato tin holds the knives and forks, and a metal crab grips white paper serviettes in its mouth. Mum would love it.

"Jake wants his mum," he says, as though he's read my thoughts.

"Oh Jake, I know you do."

"My mum," Jake says sadly. "She wasn't here."

I lean over and hug his arm. "No, but we can come back with her when we find her." He rests his head on top of mine for a few seconds, then he lifts it up as our food arrives.

Mum knows what this must be doing to him, so she must be in a very dark place – maybe one which is impossible to climb out of. That scares me. I can't bring myself to say, "She'll be back soon" now, because I don't want to lie to Jake – he wouldn't understand, and he'd expect her to be at the mobile home later.

"Hey…" Gerren frowns and looks at his plate. "Have you taken some of my chips?"

"I haven't eaten mine, so why would I take yours? Jake?" Jake's too focused on his food to answer and he's still got half of his own chips left. "Help yourself to mine, I'm not hungry and this piece of fish is enormous!"

Gerren's phone pings. He frowns at the message, "Jeez," and his face looks serious when he glances back up at me.

"Sorry, Maudie, but we're going to have to go back to the site when we've finished eating. The police are there and Brae says it's important."

CHAPTER 50

Jake

I am going home on the yellow bus. I couldn't sit at the front. Some children were in my seat. I was upset. That boy called me a baby. All the children laughed at me. I'm not a baby, I'm a Jake. They don't like me. I got all wet – a girl sprayed her drink on me. It made my skin spiky. Get it off me! It mustn't touch me. They won't stop laughing. It's too noisy. I can't stop my ears up. My head is bursting with bees. They're very angry.

That boy told those children off. You mustn't bully people! Thank you, boy. He said Jake was the best. His name is Geren. The bus driver took the children away. Maudie took the bees out of my head. Like my mum does. I can sit in the front now and drive the bus. Beep beep!

CHAPTER 51

Maudie

I'm too shattered to talk and I'm dreading what we'll find when we get back to the campsite. It's making my heart race. If the police are there it *must* be because of me and Jake. I can't bear facing Brae after all he's done for us, and I don't want him to be disappointed in me, though I deserve that for deceiving him. What's worse is I hope he doesn't get in trouble for helping us.

Gerren is staring out the window on the opposite seat, his mind elsewhere. His face is paper white.

I'm not sure any of us can take much more today, especially after some thoughtless kids on the bus were nasty to Jake. He was already disappointed it wasn't the sightseer bus. Gerren and the driver were brilliant and sorted them out. We all feel wiped out and I'm desperate to speak to Liv about seeing Mum in the cafe. Now I've got over the shock of her running off, I feel it must be a sign that we bumped into her. I'm sure now I did the right thing coming here and I'm hanging onto a hope that we'll all be back together again soon.

And if for some reason that doesn't happen, then I know I can't go home. Jake will get taken back into care and I'm not letting that happen. But if I don't go home, I'll never see Liv or my other friends or finish school. And if the police are waiting for us at the campsite, I probably won't have a choice in what happens now anyway. Argh! I'd never speak to Aunty Eve again if she puts Jake back with that woman.

I don't know what to do any more. All I know is that I have to make sure my brother doesn't lose any more than he has already – that we don't lose each other.

The bus is taking for ever. It'll be gone four by the time we get back. We're stuck in a queue that seems to be at least a mile long. Jake's fallen asleep with his arms held up on his imaginary steering wheel, his chin on his chest. Gerren's eyes are shut, but I don't know if he's asleep or pretending to be. This is all such a mess.

At last, the bus starts moving again. As we go round a corner, I see a small white van with its crumpled bonnet open and dark smoke curling up into the air. Parked in front of it is a red mini with a large dent at the back. I wonder what Liv's doing right now.

My phone pings in my bag. My shaky hands keep dropping it. I turn it the right way up and see Liv's message.

Eve spoke to Mum

The police are spreading the word
So sorry Maudie, wish I was with you
Have to babysit Theo's sister until about
7 then we can talk
Love you xxx If you NEED to talk before
that just text me and I'll find a way to call

This really is it then.

My hands feel clammy and my breath comes out in quick, uneasy bursts. I wonder if I'll be taken to the police station. I'm not leaving Jake on his own, we're sticking together.

Ahead of us I can see the entrance to the campsite with its curved white sign arched over the cast-iron gateway; *Perren Sands Camping Park*. The nearer we get, the sicker I feel. Gerren presses the stop button. He smiles at me, except it's more of a grimace.

Then he clears his throat. "You okay?"

I shake my head – I feel anything but okay.

"It'll all be fine." He turns away from me.

Gerren looks shattered. I think all my problems on top of his are too much for him to deal with.

Jake is woozy from being asleep and takes ages to get all his bits together, but he won't let us hold anything for him. At the top of the stairs, he stops and refuses to move.

"He can't do it. It's too tall."

The bus driver shouts up to us. "Can you get a move on, please? I'm running late as it is."

I hear someone say deliberately loudly, "What is it now? Really, they shouldn't bring him on public transport if he can't cope."

Tears spring to my eyes. Sometimes I think people would be happy if they could just get rid of anyone who is different. They see different as problematic, something that needs fixing. They couldn't be more wrong.

Eventually we persuade Jake he can cope with the stairs. Gerren keeps quiet and focuses on catching Jake if he slips, as his hands are so full. The people crowded downstairs watch until we get off the bus. If the police hadn't caught up with us already, every one of these people would remember us anyway. Beads of sweat roll down the back of my neck, making my hair damp underneath, where it rests on my collar.

I'm doubly stressed by the time we finally get off the bus and the doors hiss shut.

"Phew, I was terrified Jake was so sleepy he'd slip and fall on you," Gerren says, wiping the sweat from his forehead.

I can see a police car parked outside the campsite offices.

It's started to rain. Water drips off the side of the roof and runs in rivulets along the fronds of the palm leaves, pitter-patting on the concrete where it falls. I shiver with the awfulness of it all. The sky is a sheet of iron grey that presses down on my head. The shoreline has vanished, along with any hope I had that Jake and I would have more time.

My fear grows into an active panic, and as we push

through the swing doors of reception my distress threatens to engulf me. Will they separate us straight away?

There isn't anyone at the desk, but we can hear voices coming from the inner office. I can feel my heart pulsing behind my ribs. The walls of the room close in on me, so that I feel I am standing in isolation. I watch as Gerren rings the shiny brass bell on the desk. The tinny sound brings me back into the room. I feel like an ice cube has fallen down my back. I shudder. Gerren rests his arm across my shoulders, trying to reassure me.

Jake stands next to me, straining his head forward – listening to the people talking, their voices getting louder, as they walk through to where we are.

I tried so hard to do my best for Jake, to get him out of the foster home and reunite him with Mum, but it's not been good enough. I've failed him.

I don't have time to grab him and run, and I'm not sure I want to any more. The double doors through to the office swing open. I stand up straight and get ready for hell to break loose.

Brae's face as he walks through is grim, his brows drawn together and his mouth in an unyielding line.

Jake shouts out happily: "It's Father Christmas! Ho ho ho."

When he sees Jake, Brae half smiles, half frowns, clearly distracted and clearly angry with me for lying to him. "There you are, Jake. What have you done today then?"

Jake thinks for a moment before announcing – just as a tall, grey-haired man in a dark blue uniform positions himself next to Brae – "Jake had a wee. He tucked his willy in."

"Jake!"

Brae's mouth twitches, then he throws his head back and roars with laughter. After the last half hour of stress on the bus, Gerren has completely lost his sense of humour, like me, and only manages a half smile. Jake laughs loudly with Brae, stopping and starting, not quite getting it. I eye the policeman warily, though he's smiling now.

I decide to go for it. "I'm really, really sorry, Brae." I swallow the lump in my throat.

"Good grief, don't be silly. You made a great joke, didn't you, Jake?"

"Yes, he did. Jake did a willy joke."

Brae's totally misunderstood me. He doesn't realize I'm saying sorry for lying. It completely throws me, so I clamp my mouth shut and wait. The policeman winks at me.

Jake holds his frog bucket out to Brae, skimming it past my head. "Jake's got some chips." He shows me too. In the bottom of his bucket is a pile of soggy chips. He empties them on the desk.

Gerren gives a loud snort. "So that's where my chips went! I knew I wasn't imagining it."

Jake is super pleased with himself. "Jake got them for Mr Christmas."

Jake looks at me with a cheeky grin on his face and I can't help but grin back at him. He must have moved like lightning to pinch those from Gerren's plate.

"Well, thank you, Jake, I really appreciate that. I'll have them for my tea." Brae picks up a soggy chip that flops onto his thumb. "Yum!"

"Maudie, love, why don't you take Jake back to the caravan, as I need Gerren to cover for me while I sort out some trouble on site." Brae wipes his fingers on a hanky he produces from his pocket.

The police aren't here for us? Can it be true?

"Sure." I try not to look too eager to get away. "Thanks for your help today, Gerren. Jake and I had a great time. I hope you get everything sorted, Brae. We'll leave you to it. Bye!"

With that, I practically skip out of the door and into the fresh air, the cold rush filling my lungs. I hold my face up to the sky. The rain cools my burning skin, which was flushed from all the tension.

"Jake's all wet. Can you get it off him? He wants Scooby-Dooby-Dooooo!"

"You can have Scooby-Doo, Jake, and anything you want."

I'm giddy with relief. I do a little rain dance around Jake.

"Maudie is so silly sometimes."

I got away with it again. He didn't know! He... I twirl once. Didn't... I twirl twice. Know... I pirouette for the third time around my brother.

"Stop doing that. It irritates him."

I stop.

There won't be a third time lucky.

Back inside our mobile home, I put the film on for Jake and wonder whether to ring Liv now. I could just call her, but she might be busy changing Theo's sister's nappy or rocking her to sleep.

"Hey, Jake – it's sort of stopped raining so I'm going to sit outside. Give me a shout if you need me."

"No need to freak out, Scrappy!" Jake grins at me.

I go outside and pull a chair up, so that I can see the beach below.

The sun has broken through the cloud. The sand soaks up the sun, turning it gold. I sink into it and let the warmth wrap itself around me. I'm desperate to hold onto this moment of peace, but the euphoria of earlier is morphing into practicalities for the future.

I was being naïve to think everything would work out in such a short amount of time. I was hoping for a fairy-tale ending. I don't know what living without Mum might realistically mean for me and Jake. My exams start in a couple of months, but now they seem pointless when my priority is making sure Jake will be living with me instead of strangers.

I want my mum so much it hurts.

Mum loves us to pieces, but she can't see beyond her own grief for Dad at the moment. The more I open my eyes and think, the more I understand. Mum doesn't have *her* mum or Dad to turn to; they died when I was little and Mum was never close to Dad's parents. Neither of them was after they suggested Mum must have done something wrong when she was pregnant to make Jake the way he was – even though they knew he'd been starved of oxygen at birth. Dad never forgave them for that. Jake was a baby when I last saw them, so I must have been four. I remember hiding under the dining room table at Granny's house.

Jake's crying. It goes on and on and on. He's in his baby bouncer and I don't think he likes it. He wants to sit still. He doesn't like being all shaken up. He wants to lie on his back and stare at the light bulb.

Mummy and Daddy and Granny and Grandpa are standing over Jake. They're very shouty and I don't like it. I wanted to bring Jake under the table with me, 'cause he hates loud noises, but Granny told me off and said I was a naughty girl for dragging him around in his chair. She said I might hurt him.

I would NOT hurt Jake. I don't like Granny. I hid under the table.

Granny's knees are all crinkly. There's a hole in her tights. Mummy has a bruise on her leg. I don't know how she did it.

The shouting is getting louder, and Daddy is the loudest.

"Shush!" I say it underneath my breath, 'cause I don't want them to find me.

"Take that back! I can't believe you said that. How can you

possibly think that's why Jake is the way he is. Emma couldn't have been more careful." Daddy sounds like a growly bear.

"She drank." That's Granny. I can picture her cross face inside my head.

"Her name is Emma." Daddy sounds like a snake now. "Oh, come on – one glass of sodding champagne at Christmas. Give me a break."

Daddy's toe is poking through his slipper. It wiggles when he shouts.

I don't know why Mummy isn't saying anything. I peek out from under the tablecloth. She's got her hands over her ears. Jake is screaming and screaming. I want Daddy to pick him up. He's gone very purple. Daddy is waving his fist at Grandpa. Grandpa's shaking his stick at Daddy. You mustn't fight.

Granny says in her witchy voice: "We never trusted her in the first place…shelf fish and irresponsible."

I don't know what that means, there aren't any fish on the shelf, but it made Mummy cry even more. I'm too scared to hug her. I shuffle on my bottom to the end of the table and look at the grown-ups. I see some spit fly out of Granny's mouth. Daddy has gone very, very white. His voice has gone all whispery.

"Enough, I've had enough. I've put up with this for years."

Daddy's ears have gone all red. I want Granny and Grandpa to go away. I want my mummy. I try and crawl out and get Jake's chair so he can hide with me. I'll keep him safe.

"Can't you keep that child quiet?" Grandpa bangs his stick next to Jake. His arms shoot up in the air. He stops crying, then throws his head back and screams louder.

Then Mummy screams so loudly Jake makes a sound like next door's puppy. I shoot back under the table.

Mummy says over and over again, "Stopitstopitstopit!"

I squeeze my eyes shut and sing Jake's favourite song. "The wheels on the bus go round and round, round and round, round and round."

Daddy pulls my hand away from my ear. "Oh, baby, we didn't know you were under there."

He pulls me out and hugs me tight. I bury my face in his shoulder.

"We're going home, Maudie. Everything's going to be alright. Don't cry, darling."

Mummy is holding Jake tight and kissing his head over and over. He doesn't like kissing. Mummy knows that but she doesn't stop.

"Come on, Ems, let's get out of here."

"You're being foolish," Granny says. "You'll be back with your tail between your legs, as always."

Daddy hasn't got a tail. I look over his shoulder, but I can't see anything.

Grandpa doesn't say anything at all. He's looking out of the window.

Daddy takes Mummy's hand and we walk out the door.

He didn't say goodbye to them. Not then and not when he was dying.

As my thoughts tumble about inside my head it's as though I'm putting together the jigsaw pieces of Mum. She had no one to turn to and I let her down when she most needed me. She was so overwhelmed, but I didn't see it.

Mum must be so lonely without Dad.

We all need to open the Dad box. I think both me and Mum are still in denial, and all three of us need to work through it together to accept that my dear, brilliant dad is dead but we can go on without him. We can be happy again.

Jake comes out of the caravan and walks over to me. "Scooby's gone away." He bends down and puts his face in mine. "Don't cry, girl. Jake's here. You can have Jake's bag."

No one is allowed Jake's bag. He puts it on my lap.

"Thank you, Jake – that's my favourite present ever."

I hold it tight to me. It smells of Jake, a mixture of chocolate, soap powder and slightly sweaty teenage boy. He pats my shoulder.

"There, there. Jake's here."

I'm about to open his bag when he takes it back again.

"That's Jake's bag." He takes his bus picture out and turns it around and puts it back in again. "The Chase is on. Jake likes that game."

We head inside and settle down. Through the little kitchen window, the sun battles against great grey clouds that are being blown across the bay. Cascading yellow rays pouring out beneath them spotlight the parasailers battling against the force of the wind.

I glance at Jake and I'm suddenly overwhelmed with love for him and so grateful I have such a fantastic brother. He makes me realize how lucky I am, because he loves me without any limitations, a no-strings-attached love, no matter how many times I mess up.

"Release the Beast!" Jake shouts at the screen, as a very large man in a blue suit sits down on his cushioned chair and glowers at the contestants.

I stare through the little window that looks across the park to the next bay, wondering where Mum is and if she's okay. I'm sure that's the cottage we should have stayed at, in the distance. If I had binoculars, I'd be able to see right in the window. If we'd been there, we could have hidden for much longer...but then I wouldn't have met Gerren.

A thought niggles at the back of my mind, which I can't quite grasp; the cottage...someone else staying there...our last holiday with Dad before he died. I trace back to when the taxi took me and Jake to the cottage and seeing the lady in the flowery shirt. A memory clicks into place. Did she come to deliver a meal one night when we last came with Mum and Dad two years ago? Is she the lady who looks after the cottage for all the visitors? But why was she there so late on Friday if she wasn't staying there? I didn't see her properly on the last holiday as Mum answered the door and I was only half listening to them talk. We were all a bit distracted that holiday.

The more I think about it, the more confused I get.

What if it is Mum staying there?

Suddenly I can't pretend it wasn't Mum who ran out of the cafe. And the idea she might have been so close to us this whole time is like an itch I have to scratch. I'm going to the cottage to find her and confront her. But I hesitate, which is enough to send my thoughts spiralling. What if she isn't there? What if everything I've thought of saying to her goes right out of my head?

Most of all, what if she slams the door in our faces?

CHAPTER 52

Jake

My sister isn't happy. I made her feel better. She looks after me and I look after her. Scooby-Doo solves lots of mysteries. Maudie and me can solve mysteries. Scooby says we need clues. I think Mum's playing hide and seek. It was my favourite game. When I was little. We need to look for Mum. She loves rock pools. We might find her there. I need to tell Maudie.

CHAPTER 53

Maudie

URGENT! Please call me

I ring Liv straight away.

"Hello? Hello? Maudie? Are you there?"

I catch my breath. "What is it?"

"Eve rang. She's heard from your mum."

"Oh my god."

"She was rambling and a bit incoherent, but asking about you and Jake, and – wait for it – she said she saw you, in *Newquay*. She must be at the cottage!"

"Jake never gets it wrong – I knew it, Liv! And I saw Mum today, at a cafe in town. But…but she didn't want to see us. She ran away. I couldn't find her, she just vanished."

"Oh, Maudie, that's so awful. I don't know what to say."

"I nearly broke down, except I had to think of Jake. It was like I wasn't in my own body. I think I need to go to the cottage *now*. I have to find Mum, I can't put it off any more. I have to find her and talk to her."

"Yes, your mum was so worried about you and Jake when she called Eve, and desperately wanting to know if you were safe."

Mum cares about us, unlike Gerren's mum.

"Eve's driving down to Newquay tonight."

"Then that decides me. I'm definitely going to the cottage to find Mum before she gets here."

"Why don't you wait until Eve's there and go together? You could call her and have a chat. Mum said Eve will never forgive herself for sending Jake away, she just panicked."

"It's a bit late to say that now, when all the damage is done! I can't wait for Eve, I have to see Mum now."

"Of course. Let me know what happens. Love you, Maudie."

"Love you more."

I end the call. "Jake! We're going for a walk, over to the cottage we stayed at with Mum and Dad when we were here before."

I quickly text Gerren:

Phew! That was lucky with the police. Hope everything at the site is ok now. Going for a walk with Jake.

I'm about to tell him about Mum but decide against it.

I'll tell him when it's all sorted and I'm with him. I don't want to make him feel worse about his own mother.

See you soon and thanks again for today M x

I grab some supplies for us from the kitchen.

"Is Jake's mum there?"

"I don't know for sure."

"Jake's mum likes the beach. In those rock pools. Jake and Maudie find her there."

"Yes, but we need to go to the house first."

"His mum is playing hide and seek. She likes that game. Shut your eyes and count, Jake – one, two, nine, seven, fifteen. Ready or not, coming to get you!"

"That's exactly it, Jake. Here's your coat." I go to zip it up.

"Jake can do it. Jake's a teen-ager."

"Of course you can do it! Okay, we've got everything we need." I swing the backpack onto my back.

"Find Jake's mum. Jake and Maudie."

I pull my orange beanie on and hand Jake his blue one. He pulls it down so it's just above his eyes, the way he likes it.

"Let's go."

We head up the path to the main campsite and weave our way past the other mobile homes, through the field with all the tents, up to a gate that I'm sure opens onto another field that leads to the cottage. Jake likes walking, like me, though he's not too keen if it's too far or too steep and rocky.

The low boom of the sea echoes around us and a lone herring gull swoops over our heads, its white belly and black wing tips bright in the late afternoon light. It calls out a long plaintive *yeow, yeow, yeow*, which pulls on something inside me. I imagine it's guiding us to Mum. Jake stops to watch it too, and the faraway look in his eyes seems to show he feels the same pull.

The wind is bitter and our eyes are streaming with water, which flows back into our hair. I tuck my hands in my coat pockets and keep my head down. Jake walks beside me, swinging his red bag backwards and forwards.

"You're amazing, Jake, do you know that?"

"Yes, he does."

"Ha ha! Mr Modest...but you are."

"Maudie's the best sister."

That stops me right where I'm standing. "Thank you, Jake, that's really lovely of you."

"Find Mum."

"Come on then!" We grin at each other. "I know how much we've missed Mum, but I'm pretty certain we'll see her very soon now."

"See that Mum."

"You won't go back to that strange house again with that lady."

"That lady's called Wendy. She's a nice lady. Jake made a rock with her. He ate it with his pack lunch."

"Oh!" I'm thrown by this information. Jake hasn't said

anything before…but I haven't asked him. "Well, we'll get Mum back and sort it all out when we go home to our house in Shiplake. I'm sorry I didn't ask you about Wendy. I'm very proud of you, Jake."

Jake looks at me, his eyes alert and listening very intently. "Proud of Jake," he murmurs.

"I am."

He smiles and rests his free hand on top of my head. We walk along like that for a bit. I glance back over my shoulder, at the caravans arranged in a patchwork quilt. We're about halfway to the cottage.

"Jake's going to see that Mum. Jake can knock on the door. Maudie said Jake stayed there with his dad. Jake knows that. Mind that hole! Don't worry, Jake, you'll be alright. You don't want to hurt yourself. Jake can see some cows. Don't go near them, they might bite. See that Mum."

Even though it's chilly, I'm starting to sweat. I pull my hat off and let my hair fly out behind me. Jake doesn't want to take his off, despite the fact he has sweat trickling down his face, which he wipes away with his sleeve.

We keep pushing forwards through a veil of mist rising off the damp grass and strands of wool clinging to the purple heather. We reach the top of the hill and stand still for a moment to catch our breath. Straight ahead I can see the cottage, a dim yellow glow coming from one of the windows. I shiver.

"Not far now, Jake."

"Jake doesn't want to walk any more."

"A bit further."

Jake stops where he's standing and refuses to budge. "Jake can't do it. There's too many rocks."

"Take my arm we'll do the last bit together."

"Okay-okay. He can do it with Maudie."

I point in the direction of the house. "See that cottage down there, that's where Mum is. Let's go get her."

What will it do to Jake if she isn't there?

Jake starts swaying from side to side, perhaps his anxiety about Mum manifesting itself. Then he stops abruptly. "Jake has to be grown up." He starts walking.

We set off down the uneven hill together, keeping our footsteps in time.

A flock of sheep charge down the opposite hillside to where the farmer is emptying feed into a trough from a large sack. A few early lambs run to keep up on their wobbly legs.

"Ah, look at those roast lambs," Jake points out.

I laugh so much I nearly choke, all my pent-up emotion spilling over.

"What's she laughing at?"

"They're just lambs." I pull myself together. "We won't be long now." My voice sounds shaky.

We get to the bottom and walk alongside a prickly hawthorn hedge scattered with early blossom, until we reach the gap that leads over the road to where I feel sure Mum's staying. Every nerve feels hyper alert. The gate to

the cottage is swollen and warped with the damp sea air.
I struggle to move it a few centimetres. Jake leans forward
and yanks it open with one arm.

"Way to go, Jake."

"Scooby-Dooby-Doo!" He chuckles.

We go up the path; I feel sicker with each step. The
curtains are open, and a lamp is on.

"Jake's going to see that Mum."

As we approach the front door a porch light comes on
automatically, even though it's not dark yet. My heart is
thumping so loudly I swear it's drowning out any other
sounds. Jake's picking tiny balls of felt off his bag and
dropping them on the tiled porch floor.

I lift the brass dolphin knocker and bang it a couple of
times, then put my hands in my pockets to stop them shaking.
No one answers, so I knock again. I'm struggling to breathe
properly. I spot a boot rack tucked in the corner, next to a
blue, ceramic plant pot, and that's when I see Mum's black
buckled wellies on it. She's obsessed with them.

I have to lean against the front door.

I don't know if I can bring myself to knock a third time. I
could turn back now and go home, except I promised Jake.
But if she doesn't want us, I can't cope, not even for Jake.

"Is Maudie alright?" Jake peers anxiously into my face.

"Yes, Maudie's alright."

I *can* cope.

I peer round the corner, through the window. The ivy

climbing up the wall is covered in fine silvery webs. I don't want to touch them, so I push it aside with my elbow to get nearer to the window to see. A lamp throws a sombre light in the corner of the deserted room.

A blue painted wooden boat sits on a stand on the coffee table. Next to it is a cream-coloured mug. A discarded newspaper lies open on the floor next to an old leather armchair that has its back to us, so whoever sits in it can look out at the sea through the opposite window. The chair has the air of someone waiting patiently for a friend. A plate with a lonely, half-eaten biscuit rests on the arm and I can see a pair of olive-green glasses. They must be Mum's, as I don't know anyone else who wears reading glasses that look like that. She's left it all.

I wipe away my breath, which has misted up the glass. I try and see beyond the half-open door through to the rest of the house, but it's too difficult. I rap on the window with my knuckles.

"Who's there?" Jake says. "He can hear someone banging."

"It's only me, Jake." I move back into the porch. The wind picks up the red felt bobbles and scatters them over the bluebells lining the path, a garnet necklace draped over the flowers. "I'll try knocking on the door again, and if no one comes we'll go, okay?"

"See his mum. Maudie said."

"She did – and we'll track her down." I bang the door knocker hard.

"Ow! That hurt Jake's ears." Jake clutches the side of his head.

"I'm sorry, Jake, I forgot!"

Jake sways from foot to foot. I find myself doing the same thing. I'm frustrated Mum doesn't answer the door – and confused. Is she really not here or is she avoiding us?

"Mum must have gone for a walk, Jake," I tell him, even though her boots are looking at me.

I lift the letter box and peer through it down the corridor. It's gloomy, as there are no lights on here, but I can just make out Dad's chunky Fair Isle jumper on the coat rack. She's been wearing it a lot recently – practically every evening, now I think about it.

"Hello!" I call through the letter box. I already know she won't answer. "Right, Jake, let's check in the garden."

We walk round to the side gate and twist the iron ring. The gate opens with a tinny squeal, which anyone in the garden would hear. I glance across the stone terrace, over the nodding daffodils and out to the sea beyond. The only sound is the wind creaking a swing that's tied to a large overhanging branch on the tree at the bottom of the garden. "You loved that swing, do you remember, Jake?"

"Yes, he did. His dad pushed him on it. His dad pushed Mum on that swing."

"He did! You saw them too?"

"Mum wasn't happy."

Jake takes my hand. I'm so touched. We stand and watch

the swing gently rocking back and forth in the breeze. When we last came here, two months before Dad died, some days he barely had the energy to push Mum, but he was determined to do it. One day, when he couldn't manage it any more, he stood behind her and wrapped his arms around her and held her tight. She clung onto his arms and he bent his head and whispered something in her ear and kissed the top of her head. I felt guilty for watching them but couldn't stop myself. They were so happy together. I stood there and couldn't bear the thought of a world without Dad. I kept hoping some miracle cure would turn up…but watching them on the swing, I think I realized this was goodbye.

"Is that Mum okay?" Jake shakes his head. "He doesn't think so."

I take control. "Come on. We must look for her then. Hang on, I'll leave a note on the front door, in case she comes back. Then she'll know where we are."

I grab a pen and an old receipt out of my bag. I write on the back of it.

We came to find you. We've gone to the beach below the house. Maudie and Jake xxx

We have to find her, but which way do we go?

CHAPTER 54

Jake

I think Mum's sad. Inside her. At home she didn't talk to me.
I didn't hear any laughing. My mum always laughs. When Dad
went away, she didn't laugh for a long time. It made me sad.
It made my head full of mess. I couldn't unmuddle it. Me and
Maudie must find Mum and help her. We need to take her
muddle away. Then she can smile.

CHAPTER 55

Maudie

"I reckon Mum's gone down to the beach," I tell Jake as I wedge the note into the letter box.

"Jake said his mum was at the beach." He looks at me accusingly.

"Oh my god, Jake! Why didn't I think of it before? I bet Mum's gone to that tiny bay we went to on our last holiday with Dad. Do you remember it? We'd go there some evenings to see the jellyfish light up the sea?"

He gets a faraway look in his eyes, as though he's remembering those trips, like me.

The chill of evening clings to us as we make our way down the rock-hewn steps to our secret cove. The sound of the sea echoes around us, hushed by the tall wall of sea grasses that dip at our heels. At the bottom, the tiny beach curves in a crescent moon, fringed by gentle dunes.

Dad stands with his arm round Mum, breathing in the cool of the evening air perfumed with salt and seaweed. He says something to Mum, then removes his jumper and gives it to her to wear. She stands on tiptoe and kisses him.

Jake follows me to our rock, sea-worn flat by the tide. He steps carefully onto the surface and holds his hand out to help me up. The magic of this place makes him brave.

We wait. The pale sky dims and deepens to a hazy blue. Even Jake is still.

"Here they come!" Mum calls over to us.

In the distance a trail of electric-blue, luminescent lights glows in the deep ocean. It weaves its way through the waves, getting nearer and nearer. We step down from our lookout, as the drifts of jellyfish spill over the rocks, borne by the evening tide. We crouch at the water's edge and watch the graceful creatures propel themselves forward through the water; their transparent saucer-shaped bodies and the long drifting tentacles floating out behind them.

Jake points to the whirling mass, his eyes wide with wonder. "He can see them – blue, green...purple lights. Jake thinks they're dancing." His hushed voice is full of awe.

"They are, Jake," Mum sighs happily, "a ballet of jellyfish."

Dad's arm rests on her shoulders. He smiles down at her, then out to sea. I wish we could stop time and hold this moment for ever. Dad turns to look at me, as though he's heard what I'm thinking. He takes my hand. A tear falls from his eye and vanishes in the soft foam washing over our toes. Jake moves next to him *and lays his arm across Dad's shoulders. We all stand together in the waning light, not wanting to let go of each other.*

"They were so beautiful, weren't they?"

Jake nods. "Jake said those jellyfish were dancing."

"Yes, Mum loved that."

Jake grins at me. "Mum said Jake couldn't eat that sort of jelly."

"That's right." I grin back at him.

"Jake loves that beach. Jake said let's go there. To find Mum."

"You did – I should've listened to you."

I check the time on my phone. It's gone five, so we have a couple of hours before it gets dark. I feel sure Mum is looking for us there, because where else would she think to check but all the places we went to together that are near the cottage? She has no idea we're at the caravan park.

"We have to go down these tricky steps, but you've done it before, Jake."

"Jake can do it."

The steps are carved into the rock, footholds worn by time into the granite. Luckily there's a wonky metal handrail I'd forgotten about, all the way down to the bottom. Jake stalls at the top but he somehow senses my urgency because he starts to follow me down immediately.

"Hold the rail, Jake. Look at me, don't look down. We can do it, you and me. Find Mum."

"Find Little Mum. His mum needs him." He lets out a shuddery breath but keeps going. He holds his red bag in his other hand, high in the air.

At the bottom I salute my brother. "You're a star."

"Jake's not a star, he's a Jake."

"The best brother in the world."

"Best Jake."

We have to follow the bay round to the right to get to the little cove I think Mum's gone to, two bays along. The sand is smoother beyond the rocky outcrops, which makes it easier to walk. I cup my hand over my eyes and look for any sign of her. In the distance the sky is growing darker, and the clouds are melting into the sea as the light begins to slowly drain away, and suddenly I'm even more desperate to see her, as though the protective shell I've put around me has cracked open from knowing she's so near.

I scan all around for any signs Mum came this way, which is when I spot a pair of flipflops discarded on a rock. They're an old pair of mine! Why would she take them off? Were they rubbing a blister between her toes? She wouldn't be paddling, not if she was looking for me and Jake. Further along I see a line of small footsteps imprinted in the sand, curling around the piles of tangled seaweed dumped by the tide at the base of the rocks: footprints she's left behind to lead us to her.

I hurry Jake along.

Clusters of broken shells crunch beneath our feet. My eyes

hurt from the strain of squinting ahead. I follow the footsteps, which go along the base of a rocky outcrop beneath the cliff. As we get closer to the coastline the sand becomes wetter and the footprints lose their shape. Bubbles babble and pop between the sand swirls. Dad told me they were from ghost crabs hiding in their burrows. I walk back up the beach to Jake.

"Can you see Mum, Jake?" I say as casually as I can. With his eyesight he'll spot her way before me.

Jake scans the area. "He can't see her."

I need to get a bit higher up to see into the next bay. The cliff rises in a sheer drop above our heads, making me dizzy when I look up. Rocky outcrops cluster at the base, up to a low wall of granite slabs that cut off this cove from the next, which is the one we want to get to. If I get some height, I'll be able to see into the distance.

"Jake, sit on this rock and rest. You want a drink?" I swing the backpack to the ground and unzip it. "Your apple juice is in there. Listen, I need to climb up this rocky bit to try and see Mum. I won't go out of sight."

Jake's too focused on his drink to answer me.

I work my way a bit higher, avoiding the slimy looking kelp that has been combed over the large boulders. My foot slips into a small rock pool and I scrape my ankle on the dark periwinkles clinging to the side. The salt water stings.

I stop and check back on Jake. Scattered on the sand below him are some of the contents of my rucksack.

I check the cliff face. All the way up, the crevices are tufted with thick marram grass. When we were here with Dad there were sea campion and long-stemmed harebell that nodded their blue heads in the breeze. Dad knew all the names. I can still hear his gentle voice pointing out the different plants to me.

Further round, a movement catches my eye. I peer at it, not quite taking in what I see. It's Mum's indigo Berber scarf; half visible, hanging over a ledge, the silk tassels flailing in the wind.

I stare at the scarf. A dark area stains it, turning the blue to black. I pick my way carefully over to it and dab it lightly with the tip of my finger. It leaves a sticky, reddish-brown goop. I have to steady myself on the rock. I feel light-headed and sick. I wrap the scarf around my wrist and clumsily tie the ends in a knot. I can't see any sign of Mum, only some dark spots spattered over the rocks going up. I think they're blood. Why would Mum go up, the opposite way to home, if she was hurt? I feel like I've pitched forward into the cold sea. If I didn't have Jake, I'd follow the trail round right now, but I'll have to go back down first and get my phone so I can call someone for help and take him back to the site.

I slip and slide back down the rocks, knowing if Mum's injured, we don't have much time until it gets really dark. That's when I see that the tide has come in on the other side of the cove, the side we just came from.

We're cut off.

CHAPTER 56

Jake

I don't understand. Maudie says we're stuck. I'm not stuck. Uh-oh. The sea is trying to get me. Maudie says I have to move quickly. I can't do it. I don't want to get wet. I can't swim. Dad tried to teach me. I kept sinking. The water went up my nose. The sea frightens me. It's so big. It's too salty. It will swallow me and Maudie up. The water is cold and it's trying to push me over. Get it off my foot! The sea is taking the sand away. Did it take Mum away? I must save Mum. I can't see her in the sea. I can't see her on the rocks. I have to climb. I can't get up that cliff! It's too tall. Mum is very small. Like Maudie. How will they get over the rocks? It's up to you, Jake. I have to be brave. I must be Dad.

CHAPTER 57

Maudie

"Pass me the bag, Jake!"

As I reach out, he sees the scarf round my wrist and tries to snatch it off me. I lurch forwards and land hard next to Jake, forcing the air out of my lungs with a whoosh. Jake cracks up.

"Argh! Careful, Jake." I rub my knees. "Give me the bag."

He stops laughing and hands it to me. I unravel the scarf and give it to him.

"That's my mum." He solemnly puts Mum's scarf in his bag. "Jake look after her."

I scrabble frantically through my rucksack for my phone. Jake has pulled everything out and I can't see it on the beach.

"Jake drank his juice."

I know I put the phone in here.

I can see the juice carton tucked between two rocks. I empty the bag, my stomach knotting tighter every second.

"Jake, what did you do with my phone?"

"He hasn't got it."

I take a deep, steadying breath. "Can you tell me where it is?"

He shakes his head.

"I have to find the phone." I jump down onto the sand.

I can't see it anywhere. I start to get clammy with sweat. I check between the gaps in the rocks and in the bag again because I can't believe it's not there. I turn it upside down and shake it. I get Jake to stand up in case he's sitting on the phone. Then I see a dark shape in the rock pool near to Jake. I plunge my hand into the water and bring out my phone. I shake and shake it and stab at the buttons. It's completely dead.

"Jake doesn't know how it got there."

"It must have fallen out the bag when I handed it to you. Argh! I should have kept it in my coat pocket."

And why, why, why didn't I check the tide? How could I be so careless? Again.

I can't let Jake know that I'm screaming inside, because the sea is coming in fast and we're going to have to climb up the rocks to safety. We must find Mum because she's injured and needs urgent help. We can use her phone to alert the coastguard.

"We need to find Mum, Jake."

"Where is she? He can't see her."

"That's why we have to find her. Do you remember when

you were little, and you loved your climbing frame? It was red and yellow with a rope swing on the side."

"Jake sat at the top."

"That's it! You *did*, with your *Thomas the Tank Engine* bag. You have to climb now, Jake, like you did on your climbing frame." I start to move up the rocks to show him. "This is how you do it, one foot in here and put your hand in the gap to hold on. Easy, yeah? I'll help you." I take his hand. "Follow me, Jake."

He yanks his hand away and steps back. "He can't do it." He looks as frightened as I feel.

"Jake, *please* – you have to climb up. You don't want to get your feet wet. Look at the sea coming in."

He looks at the water surging towards him and lets out a low moan but doesn't move.

"Jake, you have to come with me."

"Jake can't do it. Uh-oh."

He walks backwards, shaking his head from side to side.

A wave surges up behind him and splashes up his legs, making him stumble and drop his bag in the water. He shouts, "Save his bag!"

I jump back down, reach out and grab it just as the current is about to suck it away. I struggle to stay upright against the pull. I'm shocked at the strength of the undercurrent. Jake grabs my hand to hold me up.

"Thanks," I gasp.

"Jake can't swim. Get it off him!"

I'm praying his fear doesn't make him panic. I'm praying I don't panic. I watch as my brother takes a deep, shuddering breath and stands up tall.

"Come on, Jake, you can do it," he tells himself.

We hold onto each other to steady ourselves. He pulls me towards the rocks, as the sea swirls around our feet, trying to drag us out with it. I grab onto a bit of rock. "Climb, Jake, climb!"

It's no good. He won't budge. His fear has stopped him again.

"Come on, Jake!"

A sob escapes from my throat. Jake looks at me and I can see the concern on his face. He closes his mouth, his expression becomes calmer. He takes a clumsy step up, stops, then lunges forwards and starts to climb. I half laugh and half cry at the same time.

"That's it. Put your foot here – not on the seaweed."

Jake makes an anxious sound, half scream, half moan, as he stumbles over the rocks. He grabs his bag as soon as he reaches me, his breath in short rapid bursts, as he twists the wet handles around his wrist. I pull his beanie up higher, so he can see clearly.

"Thank you," he pants.

If I can get over to the next bay, we should be able to find a ledge high enough that the sea can't reach us, if I remember this place right. If. The word is weighed down with dread. What if we can't get up there? What if I find Mum unconscious?

My mind goes into overdrive. What if she's broken her neck and is paralysed? What if Mum's dead? I force myself to stop my thoughts spiralling.

Jake mutters to himself. "The sea took the sand away. He's all wet. Jake might fall. His bag's all wet. Jake can't do it."

"It's okay, Jake, we'll do it together."

"His mum says that."

"She does, and we can too. Follow what I do. Put your foot here. You can't do it holding your bag. Can you give it to me?"

"No."

"Okay, can you put the handles of your bag over your head, like a necklace. It'll help you walk better and keep it dry."

He rocks his body back and forth, lifting one foot up and down awkwardly. We can't waste any more time.

"I'm going up." I climb. Jake stops rocking and watches me closely. I shout down to him, "Put those handles over your head. Great, now, let's go. Hold that bit there and pull yourself over."

I keep my voice on one level, firm and steady, which helps to calm us both down. I imagine Dad is in front of me, telling me what to do, encouraging me, helping me find my way. *"That's it, Maudie. Don't look down. Take it steady, now. Find the handholds."* I wish you were here, Dad. Look at the mess we're in. I can picture you raising one bushy, black eyebrow and sighing heavily, then getting on with it and sorting it all out.

I'm not sure you could get us out of this one though.

I can see a gap in the granite slabs, tucked back behind a jutting-out rock formation that reminds me of a lion's head. The cleft behind his mane is easily big enough to get through. I focus on that, praying the ledge I remember sitting on with Dad is there.

"One step at a time."

"One step," Jake repeats. "Jake must be Dad."

"Yes, Jake, that's exactly it." He's thinking the same things as me.

We make it to the gap after what seems like hours. Thank god, there is a wide sill on the other side.

"We have to hurry up now."

The sea is slapping against the rocks below us, sending bursts of spray high into the air, then billowing back with a rush. The water came in so fast. The seagulls are screeching furiously above us, beating their large wings. Every so often they dart down, making Jake duck. I'm so scared they'll make him lose his balance. I cling onto a rock hold and swing my rucksack above my head to frighten them off. They squawk angrily at us.

"Shut up, birds," Jake says testily.

I hold my hand out to Jake, to help him through, but he refuses to go any further again. I want to howl, right here, right now. I can't vanish through the hole leaving Jake. If he can't see me, he'll think I've left him.

I step up a bit higher and make sure he can see me and take in what I'm saying. "I need you to look at me, Jake, it's important. We have to squeeze through this hole, so the sea can't get us. We'll be safe on the other side." He looks away but turns straight back, making himself focus on what I'm saying. "We can't get high enough this side. The sea will reach us, and I don't want that to happen. Okay?"

"Sea get Maudie and Jake. Okay."

"I'll go first, you follow. You have to bend your head."

The ridge on the other side is wide enough for both of us. I shake with relief. I poke my head back through the crevice. "Ready?"

"He doesn't like it."

But Jake lowers his head and comes through. We both stand trembling on the ledge together. Jake's breathing comes in short rapid gasps, matching the frantic pace of my heart. I scan the crag to try and work out the best way to go from here.

I see a line of dark red spots on the rock ahead. Blood. Mum must have gone that way; I'm dreading what we might find when we get to her. This cove is set much deeper back, so there is still flat sand to walk on if we get a move on.

"We're going down again first, Jake."

He follows.

We can do this.

Together we walk across the sand, me scanning the cliffs

for our best route up and for any signs of Mum. I can't see any footprints on the beach, but then I notice two rough, uneven channels with strange, paw-like tracks running either side, trace fossils in the sand.

I get it! Mum was crawling.

She isn't in a good way. I follow her tracks, which stop at the base of the next outcrop of rock.

"Mum's around here." I point to the cliff.

"Jake's trying to see her."

I can't think about where this will end or what will happen to us. I'm kicking myself I didn't tell Gerren what I planned to do – he'd know the tides and would've warned me. Our only hope is Liv, who knew we were going to the cottage. But how long until anyone realizes there's a problem? I feel floaty and detached.

Jake grabs my arm and shakes me.

"That's Jake's mum."

"*Where?*"

I strain to see. I follow where Jake's pointing and can just make out a shape, partly behind a rock at the bottom of the cliff. It's only when it moves slightly, I realize Jake's right. I'm euphoric, then dizzy and my heart seems to stop then race.

"MUM!" I scream across the beach. "MUM!"

"MUM – JAKE'S MUM!" he shouts as loud as he can.

I grab Jake's arm and we make our way over as fast as we can, slipping on the seaweed and half falling between the rocks. Jake doesn't say another word until we reach her.

"Jake found her! Jake's mum. She's back." He goes to pat her head, but stops when he sees the blood matted in her blonde hair, his face confused. "She can't hear you, Jake. Oh dear. Mum's hurt."

"It's okay, Jake, Mum will be okay. Take her hand that side."

He does as I say, holding it between both of his. "It's too cold."

I want to throw my arms around her and never let go, but am too afraid to hurt her more. I take her other hand and hold it between mine. It's icy. I breathe warm air onto it. Jake sees what I'm doing and does the same.

"Mum, please be okay, please wake up, please. I love you so much." I cup my hands round her face.

"Jake and Maudie are here. Jake loves you too."

She finally looks up. "Maudie...you came. Jake. My Maudie...my Jake. I was wanting to see you...so...much. I prayed you'd come." She smiles weakly, tears filling her eyes. Her face is unnaturally white, and her lips have a tinge of blue. Jake crouches down beside her.

"Mum." I swallow, holding myself together. "Are you okay? Does it hurt badly?"

"A bit...awful headache."

"Oh no, Mum's got a headache. Jake needs to get medicine."

"Oh, Jake..." Her eyes are glazed. "Your...your hair... Maudie."

"Temporary. Don't talk, Mum."

Her coat is undone, and the ends are soaking up sea water from a rock pool. I remove them and sit beside her on the rock and carefully wrap my arms around her. She feels so small. Her hand reaches up to touch my face, but she doesn't have the strength and it flops back down beside her.

"Jake, sit the other side of Mum, we have to warm her up more before we can move her. That's it. Can you move, Mum?"

She slowly shakes her head. "I'm not sure. I…I slipped. I'm sorry, Maudie…so s-sorry."

"Shushhh. We need to get to safety. Where's your phone? The tide is coming in fast and we're already cut off."

"Cut off?" Mum looks frightened.

"We'll be fine. Let me get your phone out."

I go through her pockets. She searches too, but her hands are weak and clumsy. "Let me do it, Mum. I can't find it – did you drop it?"

She frowns. "Oh no…I left it at the cottage. You weren't answering your phone…it was dead…I tried and tried until there didn't seem any point."

"My proper phone is still at home. Mum, we have to move up higher, *now*."

"We won't get Jake up the rocks."

"We'll manage."

Jake puts his face near Mum's. "Jake already did it."

"That's a-amazing, Jake." Mum tries to smile but ends up grimacing.

"Don't talk, Mum." I sound confident, but inside I'm terrified. "Can you stand up?"

She tries but her knees give way. "I'm so tired. I can't keep my eyes open."

I remember being told once not to let someone go to sleep if they have a head injury. Funny what sticks in your head. "Stay awake, Mum. Mum! Look at me. You must stay awake. I think you have concussion. Come on, Jake, we'll climb up here together. Alright, Mum?"

She nods but her head falls forwards, her eyes closing.

"Wake up, Mum, *please*."

"Wake up, Little Mum! It's okay. Jake's here. Jake can look after Mum. Wake up, Mum! Jake's here."

The bag around his neck rests on Mum's head as he tries to help her up. I gently move it.

"Jake missed you," he says to Mum.

She struggles to lift her head up. "My Jake." She desperately tries to keep her eyes open. "I missed you too."

The sound of a wave crashing onto the rocks warns me we don't have long to get to safety, somewhere where we can hopefully be seen. There's no way Mum can walk, let alone climb. I'm too small to lift her by myself.

"We're going to have to carry Mum between us. You take her legs and hold on really tight."

"His mum needs a doctor."

I manoeuvre my hands under Mum's armpits and gently rest her head on my chest, praying I'm not hurting her.

She groans slightly. "Ankles, Jake." I smile at him encouragingly. He grips his hands around them; they look so big. A wave surges over the sand, splashing Jake's legs. His panic moves him forwards.

"Oh no, he can't do it. Mum's cold. Jake has to help her. Jake can't breathe prop'ly. Help Maudie. Be Dad, Jake."

Mum's dead weight strains the muscles in my arms, making them burn. I grit my teeth and focus on navigating the footholds backwards. I can see where the dark line of the water's edge finishes, and the dry rock begins. There's a small cavern and a longer ledge running in front of it a bit further up. It's our only hope.

I'm not sure I can do it – my arms are shaking violently.

"Stop, Jake, I have to rest a minute." I breathe in deeply through my nose and out my mouth. "Okay, let's go."

It's no good, my arms are so weak I can't lift Mum up again.

CHAPTER 58

Jake

"Noooooooooooo!"

Maudie screamed. My ears popped. She can't pick Mum up. Her arms are too little. Mum won't open her eyes. I can't push them open. She's coughing. It's bad. She needs cough syrup. It tastes of blackcurrant. That wave nearly hit us. Go away, wave! Leave us alone. What can I do?

I hear Dad's voice. In my head. "You can be a fireman, Jake." I watched the firemen on the telly with Dad. They were brave. "You can carry your mum, Jake. You're strong. Do a fireman's lift."

Okay, I'll try.

"Atta boy, Jake, you can do it."

I can, Dad, I can.

CHAPTER 59

Maudie

Enough. I need to get a grip. My scream of frustration has startled a small colony of kittiwakes, which circle above our heads, their ink-dipped wings flapping furiously as they call a warning to one another. I spit the bile that sicked up into my mouth onto a rock. I rub my arms to get the circulation going.

"That's dis-gusting." Jake gives me a black look.

As I grit my teeth to move Mum again, Jake slowly reaches down and picks Mum up and heaves her over his shoulder.

"Jake's a firefighter," he announces proudly.

"That's brilliant, Jake."

The momentary elation is replaced with fear as I manoeuvre myself around him to guide him up the rock. I pray Mum's head won't knock too hard against Jake's back. My heart is hammering in my chest. I have to believe we can do this.

Slowly, slowly we move up the rock face. "Don't look down, Jake, just listen to me." I wipe the sweat out of Jake's eyes, so that he isn't blinded. I yank his hat off, as it keeps slipping down. His hair is plastered flat to his head. His knuckles are white from gripping Mum so tightly.

By the time we get to the hollow in the cliff, we're both sweating buckets. I help Jake up onto the ledge, terrified he might fall backwards. We stagger into the shelter, and just manage to lower Mum down to the floor as she slips off his shoulder. Mum grunts and her eyelids flutter open.

"Where...where are we?" She looks around the shelter, confused.

"Jake carried you, Mum. We're on a ledge a short way up the cliff, in a kind of half-cave. Can you sit up if I help you? We can rest your back against the wall."

Jake hovers by me, breathing heavily from all the exertion.

"Help me move Mum, that's it – pull." I take my jacket off and roll it behind Mum's head for support. "Sit, Jake, you'll be safer."

He shakes his head. "It's too dirty. He doesn't like it here. It's all stinky."

The tiny cavern is covered in dry gull droppings and the walls have dark water streaks etched into them by time. The acrid smell stings my nostrils. I take my shirt off, gritting my teeth against the cold, then put it on the floor for Jake to sit on. Jake moans about it, but I manage to get him to sit with his back against the wall, close to Mum, so they feel solid and safe. He puts his hand out for his bag.

"You were incredible, Jake – you saved Mum."

She stirs. "So proud of you both," Mum whispers.

Jake puts his face next to Mum's. "Jake was a fireman." When she doesn't respond, he looks around the shelter. "Jake doesn't like it here."

His eyes dart around the walls, and open wide, taking it all in. He clutches his bag to his chest.

"It won't be for long." I sound like we're waiting for a bus my voice is so calm.

Mum's hand slips out from under her and rests on Jake's leg. He gradually loses his panicked look.

I get my water bottle. "Mum – you need water." She opens her mouth and I tilt the bottle for her to drink. Some of it spills down her front. Her eyelids flutter open and shut, then open again. She twists herself round to see me properly, which exhausts her.

"Maudie…" Her voice is very faint. "It wasn't you and Jake I was running from…it was me. I'm—"

"You don't have to do this now, Mum."

She nods. I kiss her gently on her cheek. It feels clammy. I wet a crumpled tissue from Mum's coat pocket and gently clean around the gash on her head; I don't want to make it bleed again. It's deep and will need stitches. She must have hit it hard.

"Jake wants some apple juice."

"You drank it, remember? I'm sorry, all we've got is this."

333

He takes the cup of water I hand him, knocks it back, screws his face up in disgust. "That's nasty."

"Listen, Jake – I'm going outside to see if I can spot a boat that could get us help. You look after Mum and don't move, okay?"

He yawns widely. "Okay. Jake won't move."

I wrap him in a hug and hold him tight until he pushes me off.

Outside a low sun hangs over the sea. The wind coming off the water is damp with salt spray. I wrap my arms around my body to stop myself from shivering. I've no idea what the time is now but the light is fading. I need something bright to attract attention but I'm only wearing my orange beanie, which is useless as it's so small. We're completely invisible to anyone.

A shadowy feeling of hopelessness threatens to fold in on me. We don't have any choice but to wait it out here until someone notices we're gone and comes looking for us. I don't know how Jake will cope with being on this ledge and I don't know how bad Mum's injury is. There's no way I can leave them by themselves, even if I could climb to the top. We might have to spend the night here, which petrifies me.

Jake's nodding off to sleep when I go back inside. Mum's head has slipped onto his shoulder. I don't know if I should keep her awake but decide to let her rest and wake her up in a bit. I'm glad Jake will be free from the terror that's threatening to drown me, if only for a bit.

Jake coughs and places his bag across his legs. It's staring me right in the face. I can use Jake's bag as a distress signal, as it's much bigger than my beanie.

I crouch in front of him. "Jake?" He half opens his eyes. "I need your bag." That makes him sit up, jolting Mum's head. She doesn't make a sound.

"It's Jake's bag. His bus lives there."

"I promise you can have it back. I need to make a flag so we can be seen up here."

He frowns, trying to take in what I'm saying. I reach out my hand to take it, but he won't let go. "It's Jake's bag. Don't touch his bag."

Mum struggles awake. "Let Maudie have your bag, Jake. It's important. Can you be brave?"

Jake grimaces. "Oh no, Jake. Maudie needs it. It's not a flag. It's a bag. It's all wet." He shakes his head, but he takes his damp bus picture out, then a tiny cowrie shell, which he puts in Mum's lap. "Jake's got a cow shell. From Ben."

It's beautiful. Mum curls her fingers around it. I didn't know he had that. I realize there could be a lot I don't know about Jake and I feel ashamed – but there's plenty of time to change that. He's doing things independently, which is great. I need to let him do more.

Next out is his bus key ring from Liv and finally some squashed chips covered in red fluff. He hands me his bag.

"Thank you, Jake, I'm going to buy you lots of bags when we get out of this."

"Jake likes this bag, thank you."

Mum's eyes are shiny with tears. "You're so grown-up, Jake."

"Yes, he is. Jake likes beer. He had a pint."

"Of beer?" Mum's eyebrows shoot upwards, making her wince with the pain.

"No, a Coke – though I think he'd have liked a beer," I tell Mum, as I undo my shoelace and tie it through the bag's handles.

"Jake can eat his chips. He borrowed them."

I take his bag outside to secure round a sticking-out bit of rock. I wedge a loose stone on top of that, so it can't blow away. It flaps in the wind, a small beacon of hope in the gathering dark.

The low boom of the waves on the rocks below tells me the tide is getting much higher. It will be several hours, most of the night, before the beach is clear again.

I glance back at my mother side by side with Jake. "I'm so sorry, Mum, for everything." I'm not sure she can hear me, as her eyes have closed again.

I wish I'd realized she felt so lonely. A lot of Mum's friends seemed to vanish after Dad died. "Guess they don't know what to say to me," she told me once. It must have hurt Mum a lot. She had all these feelings and emotions she didn't know what to do with. We've all been pretending we're fine, Mum more than anyone – except she didn't have the time to grieve because all she did was cook, clean, work and look after me and Jake. She kept going until she fell apart, but now I see she deserves to be more than just our mum.

A spark of understanding lights up in my head about myself; I don't have to be the perfect daughter or perfect sister either. I wanted to be the best at everything, so Mum and Dad didn't have to worry about me, as they had so much to deal with: medical appointments for Jake and then for Dad; people's judgements, which often meant they had to fight for what they felt was right for all of us, most of all against Dad's parents. I feel like maybe I grew up so quickly I got confused along the way, but it's okay to get things wrong because that's how you learn to get them right. Liv tried to tell me this so many times. I can hear her voice loud and clear inside me. *"We're pressurized by our culture of perfection. You don't have to cave in to that, it's bullshit. You're allowed to be free, to be who you are without those expectations. Especially you, Mauds. You seem to think you can't be anything other than perfect. It's you who thinks that – not your mum and dad and not Jake. They love you for who you are – unreservedly – and so do I, even though you drive me up the wall sometimes."*

She's right, and being in Cornwall with Jake these last two days has opened my eyes to that a bit more. I've been anything but perfect since we've been here – in fact, I've made some big mistakes – but it hasn't changed the way Jake feels about me. He's coped with it all, way better than I expected: so perhaps it's time to stop keeping such a tight hold on him and allow him to grow more. We've both learned from my mistakes, and that's been good for us. I can see clearly now that it's more than enough being me, it's more than enough being Maudie, flaws and all.

I shiver in my T-shirt, my teeth clattering together. A lone gull sits above my head, calling out in alarm. Jake cries out in his sleep, "Don't hurt him!"

I go back inside the hollow and squeeze myself next to him, soaking up the warmth radiating from his body. I stroke his arm in a gentle rhythm and sing Mum and Dad's favourite song, the one they danced to whenever they heard it on the radio. Hopefully Mum can hear it too. Jake sings with me in his half sleep.

Any time their song came on the radio Dad would grab Mum and sway her around the kitchen, oblivious to my eye-rolling.

Jake is drifting back to sleep. I need to go outside and keep watch.

The sun slants across the corner of the ledge, edging it with gold. The sea stretches for miles in front of me. The light is changing, and the setting sun fringes the horizon with burnt orange. Clouds scud across the darkening sky.

My view is cut off by the cliffs curving round on either side, so I hope and hope that a fishing boat heading for the harbour or someone sailing round the coast might go by and see our flag before the sun sinks below the horizon.

I wonder if Liv has tried getting hold of me again. I know she'll be worried when my phone is dead. We used to think we had twin telepathy, as we always thought the same things and sometimes even said the same things at the same time. I close my eyes and tell her we're in trouble. I imagine the thought flying over the water to her.

Please hear me, Liv, I need your help.

I wish Gerren was here, sat next to me, keeping me strong. I'm sure our connection was more than just our runaway mothers. He's stuck by me with Jake the last couple of days, when lots of guys would have run a mile. He didn't tell Brae I'd lied to him, he kept my secret safe and he stood up for me and Jake on the beach, when he barely knew us. My heart hurts thinking about him. I tuck my arms round my knees and rest my head on them.

"Maudie," Mum calls me. Her voice sounds a tiny bit stronger.

I go back inside the shelter. "I'm here, Mum. How are you feeling? I'm worried about your head."

"It hurts…but it's more of a low thud now than a sharp knife."

Jake is out of it, a faint snore rattling in his throat. I kiss the top of his head. Mum looks at us so lovingly I nearly break.

"Sit next to me, Maudie." Her green eyes are troubled in her pinched face. "I'm…I'm not going to make excuses for what I did…but I'd like to try and explain, if I…may? While Jake's…Jake's asleep."

"Okay." I hesitate, but she reaches up and holds my hand. "Please?"

I nod.

She pats the ground beside her and tugs weakly at my arm to sit. She shuts her eyes. I think she's gone back to sleep again, but then she starts to speak.

"I'd been pretending for so long that everything was alright…but it wasn't. I just kept going on automatic, until I couldn't any more, and I…just fell apart." Her voice is strained, and her chest rises and falls rapidly from the effort of talking.

"Mum, don't—"

"No, let me speak." She wipes a tear off her face with a trembling hand. "The trouble with ignoring the pain inside you…is that in the end it catches up with you… And it did, tipping me over the edge. It all came out at once in a confused mess. The day I left, it was your dad's and my anniversary. I couldn't bear it – we should have been celebrating it together. I felt like my brain was shutting down, but my head felt full of angry bees, buzzing incessantly…tormenting me."

"Yes, I get it – that's how my head's felt a lot recently, Mum. Too many emotions pushed away that felt like they were shouting for attention, but got knotted up together, so nothing made sense and nothing could get out. I didn't know where to begin."

Mum nods, recoiling at the pain it causes her. "Yes, that's exactly it. Then I stopped caring…like a switch had turned off inside me. I f-felt empty, blank, which was scarier than feeling too much. I'd wanted to stop hurting, but when I couldn't feel anything at all, I was desperate to have it back. It was like…like I was betraying your dad without it. But it did come back, ten times worse…and that's…that's when I had to go. I thought down here, on my own, I'd be able to sort it out. But all I did was bring my grief down with me and put it in a different setting. I know…I know what your dad would have said to me—"

"It's just a matter of geography," I fill in. "He loved quotes, didn't he?"

"Yes…we used to tease him so much." Mum gazes off into the distance for a moment, remembering. She sighs deeply, holding herself together.

"I think none of us can actually believe Dad's not here. We can say the words, but they don't mean anything. But we have to face up to it, Mum."

Mum smiles weakly. "Yes, together. I never could have imagined your dad wouldn't be with me until we were old. I walked out of the sun into the darkest shade when he died." Her breath is shallow. "I'm…I'm okay." She squeezes my hand. "Your dad made the tough times bearable…he made me laugh – all of us. And there's so much guilt. I didn't get the chance to say all the things I wanted to before he died." Mum's face creases in pain. "The grief was so big that I couldn't find the words."

"Mum, please – I'm worried you'll make yourself worse." Her forehead feels too hot.

She grips my hand tightly and says fiercely, "I'll never forgive myself for walking out on you and Jake, or that I made you invisible because I was so focused on just getting through each day." Her voice cracks. "I knew you were hurting, but because you never complained I told myself you were coping, when I knew you couldn't have been.

"I could barely hold it together myself, so I let...let you deal with it all by yourself. I hated myself for that. I was the parent, but I failed you as your mother." Her eyes shut momentarily. A tear escapes from underneath her lid. "I couldn't bear to even look at myself in the mirror. Can you e-ever forgive me?"

I nod, because I can't speak. All the hurt I've buried spills out of me in great, heaving sobs. Mum wraps her arms around me.

"I'm so sorry," she says, over and over again.

Our crying gradually fades, as Mum quietly rocks me in her arms. "I've got you, sweetheart, I've got you."

Jake snorts, which wakes him up momentarily. Mum whispers to him to settle him down again.

"Best he sleeps," she says.

"When we get back, Mum, things can be different. Jake has grown up so much over the last few weeks. I think that's because he's had a bit more freedom. You need time for you and it's alright to want that. All you do is look after us and work. I don't remember the last time you did anything for yourself and I'm so sorry."

"You don't have to say that, darling. None of this is your responsibility." Her words are vehement. "I've expected too much from you."

"I love Jake and I want to help keep our family together, but I've realized I don't have to try and be perfect any more, and neither do you. We both deserve time to think our own thoughts and just be us. Jake could spend more time with other people. I think he'd really like that."

Mum shuts her eyes. Her lip trembles and she struggles to speak.

"Your dad would have hated that."

"I know. Do you remember when Jake started his new school, and that teacher—"

"—asked if we had considered Jake going into a care home?"

"Dad went ballistic."

I can see his face now, almost purple with rage. Mum tries to sit up straighter. I help her.

"He made me promise that I'd never do that," she continues, "especially after Eve had suggested the same thing. I...I don't think he ever really forgave her. He made me promise that if any...anything happened to him, I'd always keep Jake at home, always look after him, just us."

"He made me promise that too, just before he died. He didn't need to say that, did he? Of course we wouldn't. But if he could see us now, Mum, I think he'd understand we need to change. I think we need to let Jake grow up a bit. We'll never send Jake away, but he's loved being a bit more independent."

Mum looks at me, wide-eyed. She glances over at Jake. "I need to let you both be... It's hard. I just want to protect you both."

I rest my head on her lap and she strokes my hair, like she used to do when I was little. Her hands remind me of a tiny bird's claw, she's lost so much weight.

I look up at her sad face. "We need to say goodbye to Dad. Properly."

Mum's voice is husky. "Yes, that's important for all three of us."

"I think the three of us should scatter his ashes in our special place, down here, where we saw the jellyfish illuminating the water with their blue light. Dad was so happy there."

Mum squeezes a yes on my hand. "And at peace."

In the background is a faint droning sound. I sit bolt upright. "Can you hear that, Mum?" I stagger to my feet. It gets louder. "A boat!"

I run outside. A small red and white speedboat races across the bay, its outboard motor whining and buzzing, its bow riding high, two people standing up at the helm. I wrench the bag from the rock and wave it from side to side above my head in a big loop. I know they can't hear me, but I shout and scream, "HELP! OVER HERE!" over and over again.

For a moment I think it's coming in, but it flashes across the water and into the next bay. The light is too dim. But I wave until the sound of the engine is no more than a faint buzz.

CHAPTER 60

Maudie & Jake

The light has gone, outside. The sun sank below the horizon. We watched it blurring into deepest blue and with it went our hope that anyone would rescue us until the morning. Mum is asleep for now, wiped out after the exertion of talking to me. She's curled up on the floor, her face squashed against her arm. I'm with Jake – I don't want him to be scared, because he hates the dark. We're using Jake's bus key-ring torch, taking it in turns to shine it on our faces. The light comes out of the headlamps. Liv said it might come in handy. Little did she know.

"It's Monday tomorrow, Jake. We need to get you a new magazine."

"Can he have a red bus?"

"Of course."

"Jake has brie cheese for lunch on Monday."

"*Bonjour!*"

"*Bonjour!*"

We both say it at the same time. It always makes Jake laugh. Dad started it years ago and thought it was hilarious. Mum would shake her head and mutter, "Will you ever grow up?" But she'd laugh too.

I can speak French. Bonjour – juma-pel Jake. I went to France on holiday. Dad ate some snails. Yuk! Maudie teased me. She put a snail on my plate. I teased Maudie. I put it on her head. I can't have cheese now. We're in a dark cave. It's very cold. The wind is shouting round the walls. Maudie has fog coming out her mouth. I can see it in my bus lights. I can't go home. I have to look after Mum and Maudie. Don't worry, Dad, I will.

"Jake's hungry. He hasn't had his dinner."

"You ate your chips."

He tuts at me. "They were all furry."

I unwrap my granola bar. "Here, I'll remove the nuts and you can have the rest. Here you go." I shine the torch on Jake's hands.

Maudie's put all those nuts on her lap. I hate nuts. They hurt my teeth. Hurry up, Maudie, I'm hungry.

He grabs it from my hand. "Thank you. Jake likes raisins." He stops before he eats any. "Mum can eat it." He passes the bar back to me. I'm too moved to say anything. Right under our nose Jake has been growing up. I see now that perhaps we've been a bit overprotective. We must learn to let go – and help him on his way. Jake will always be with us at home, but the world is calling him and we must let him try it out.

I pull his coat over our legs and tuck it under our arms. The damp in here is seeping into our bones. I watch Jake's face in the shadows. My brilliant brother, who I'd walk to the ends of the earth for.

Mum sighs. I pull out a strand of hair that's caught in her mouth. She whispers something in her sleep, but it gets lost in the wind whistling round the cavern.

I've ripped my bus leaflet up. I couldn't help it. I don't like the dark. Maudie told me not to be scared. She said she would chase away the monsters in my head. I'm going to chase them away. Maudie said she'd get me a new bus magazine. She's the best sister. She makes me happy. Mum makes me happy. Dad makes me happy in my head.

Jake taps my arm. "Dad took Jake to football on Saturday days."

"He did, Jake," I smile, "and you both wore stripy scarves."

"Dad's not here."

"No, but he's in here."

I place my hand on his chest and feel the *thump, thump, thump* of his heart.

"Don't be 'diculous. His dad's not in there."

I start to giggle, and Jake joins in until we're both doubled up with laughter. Mum smiles in her sleep. Jake's the first to stop.

"Jake can hear something."

I strain my ears. Then I hear it, a dull *whump-whump* behind the wind and crashing waves. A beam of light cuts across the opening. A dark grey shadow swoops across the sea in front of us. A group of gulls take off the side of the cliff, circling wildly, caught in the bright glare from the beam of light shooting out the front of the helicopter.

"Stay there, Jake!"

I frantically wave the red bag in the air, hoping the colour will catch in the light. The helicopter hovers for a moment, then swoops around and away before swinging back in nearer to the cliff. I can just make out a man in a helmet, goggles and a flight suit, with a rope tied round his waist. He's perched in the open doorway of the helicopter.

I move back and stumble over Jake's feet, not knowing he's behind me.

He catches me as I fall.

We stand just inside the shelter together, side by side.

Jake holds his hand up and salutes the pilot.

CHAPTER 61

Jake

That light on that helicopter was too bright. It hurt my eyes. The man came to rescue us. He fell out the helicopter. On a rope. They took my mum on a stretcher. Leave her alone! I didn't want them to take her. We just found her again. I didn't want to go in the sky. I screamed. That man gave me some medicine. To calm me down. I was very frightened. Maudie helped me. They tied me up with her. The man on the helicopter pulled us up, up, up into the sky. I had thunder in my ears. The wind pushed us. I was swinging in the air. Maudie cried, so I kissed her head. She was scared like me. Mum was asleep in the helicopter. The doctor gave her an injection. "Don't worry, Jake, your mum will be fine." Maudie held her hand. I held her hand. I fell asleep.

CHAPTER 62

Maudie

"We're going to be fine, Mum," I whisper in her ear.

A paramedic is looking after Mum, who is wrapped up in a silver thermal blanket, like me and Jake. I'm pleased he's too sleepy from his sedative to be upset by that. His red bag pokes out the side of his blanket, clutched in his hand. Mum has an intravenous line to give her fluids. Her eyes are shut; she's peaceful.

I start to cry, the stress and fear of the last few hours finally breaking me down.

Jake half opens his eyes. "It's okay, Maudie. Jake's got you. Shush, don't cry," he murmurs before shutting his eyes again.

The helicopter lurches to the side and the pilot's voice crackles through the intercom.

"We're coming in to land."

As soon as the helicopter settles and the propellers have

stopped spinning, the exit door is opened and outside are a team of medics waiting to whisk Mum away on a trolley into the hospital. A couple of nurses help Jake into a wheelchair, and I walk next to him to go down to be checked.

We disappear through the doors, which swing together with a loud slap.

Jake is transferred to a bed until the tranquillizer has worn off. He's deeply asleep now, but I want to make sure I'm next to him when he opens his eyes. I hook his bag over his arm and tuck it on the bed beside him. I watch his chest rise and fall. My eyelids open and close.

It seems like no time at all has passed when I'm woken up by the doors behind me whooshing open, startling me awake.

"Maudie – thank god you're alright." Eve hesitates by the doors before rushing over and enveloping me in a hug. When I don't respond she steps back, unsure what to do. "Is Jake okay? I've just seen the doctor and he said your mum is going to be fine, but she took quite a blow to her head. She has concussion and will have to stay in until they're sure she's safe to leave. She's out of it still, so we can't see her until she wakes up. I wanted to see you."

Her words tumble over each other.

I don't answer, unsure how I feel and slightly resentful I didn't get to hear how my mum was first. Eve pulls a chair up next to mine.

"Is Jake alright, Maudie?"

I nod, but I can't bring myself to look at her yet.

Her hand rests on mine on the hospital bed. I don't move it.

"Maudie, look at me please."

Reluctantly I turn to face her. Eve's eyes are very red; she's obviously been crying, and her fingers nervously twist the ends of her pink scarf.

"I know how much I hurt you and I hate that I did, but I didn't mean to. I'd do anything to wind time back and start again, because I'd do it completely differently."

"Hindsight is a great thing, as Dad used to say."

"I know. I don't think he liked me very much."

Eve looks so miserable I relent a bit. "He did like you, he just couldn't forgive you for suggesting Jake went into care. He understood for some people it's the best option, but just not for him and Mum with Jake."

Eve nods. "That was blinkered of me. I was trying to help your mum and dad. They looked so exhausted and beaten. I was wrong."

"They were exhausted, but never beaten. That makes Jake sound like a burden, and he's anything but. He's just Jake, their son, my brother. We'd never be without him.

"What did beat them down was having to deal with the way some people react to Jake. They coped when they had each other, but when Dad died everything got too overwhelming for Mum. You thought she was running from

Jake, but she was running from her grief, and she was running from herself, Eve. She told me that on the cliff."

Eve nods sadly. "I see that now. I'm so sorry I put Jake into care, Maudie. I panicked, but these last horrible days I realized I shouldn't have separated you two. You'd both lost enough, and I could've helped you instead of making more stress for you. I was nervous and a bit frightened, because I'm so useless with Jake, but I'm going to try hard to be better."

She can't say any more, she's so distressed.

"You're not useless with Jake, Eve – he loves you. But it'd help if you saw all of us a little bit more, if you could."

She tries to control her sobs, but they come out in a loud snort, which makes us both laugh. I fling my arms round her and we hold onto each other, not wanting to let go.

When we finally do, Eve points towards the doors. "There's a really cute guy sitting in the corridor. I think I heard him tell the nurse he's waiting for you."

"Oh, that must be Gerren!" My heart soars at the thought that he's outside. "I don't know how he knows we're here."

I thought about him when we were stuck in that cold cave, not knowing what was going to happen to us. I so hoped I'd see him again.

"I think the whole of Cornwall must know about your dramatic sea-rescue by now," Eve tells me. "Would you like to go and see Gerren now?"

"It's okay – I need to be with Jake when he wakes up, or he'll be scared."

"I'd like to do that, if you think it would be okay."

I'm reluctant to let her, but seeing Eve's hopeful expression makes up my mind.

"Yes, it would be – more than okay."

Eve pulls her chair up closer to Jake. I smile at her as I go out.

Gerren is asleep on a chair in the corridor, his chin resting on his chest. I'm so happy to see him. He must sense me standing in front of him, because his head shoots up and he opens his eyes. Gerren leaps out of his chair and wraps me in a hug, before pulling back and looking at me closely, his face creased with concern.

"Thank god you're alright! You are alright, aren't you? You must've been terrified, especially when the sea cut you off."

"I'm okay, just. Shocked more than anything, but all in one piece."

"And Jake, your mum?"

"Jake's fine, he was amazing. He carried Mum up the rocks to safety, even though he was petrified himself. Mum has concussion and has to stay in here until they think she's safe to go home, but she's going to be okay." I bite my lip to control my emotions.

Gerren hugs me again. "That's so good to hear. Where's Jake now?"

"They had to sedate him to get him up into the helicopter, so he's sleeping it off. My Aunty Eve is with him in case he wakes up."

"That's really cool, Maudie. And how are things with your mum? Did she say anything to you?"

I want to tell him everything, but I suddenly realize I want to get out of here for a bit. "Do you fancy a walk?"

"Yeah, good idea." He glances at his watch. "We could watch the sun come up, as it's nearly seven o'clock."

We make our way across the hospital car park, through the town, which is starting to wake up ready for work after the weekend, and down to the beach. We walk in silence, not needing to talk.

I glance up and a smile twitches across his face.

"For someone who was trying to stay hidden, you topped it with a spot on the main news."

"You're kidding?"

"I saw you on the waiting room TV. Local news wants to talk to you too."

"I hope not!"

He takes my hand. His skin is rough against my palm. I don't want him to ever let go. The morning sun casts a soft amber glow across the sky. It shines softly on the deep-blue water, dappling it with threads of gold. In the shadows, a cluster of lemon sea spurge bobs slightly in the breeze. We go down the rocky bank onto the night-chilled sand. I glance up at the rust-coloured cliffs and a shadow momentarily sweeps over me. Gerren hugs me and the shadow slips away. We both take our shoes and socks off and leave them high up the beach.

"Race you!"

Gerren takes off towards the sea, leaving me trailing behind. When I catch up, out of breath, he's looking at his watch and grinning from ear to ear.

"What took you so long?"

I kick water at him, and we have a mock fight, until he picks me up and swings me round. We're both drenched, but I don't care; it feels so good to be silly and let go of all the tension of last night. He puts me down and his face becomes all serious.

"I was so worried about you yesterday, when you didn't answer my calls and you weren't at the caravan. Then when Liv got through to Brae, because you weren't answering her either, we all guessed something was wrong. It's lucky you'd told her you were heading over to the cottage." Gerren pulls me even closer.

"My phone ended up in a rock pool. I can't believe Liv managed to track down the campsite, though!"

"She did some pretty cool detective work. I drove to the cottage, but when I saw your note on the door and that you hadn't come back yet, I knew something was seriously wrong and rang the coastguard."

Tears well up in my eyes. He cared that much about us. "I...I don't know how to thank you, or Liv."

"There's nothing to thank us for. I wanted to help. And it all made me realize how much I care about you. You know, in the cafe when you told me your mum had run away from you, I wasn't sure I could cope. It triggered all the feelings I thought I'd dealt with."

"And yet you stayed with me and Jake."

"How could I dump you? You were so damn brave, doing what you did."

A flock of seagulls explodes in a squawking cloud from the cliff, startling us for a moment. We watch them settle back on their rock and start to walk slowly along the water's edge.

"You know, Mum apologized for running away and explained how everything had completely overwhelmed her. I'm sure things will be better now."

"I'm glad." He grips my hand tightly and I can tell how much he means it.

He picks a shell up and looks at it closely before tossing it out to sea. I hadn't noticed we'd walked the length of the beach. We climb up the low wall of rocks stopping us going any further and find one to sit on that isn't covered in purple mussel shells. We sit close together, our thighs touching. For a while we don't notice anything else around us, not the rising sun, not the sea nor the boats bobbing on the water.

Eventually a dad clambers over the rocks with his two small boys, fishing nets in their hands, and breaks the spell.

"Does your dad come down here?" I realize I haven't asked much about his family.

"Whenever he can. He works long hours, project-managing building work."

"Where does he live, you live? I'd forgotten you don't actually live here."

"Basingstoke."

I sit up straight. "You're kidding! We live in a place called Shiplake, just outside of Reading. That's not far from Basingstoke, is it?" I can hear the excitement in my voice. I sound thirteen again. I lower the squeak and try to say as casually as I can: "Maybe we could meet up sometime? You know, for a drink or something?"

"I like the sound of the something," Gerren half jokes, that smile twitching across his face again. Then he looks at me seriously. "I'd love to meet up with you. Just try and stop me."

Gerren lowers his head, so that I can feel his warm breath on my skin. I turn towards him and he leans in and kisses me, very gently.

"I'm glad you kidnapped Jake."

CHAPTER 63

Jake

Mum came out of hospital. I'm going to have one more holiday day, with my family. At the cottage. Maudie said Mum must get a bit better before we go home. Father Christmas took me to see Beth. She's very smiley. I like her. She gave me a new mug to drink my tea in. It has a blue turtle on it. I helped make Cornish pasties. I cut the potato into bits and mixed the egg up. I didn't do the onion. It hurt my eyes. They were full of water. I put the pasties in the oven. "Be careful, Jake, don't burn yourself!" I ate my pasty for my tea with some carrots. Father Christmas said Ge-ren likes Maudie. I said he mustn't kiss his sister. Father Christmas did a big laugh. It made his belly wobble. Beth did a laugh too. She said Ge-ren was a lovely boy. She said I was a lovely boy too. I am. When we go home, Eve is going to take me bowling on Sunday. With her boyfriend. I'll win. I can go back to school on Wednesday. I like school. I can play the drums. In the music room. Derrick always tells me what to do. I'm going to put Derrick on the time-out step.

CHAPTER 64

Maudie

Eve's car is packed up and ready to go. Mum can't drive yet. Her car wasn't at the cottage because she'd broken down just outside of Perrin Sands and it had to be towed to the garage. That's why she'd arrived so late at the cottage, after she'd booked it with Liv's aunt using a fake name so no one would realize she was there. She'd headed up to the Lake District first after she left home, but felt drawn to Cornwall despite what she'd said about never going back. Because we'd been so happy here with Dad. We'd missed each other by minutes the night we all arrived.

I'm not sad we're leaving, because me and Liv are coming back down after exams, with our gang. Liv, who helped save our lives. I can't wait to see her.

Jake is in the garden on the swing, by himself. He looks lost in thought. His red bag is hooked over his knee. I go through the French windows and outside. A row of bright daffodils breathes clouds of yellow into the morning sun.

The wind has dropped completely, and everything is still. The only sound is the faint buzz of an early bee on the neat primroses round the bottom of the oak tree.

"Hey, Jake, what are you thinking about?"

"Jake's dad. Mum said he was the best dad. Jake knows that."

"He was, Jake…though it was so annoying when he used to take his socks off and rub his feet together. It made that awful raspy sound."

"It made Jake's teeth fuzzy."

"Yes! That's exactly it. He always did it while we were trying to watch the telly."

Eve's voice calls from inside the house. "Breakfast, you two!"

Jake is up off the swing and halfway across the garden before I've even moved.

"Beans on toast on Tuesday. Jake's favourite." He disappears through the French windows.

I go over to the kitchen window and poke my head through. It worries me that Mum's still so pale, with large, dark shadows under her eyes, but her face lights up when she sees me.

Eve holds a large plate up. "I've made everyone's favourite waffles."

"Great – I'm starving!" I grab a plate.

"Jake doesn't need beans. I can have waffles on a Tuesday if I want them," he says self-importantly.

Mum looks surprised.

"We both had to make changes down here, didn't we, Jake?"

"Jake had to have sausages instead of cheesy pasta. On the barbecue. No problem."

Mum nearly falls off her chair.

I watch Mum, Jake and Eve talking around the breakfast table. Their laughter drifts out of the open window. It feels like a sign of hope, that things will get better and all of us will work together now.

I pinch myself. We did it! Jake and I brought our family back together. We couldn't have done any of this without each other.

There's a knock on the front door.

Eve raises her eyebrows at Mum, who shrugs.

"I'll get it!" Jake wraps the handle of his bag around his wrist and sends his chair flying he gets up so quickly and goes to answer the door.

"Well, if this is what happens when I'm gone for a bit, I'll have to plan a minibreak." Mum laughs. "Is he okay though?" She tips her chair back to try and see what Jake's doing.

"He's fine, Mum, let him do it. And I think it's a great idea if you go away. You deserve to do something nice for yourself. Perhaps...perhaps we could do something together?"

Mum reaches across the table and places her hand on top of mine. "I'd love that, but who'd look after Jake?"

"Maybe he could go and stay for a couple of days with the

lady he was fostered with. He told me a few things they'd done together. I'll tell you more about it when we're home. I think he really liked her."

We can hear Jake talking animatedly in the background. He comes back into the kitchen with Gerren and Brae.

"Jake said Brae could have some breakfast," he declares loudly.

Gerren sits next to me and whispers, "He didn't ask me, just Brae, though he said I could have a cup of tea." He grins at me.

"Don't bother getting up," Brae says to Eve, "we just thought we'd come and say goodbye before you leave today. And I have a small proposition to make to you all."

Eve pulls a chair out for Brae and places some food in front of him.

"Thank you, don't mind if I do." He directs what he says next to Mum, between a bite of food. "Beth, my sister, and I were talking last night, and we were wondering if you'd consider coming to use our family caravan here on the site – in the school holidays, if that works best for you all. Maudie and Jake have been staying there these last couple of days. You see," he clears his throat, "we realize you could do with a break, and me and my sister so enjoyed spending time with Jake, we thought it would be nice to do it again."

He looks anxiously from Jake to Mum and to me.

Gerren squeezes my arm. "And hopefully I'll be down here too, and we can get even more time together."

"I don't know what to say." Mum looks like she can't believe it's true.

"Yes please." Jake leans over and shakes Brae's hand. "Jake wants to do more cooking and have more presents."

"Jake!" Mum tells him off, but everyone falls about laughing.

I look round the table and for a moment I'm overwhelmed. I came down here having lost nearly everything, and now I'm going home with so much more: new friends, new understanding, and the opportunity to build up our broken family. Also, I realize, I can have a boyfriend and be there for Jake and Mum still. And I know that no one can ever replace Dad, but having these people around us, supporting us, gives us all a second chance at happiness – and everyone deserves a second chance.

I can't wait to get home and tell Liv.

EPILOGUE

Maudie

The air is perfumed by honeyed clusters of pink sea thrift, bobbing about on top of their upright stems. The sun is so bright that the sea is nothing but sparkles. Jake is holding on tightly to Dad's ashes in their polished wooden box, and Mum holds onto his arm. Jake bends down to speak to her.

His words carry on the wind to me: "Is Jake's mum okay?"

We've come back to Cornwall, three and a half months since we were rescued – back to the place we were last all together as a family, with Dad. The place where we were happier than we had been for a long time, even though we knew Dad was dying; our special beach, the one we called Jellyfish Cove.

For a moment I listen to the sea holly rustling in the breeze.

"Why did you have to die, Dad?" I whisper, knowing it's time for us all to face up to the fact that Dad isn't coming back. We can't tell him all those things we never got to say, and that's just the way it is. We will say them now, when we scatter his ashes and finally let him go. We're ready for it now.

So much has happened in those months since we took Mum home. Jake's stayed with his foster carer for a couple of nights. Mum and I really like Wendy, she's so calm and has a great sense of humour – not that she was amused at me kidnapping Jake, but she understands why I did it. Liv and I got through our A levels relatively unscathed and are still waiting to hear if we've got into our chosen art college. We are working flat out on our portfolios for the foundation course, wherever that might be. Mum has taken up life drawing, something she always wanted to do, and Gerren has become a big part of our lives. He and Jake watch football together on Saturday evenings, with bowls of lasagne balanced on their knees, just like Dad and Jake used to do. While they do that, Mum and I sit in the garden and talk or sometimes we enjoy being silent, when it means more than any words we can say.

But most importantly, we've been going to family therapy – we couldn't navigate our grief by ourselves, so the three of us go every Wednesday evening and finally we are learning to untangle the agony and despair that has consumed us for so long.

Mum walks over to me.

"Ready, darling?" Her hand is strong holding mine as she leads me over to Jake.

It's low tide and the waves lap gently at the water's edge.

We stand together, looking out over the sea to the horizon that anchors us to this moment.

"Who'd like to speak first?" Mum looks from me to Jake. "Jake, would you like to speak about your dad?"

"Okay, Jake will." He steps forwards. The water rolls quietly over his bare feet. "Get that water off him! No, it's alright, Jake, it won't hurt him."

Mum rubs his back gently to reassure him. "What would you like to say?"

He hesitates, then begins. "Jake misses Dad. Jake loves him. Dad took me on buses. Dad looked after me. He was the best dad."

He hands Mum the urn, then he slips his hand in his pocket and takes out a crumpled photo of him and Dad laughing together.

"Jake can't see his dad." He holds his photo against his chest. "But his dad is in here." He holds his hand on his heart. "Maudie told me. Dad is in Jake's head too. Jake can see him. Bye bye, Dad. I. Love. You."

Mum grips the urn, tears splashing onto the lid. She reaches out a hand and cups it round Jake's face, then turns and holds mine too. Her face is blurred through my tears.

Mum takes a deep breath. "I miss you so much, my darling. You were the best husband, best father and my best friend. You made this world a better place for all of us to be in. You're right here, in my heart; you always will be. It's time to move on, and I don't want to do it without you, but I know we're going to be alright… So you don't have to worry. I love you."

Jake takes a crumpled tissue out of his pocket and gives it to Mum.

We both look at Mum, and each other. Her simple but beautiful words express what we all feel about Dad. And remind us that we will be alright. A soft sigh escapes my lips that echoes the hushed murmur of the sea in a shell.

Mum hands me Dad's ashes. A wave washes back from my feet, making the sand pull and sink away from under me, before rushing back in and nearly toppling me over. I can almost feel Dad laughing and see his eyes shining with glee. It gives me the strength to speak.

"I miss you, Dad. I love you with all my heart. You were my everything. I'll never get over losing you, but you'll never truly leave me, because I'll carry you with me, inside me, until the day I die."

Mum takes the lid off the urn. We walk out into the water, side by side, Jake lifting his feet high. We scatter Dad's ashes and finally let him go. We watch them being carried away on the current, tumbling with the fishes, away to the horizon.

"Bye, Dad," I whisper to the wind.

We turn and walk up the path together, ready to go home.

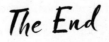

The End

Author note

To my readers,

I wrote my book, *What the World Doesn't See*, because I wanted to give my brother a voice that he couldn't have for himself. I hoped by doing so that it might give a voice to others like him too, or that readers might recognize in him either themselves or someone they knew. As a child I never saw anyone with severe learning disabilities in a book, which made me very unhappy, because my brother filled our lives with love and laughter.

I don't think I can find the words to say how special my brother Guy was to us or to do justice to his life. But what I do know is that he made a big difference to the lives of those of us who loved him. I write this letter with huge sadness, because my wonderful brother died unexpectedly last year, before this book was out in the world. My family is heartbroken – there is an enormous Guy-shaped hole in our lives we can never fill.

My brother couldn't easily communicate what he wanted from life, and what he was feeling. His needs were complex, and he required twenty-four-hour care. He had limited speech. Because of this I know I can never fully understand how he felt and can only record what I observed and learned over the years, having such a close relationship with him. My brother Guy would not have been able to achieve some of the things that my character Jake does in this book. Jake is not a voice for everyone like him, and I don't claim that he is the voice of any particular condition. There is enormous diversity within every person's disability – we are all individuals with different needs and experiences.

Being born in the 1960s meant that my brother was labelled "mentally retarded" or "mentally handicapped" – terms we always hated. It wasn't until he was a teenager that the term autism was used for his diagnosis, and we were told he was "severely autistic". For the doctors it meant they could be more specific with his care. It was only later that our family came to understand that his diagnosis may have been more complicated than we realized.

I remember my mother telling me that Guy was born at forty-three weeks, so three weeks overdue, and that when he was born, he was dry, blue and had clearly been starved of oxygen, perhaps causing some brain damage. In those days his conditions weren't researched in the same way they would be now. But to me he was just Guy, my brother, and not a diagnosis or a label.

I adored him from the moment he was born, and he had me willingly wrapped around his little finger. As a tiny baby I always wanted to feed my brother, so Mum would prop him up on me with some pillows and let me give him his bottle. He'd never look at me but stare at the bright light bulb on the ceiling above him, unblinking. I tried it myself but couldn't last more than a few seconds without my eyes watering. I was in awe of this skill that my brother had, little realizing at the time that this already signalled to Mum and Dad that something was wrong; that and the screaming that went on for hours, seemingly without taking breath.

Life wasn't easy for Guy; the world was difficult for him to navigate – it could confuse and terrify him, often causing meltdowns. We didn't always know what might have triggered these, because he couldn't tell us, but it could be something seemingly insignificant to us, like a bit of fluff on his arm, a look from a stranger, or stairs, which meant that our routes had to be planned to avoid these obstacles.

But most of all I remember the laughter and the joy that Guy brought. He had perfect comic timing and knew when to use it with full effect, often in the most public of places. And the bags. He adored his different coloured felt bags, with his favourite bus or train magazine settled neatly on the bottom. He died in hospital with his bag next to him, tightly clutched in his hand. It was buried with him, where it belonged, by his side.

I always knew that one day I would give my brother a voice, because people with disabilities are the most under-represented group in fiction. I wanted people to see that his life is not unworthy of story and that we need to look beyond disability to the whole person. He was a fully rounded individual with emotional complexities just like anyone else. I have kept my character Jake's speaking voice in my story the way my brother spoke, in third person. We tried to teach him in the first person, but Guy wasn't having it.

My brother's life has fuelled my desire to help dispel the myths of disability because I need to make it clear that it was a joy to have him as my brother and he enriched our lives. To me he was a superhero. I know I wouldn't be the person I am today without having known him. I say this knowing that my brother and other disabled people aren't put on this earth to teach us anything at all, they are simply human beings; but my brother did this for me. When you have a brother like mine you understand what life is about: kindness, empathy and love. One of the last things my brother said to me just before he died was, "You alright, Mel?" I think that says it all.

Guy made the world special just by being in it. I hope this

book will show everyone who reads it, what the world doesn't see.

With thanks,

Mel Darbon

Acknowledgements

My thanks begin with all my family, as I couldn't do this without them. To my darling husband Mike, a special thank you for your endless love and support. Also, to my wonderful son Harry, your unwavering belief in me and my writing means the world, as do your words of wisdom and insight. My beautiful daughters, Aimée and Phoebe, thank you for opening my eyes. To Maudie, for allowing me to borrow your name for my main character and helping shape the person she was to become.

This book wouldn't be the book it is today without my amazing editor Sarah Stewart, who helped guide me through all the ups and downs of the editing process. The first draft to the final version was a roller-coaster ride, but you kept me going with your constant words of encouragement and abiding belief in this story's importance.

Thank you to the Usborne team for your passion and

dedication, with special thanks to Will Steele for the stunning cover design and Adams Carvalho for the wonderful cover illustration. My thanks also to Sarah Cronin for the page design and not forgetting Fritha Lindqvist and Beth Gooding for your hard work and passion on the PR campaign.

Thanks as ever to my very own special agents, Rachel Hamilton and Ben Illis. Your care and conviction, plus your incisive editorial notes, have been above and beyond the call of duty and have meant the world to me.

Thanks to all my lovely writer friends, writing community and MA WYP Bath Spa colleagues – you know who you are – for your writing wisdom and inspiring chats. To my dream team, Miranda and Jas, for your constant advice, thoughts and support, a huge thank you and the promise of a glass of champagne...or two. To dear Lu for always being positive and encouraging, as well as for your input on this book. We certainly had some laughs!

To my wonderful sensitivity readers; Fox Benwell, Adam Murphy and Emma Ferrier. A big, big thank you for opening my eyes and helping me put your shoes on. I am ever grateful.

To Liz James, for your generous help with understanding social work and care issues.

Angela Jones, for always being ready to listen and offering help and advice. Diolch!

To Annie Everall, Miranda McKierney and Carole Estall (The Reading Jackdaw), many, many thanks for your tireless support.

My special thanks to the students at Pathways, Henley College, for helping shape my character, Jake. I loved my time working with you.

To the Learning Disability Community, my thanks for allowing me to try and speak up for you all. It doesn't matter how slowly we go, as long as we don't stop.

Finally, to my darling brother Guy, the inspiration behind this story, the biggest thank you of them all. I hope I've given you the voice you deserve. I miss you every day.

About the author

Mel Darbon spent a large part of her childhood inventing stories to keep her brother happy on car journeys. She has worked as a theatre designer and freelance artist, as well as teaching young adults with learning disabilities and running creative workshops for teenage mums, young offenders and toddlers. She is a graduate of Bath Spa's MA in Writing For Young People, where she found a channel to give voice to those who otherwise might not be heard. Her first book, *Rosie Loves Jack*, was selected for World Book Night and Empathy Lab's "Read for Empathy" collection.

Also by Mel Darbon

"A pure joy from start to finish."
Brian Conaghan Costa-winning author

ROSIE
LOVES
JACK

Mel Darbon

* A World Book Night title

* The Sunday Times Culture's YA Book of the Year

* Nominated for the Carnegie Medal

* Shortlisted for the Branford Boase Award

* A Malka Penn Award for Human Rights
in Children's Literature Honour Book

*"They can't send you away. What will we do?
We need us. I stop your angry, Jack.
And you make me strong. You make me Rosie."*

Rosie loves Jack. Jack loves Rosie. So when
they're separated, Rosie will do anything to find
the boy who makes the sun shine in her head.
Even run away from home.
Even struggle across London and travel to
Brighton, though the trains are cancelled and the
snow is falling. Even though people might think
a girl like Rosie could never survive on her own.

Love this book? Love Usborne YA

Follow us online and sign up to the Usborne YA
newsletter for the latest YA books,
news and competitions:

usborne.com/yanewsletter

 @UsborneYA

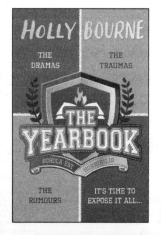

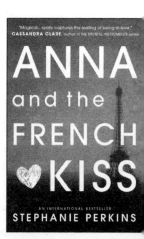